sammy KEYES
and the WEDDING CRASHER

OTHER FAVORITES BY WENDELIN VAN DRAANEN

Sammy Keyes and the Hotel Thief
Sammy Keyes and the Skeleton Man
Sammy Keyes and the Sisters of Mercy
Sammy Keyes and the Runaway Elf
Sammy Keyes and the Curse of Moustache Mary
Sammy Keyes and the Hollywood Mummy
Sammy Keyes and the Search for Snake Eyes
Sammy Keyes and the Art of Deception
Sammy Keyes and the Psycho Kitty Queen
Sammy Keyes and the Dead Giveaway
Sammy Keyes and the Wild Things
Sammy Keyes and the Cold Hard Cash
Sammy Keyes and the Wedding Crasher
Sammy Keyes and the Night of Skulls
Sammy Keyes and the Power of Justice Jack
Sammy Keyes and the Showdown in Sin City
Sammy Keyes and the Killer Cruise
Sammy Keyes and the Kiss Goodbye

How I Survived Being a Girl
Flipped
Swear to Howdy
Runaway
Confessions of a Serial Kisser
The Running Dream

sammy KEYES
and the WEDDING CRASHER

WENDELIN VAN DRAANEN

A YEARLING BOOK

This is a work of fiction. Names, characters, places, and incidents either are the product of the author's imagination or are used fictitiously. Any resemblance to actual persons, living or dead, events, or locales is entirely coincidental.

Text copyright © 2010 by Wendelin Van Draanen Parsons
Interior illustrations copyright © 2010 by Dan Yaccarino
Cover art copyright © 2011 by Karl Edwards

All rights reserved. Published in the United States by Yearling, an imprint of Random House Children's Books, a division of Random House, Inc., New York. Originally published in hardcover in the United States by Alfred A. Knopf, an imprint of Random House Children's Books, New York, in 2010.

Yearling and the jumping horse design are registered trademarks of Random House, Inc.

Visit us on the Web! www.randomhouse.com/kids

Educators and librarians, for a variety of teaching tools, visit us at www.randomhouse.com/teachers

The Library of Congress has cataloged the hardcover edition of this work as follows:
Van Draanen, Wendelin.
Sammy Keyes and the wedding crasher / Wendelin Van Draanen. — 1st ed.
p. cm.
Summary: When her history teacher begins receiving death threats and her own name is near the top of the suspect list, eighth-grader Sammy is determined to find the real perpetrator, but she is distracted by her mother's relationship problems, her almost-boyfriend inexplicably avoiding her, and her duties as a reluctant bridesmaid.
ISBN 978-0-375-86107-9 (trade) — ISBN 978-0-375-96107-6 (lib. bdg.) —
ISBN 978-0-375-89734-4 (ebook)
[1. Teachers—Fiction. 2. Weddings—Fiction. 3. Schools—Fiction.
4. Mystery and detective stories.] I. Title.
PZ7.V2857Saqs 2010
[Fic]—dc22
2010006916

ISBN 978-0-375-85456-9 (pbk.)

Printed in the United States of America

10 9 8 7 6 5 4 3 2

First Yearling Edition 2011

Random House Children's Books supports the First Amendment and celebrates the right to read.

Dedicated to
Lillian "Wild Ride" Penchansky
(Officer Borsch has got nothin' on you!)

***

Special thanks to
"The Cammy Crew" for their patience and steadfast fanship,
and to my gentle backseat drivers,
Mark Parsons and Nancy Siscoe—I'd be lost without you!

sammy KEYES

and the WEDDING CRASHER

PROLOGUE

In the beginning I thought it was funny. I mean, having Mr. Vince for a teacher is not exactly a sunshiny way to start your day. It's more like being trapped in a room with a dark, threatening cloud rumbling around you.

It's not just that Mr. Vince acts like he hates us, it's also that he's gross. Everyone knows he chews tobacco because we've all seen him add to the little cup of nasty brown spit that he keeps in his desk drawer. Plus, he has a disgusting scratching habit. You name it and we've seen him scratch it—his head, his neck, his stomach, his crotch. It's unbelievable.

So when the pranks began, I had to laugh. But pretty soon I realized that the prankster was serious.

Serious and dangerous.

ONE

I was almost looking forward to eighth grade starting. Not because I missed getting up early or couldn't wait to be saddled with homework again.

Please.

No, I was looking forward to school starting up again for the only reason anyone in junior high looks forward to it.

I'd get to see my friends every day.

My best friend, Marissa, was ready, too. Her family is in crisis mode, and I think going back to school seemed like a way for her to escape all that. Plus, we'd be eighth graders instead of lowly seventh graders, and last year's stress of being at a new school would be totally gone.

But then the first day of school arrived, and I got my final schedule.

"No!" I cried when I saw it.

"What?" Marissa asked.

"I've got Mr. Vince! For homeroom *and* history!"

"Eew," she said as she inspected my schedule. "Bad way to start the day."

Then I leaned over to see her schedule and saw that we

only had one class together—drama, at the very end of the day. "No!" I cried again. "This is the worst schedule ever!"

Our friends Dot and Holly joined us, and I found out that they had three classes the same as Marissa . . . and that all of them had some guy named Mr. Jefferson for history instead of Mr. Vince.

"This is so unfair!"

"Maybe you can get switched?" Marissa said.

So I marched right up to the office. It wasn't *just* that I had only one class with Marissa, it was that I had only one class with Marissa *and* they'd stuck me with Mr. Vince.

Mr. Vince!

Let's just say that there was no way I would survive the year with Bad Mood Bob. And that's not just because he hates kids. He may teach history, but he and I *have* history. Last year he covered up a total sabotage of my softball team by one of his players so his team could play at the Sluggers' Cup. That may not seem like a big deal to you, but in Santa Martina, the Sluggers' Cup is *huge,* and since I was part of why his little shenanigans backfired, anywhere near him is now definitely enemy territory.

So, yeah. As Grams would say, I had good grounds to demand a change. Trouble is, when I got to the office, I found out from the office lady that my counselor couldn't see me. "She's swamped, sweetie," Mrs. Tweeter said with a tisk. She leaned forward and whispered, "She's new this year, so have a little patience, all right?"

"But she put me in Mr. Vince's class!"

Her eyes did some rapid-fire blinking over the tops of

her reading glasses, and I could tell she was remembering the Sluggers' Cup fiasco. "Oh my."

"Exactly!"

She took a prim breath and a little step back. "Well, Mr. Vince *is* a professional, dear. And if you stay on your best behavior—"

"No! This will never work!" I looked past her to the vice principal's office door. "Can I please see Mr. Caan? He'll straighten this out."

"Hmm. I *would* see about that," she said, drawing out the words, "but Mr. Caan no longer works here."

"He what? Wait. Why not?"

"Didn't you read the August newsletter, dear? He's now principal at the high school. Mr. Foxmore is our new vice principal."

"Mr. Caan is at the *high* school?"

"That's right, dear." She gives me a cheery smile. "So you'll reunite with him next year."

"Well, what about Dr. Morlock?" I ask. "Can I see him?"

She looks at me like, You're kidding, right? because Dr. Morlock is a totally absentee principal. I only saw him about three times last year, but one of those *was* at the Sluggers' Cup tournament, so he knows about me and Mr. Vince.

"He's not even here?"

"He was, dear, but he had a meeting." She reaches to answer the ringing phone. "I'm afraid you'll have to wait your turn to see Miss Anderson, just like everyone else. I'm sorry."

I left there so frustrated that even the janitor noticed. "Hey, hey, hold on now, Sammy," he said, catching up to me. "What's wrong?"

"Oh, hi, Cisco," I said, feeling bad for blasting right by him. I mean, Cisco may be "just" a janitor, but he's the coolest adult at school. He can talk about music or movies or sports, and he knows all the kids by name. So instead of answering "Nothing" like I would have with most other people, I said, "They put me in Vince's class, and nobody in the office seems to get why that's a disaster."

"Oh boy," he says, and I can tell that he *completely* gets it. He glances back at the office. "A lot of changes around here, man. Not all good, that's for sure. I coulda told them what to prune and what to transplant if they'd asked me, but of course they didn't."

I laugh and tell him thanks, and just knowing he understands why I'm unhappy makes me feel better.

A lot better, actually.

"Don't worry," he says with a wink. "Things'll work out."

After that I just tried to tell myself that my schedule *would* get changed. Things *would* get better. After all, they couldn't get much worse, right?

But when I walked into history third period, I found myself face to face with Heather Acosta.

"Hey, loser!" she sneered.

I stepped around her and found a seat, but wow. Talk about a rash of bad luck. I mean, anywhere near that vicious redhead is like being surrounded by poison oak. Get too close and your life will be covered in itchy, oozy bumps. Stumble in and you might actually die. The only real solution is to avoid her, but she makes that difficult.

Very difficult.

For one thing, she's sneaky. Some days she's shiny and green, and people think she's, you know, a blackberry plant or some sweet little meadow clover.

Don't let her fool you. She's always poison oak, and when she finally shows her true colors, you'll just want to go drown yourself in calamine lotion.

So I steer clear.

Really, I do.

Trouble is, she likes to brush up against me.

Likes to camouflage herself in front of our teachers.

Likes to surround me and make my life as painful as she possibly can.

So after she calls, "Hey, loser!" she says, "I saw my brother hanging out with a hot girl at the high school yesterday. He is *so* over you!"

See? It's hard to ignore her. Especially when she says things you're secretly worried about. I mean, Casey isn't *officially* my boyfriend, but Marissa has been saying that it was inevitable for so long that I'd started to believe it.

I *wanted* to believe it.

But he's in high school now.

And he's still my archenemy's brother.

Whose dad is secretly going out with my soap-star mother.

Which makes everything . . . complicated.

And messy.

And not at all inevitable.

And on top of all that, I haven't heard from him since he called me during his high school orientation, and that was over a week ago.

But anyway, as if having Heather in Mr. Vince's class wasn't painful enough, it turns out I also have her in science and drama.

Half of my classes!

Why not just move her in with me?

But after two weeks of trying to get my schedule changed, Miss Anderson told me that there's nothing she can do about it. Dr. Morlock is never around, and the new vice principal refuses to see me, which makes me really mad. I thought about following him to his car after school and making him hear me out, but I don't even know what he looks like!

Grams tried talking to him on the phone, but she couldn't get anywhere with him, either. And when Mr. Foxmore began asking questions about why *she* was calling instead of my mother, Grams gave up. "Why didn't I say I was Lana?" she moaned. She fluttered around the kitchen like a trapped little bird. "I'm sorry I botched that, Samantha. He made me so nervous! Maybe you can get your mother to call?"

I just rolled my eyes and snorted.

Like Lady Lana would want my sorry little scheduling problems to interfere with her soap-star life?

No, the bottom line is, I'm stuck with Mr. Vince for homeroom and history, and I'm stuck with Heather Acosta in history, science, and drama. "Oh, that's harsh," Cisco said when he asked me how things had turned out. "But that's what's happening around here, man. People don't *listen*."

"It's nice that you do," I told him.

"Too bad that's all I can do." He smiled and pushed his cleaning cart along. "Except clean up your messes."

"Hey! I throw out my own trash."

He laughs and waves. "I know you do, Sammy." Then over his shoulder he calls, "Believe me, I pay attention!"

Now, there *is* one good thing about my schedule, and that's Billy Pratt. Billy is also in history, science, and drama and totally makes those classes. For one thing, he's a good friend, but he's also like a chimp in a cage of hyenas.

A macaw swooping through a murder of crows!

A clown fish in a school of sharks!

He's so . . . Billy.

And although most teachers don't appreciate his hyper sense of humor, I sure do. Especially after it finally kicked in again during the third week of school.

"Are we gonna reenact battles in here?" he asked Mr. Vince on Tuesday.

"No, Mr. Pratt," Mr. Vince said with a frown.

"Are we gonna set up encampments in here?" he asked on Wednesday.

"No, Mr. Pratt. But you can set up camp in the principal's office, if you'd like."

"Are we gonna have guest speakers in here?" Billy asked on Thursday. "We could *really* use some guest speakers in here."

This made Mr. Vince scratch his hip, and eye him with

9

a frown. "Are you implying that my class is boring, Mr. Pratt?"

Billy gave a little shrug. "I'm implying that we could *really* use some guest speakers in here."

Mr. Vince scratches his other hip as he looks around the classroom. "How many of you think we need guest speakers?"

Billy's hand shoots up, but everyone else just looks around at everyone else.

"Aw, come on," Billy says to us. "Flap your chicken wings in the air already. Don't you want to listen to some old Civil War dude? Or Rosie the Riveter? Or slaves that were hunted by hounds?"

Jake Meers' hand inches up. "I would."

David Olsen's follows. "That would be cool."

Soon almost everyone has their hand up, including me.

Well, not Heather Acosta, but that's because she's being her sneaky little shiny-leafed self.

Mr. Vince shakes his head and mutters, "I'm dealing with a roomful of retards." Then his face pops full of blood as he screams, "Those people are all dead! Dead, you hear me? They've died! They're DEAD!"

Billy jumps out of his seat. "We should have a séance!"

"GET OUT!" Mr. Vince yells, pointing an angry finger toward the door. "Go to the office NOW!"

So while Billy collects his stuff and trudges out the door, Sasha Stamos turns around in the seat in front of me and whispers, "I can't believe he called us retards. Doesn't he know that's offensive?"

I smirk. "He *lives* to be offensive." Then I add, "This

place takes some adjustment, huh?" 'cause Sasha was home-schooled until just this year.

"Well, my little brother's autistic, and I shouldn't have to *adjust* to such an ignorant teacher." Then she gives me a we'll-just-see-about-*this* look and turns back around in her seat.

The trip to the office doesn't seem to dampen Billy's spirits, though, because on Friday he comes into history wearing a hodgepodge of clothes that sort of adds up to a Civil War soldier's uniform, including a blue hat with crossed rifles on it.

The hat comes off, though, when Billy notices a short man with soft features and receding red hair standing in a back corner of the classroom.

I catch Billy's eye and grin like, Guest speaker? But he shakes his head and gives me a warning look that means one definite thing.

Be good.

The tardy bell rings, and Mr. Vince immediately clears his throat. "I'd like to apologize," he says, looking down at his shoes, "for using the word *retard* yesterday. It was in poor taste, and I shouldn't have done it."

He glances up from his shoes and sort of vultures a look at the class.

We just stare at him, not making a peep.

"I'd like to put the incident behind us, so please accept my apology."

We just stare at him some more.

Then suddenly he calls, "Mr. Foxmore, stay a minute, would you?"

We all whip around to see that the man with the receding red hair is in the middle of slipping out the door.

Now, through my head are flashing a million thoughts.

That's Mr. Foxmore? The new vice principal? The new discipline guy? The new Mr. Caan? The guy who flustered Grams and refused to see me?

It can't be!

He seems so . . . soft.

And he's *short*.

And his suit is all rumply!

I mean, if he can't even control his suit, how's he ever going to control eight hundred junior high kids?

But then it hits me that he just got Mr. Vince to do something that Mr. Caan—who looks and acts like a pro wrestler—had a really hard time getting him to do.

Apologize.

Sasha Stamos turns around and whispers, "My mom called the school about it yesterday!" She seems very proud and super excited, but then hesitates and adds, "Don't tell anyone, okay?"

I nod, and as Mr. Foxmore comes back inside the classroom, Mr. Vince reaches for the rope at the bottom of the projection screen, which is pulled down in front of the whiteboard. "I'd like to know," he says, looking around the classroom, "which one of you thought you could get away with this?"

Then he yanks the rope, rolling up the screen and exposing a big, bold, red-lettered message on his whiteboard.

A message that says, DIE DUDE!

TWO

I don't know why I thought it was funny, but I did. I mean, come on. How seriously can you take a death threat when it has the word *dude* in it?

So, yeah, I laughed. It just kind of came out. And other people laughed, too, so it wasn't only me.

But Mr. Vince?

Oh boy.

He took it *really* seriously.

"You think this is funny?" He looked right at me. "Do you know you can get *arrested* for something like this? Do you know it's a *felony*?"

"A felony?" I blurted. "Writing on your board is a felony?"

The rest of the class snickered, but I was already kicking myself.

When am I ever going to learn to keep my stupid mouth shut?

But off it yapped, anyway. "Hey, quit staring at me like that. I didn't do it!"

"Yeah? Then who did?" he asked, looking around the room. "Death threats are felonies!"

Everyone sort of shrank back because he was definitely turning red around the edges. Then, over on my right, Jake Meers says, "Why do you think it was one of us? Someone could've put that up at break. Or earlier."

"Yeah," David Olsen adds. "Like, did you use the board in first or second?"

Mr. Vince just stares.

First at Jake.

Then at David.

"Perhaps you should just erase the board and get on with class," comes a quiet voice from behind us.

Everyone turns to look at Mr. Foxmore.

His gaze is cool.

Calm.

Mr. Vince says, "But—" and in that instant Mr. Foxmore's look sharpens, an eyebrow arches, and his head cocks slightly.

It's a total ninja move, but just of his face.

Mr. Vince hesitates, then picks up an eraser and wipes the message away. When he turns back around, Mr. Foxmore is gone.

The vibe in the room was really weird after that. It was quiet and *seemed* calm, but the air was hot and angry. Like any second there'd be a downpour of hatred.

We were all glad to escape to fourth period, and by lunchtime the whole school knew about the message, and everyone had different theories on how it wound up there.

"You swear it wasn't you?" Marissa whispered to Billy, who was sitting at our lunch table.

"Why does everyone ask me that?" Billy said. "I'm the poster boy for peace, love, and understanding."

I laughed. "More like the poster boy for pranks, laughs, and under-studying." I shrugged. "And who cares, anyway? Vince made a huge deal out of nothing. A felony? Come on!" I laughed again. "I'm just glad that it wasn't me!"

After lunch, though, I found out that Heather Acosta also had a theory. "I know it was you, loser," she said, slithering up to me during science.

"Oh, right," I snorted, and that's when it crossed my mind that *Heather* might be the person who'd written the message.

Now, maybe I should have suspected that right away, but it was actually counter-intuitive. I mean, Heather was on Mr. Vince's softball team last year, and let's just say they're peas in the same rotten pod. But Heather also has a history of setting things up so people she's mad at get blamed.

Usually, that's me.

The thought really bothered me, but when I told Marissa about it in drama, she whispered, "Look, stop worrying. It's over. Erased. Just forget about her, okay?"

Obviously, this was something she had no problem doing because, just like that, she switched subjects. "Do you want to go to Hudson's with me after school?"

I blinked at her. Hudson Graham is *my* friend. He may be seventy-three years old, but I've been dragging Marissa to his house for iced tea and good advice for over a year, and now *she's* inviting *me* to go with *her*?

"Why are you going to Hudson's?" I asked, still trying to wrap my head around the change.

"Because Mikey hangs out there after school." She tossed me a scowl. "Mom says I have to either go straight to Hudson's or straight home, and it's *way* better than going home."

Something about this made me sort of, I don't know . . . fold up on the inside. Not collapse or anything like that. Just kind of . . . close in. I mean, I knew that Marissa's little brother had gone to "camp" at Hudson's during the summer while their parents tried to straighten out their problems, but I figured when school started up again, that would be over.

Obviously, it wasn't.

And the thought of Mikey and Marissa hanging out there, like, *permanently,* bothered me. I didn't *want* it to bother me, and I couldn't really explain *why* it bothered me, but still, it did.

Maybe it's because I'd finally gotten used to things. Hudson had helped me adjust to having an absentee mother, and to living secretly with Grams in a building full of old people, and to being in junior high school, and . . . and to believing it was okay to like my archenemy's brother. And now, just when I thought things were settling down, everything was changing again.

I wanted it to *stop*.

I wanted to go back to having Marissa in my classes.

I wanted to go back to having Hudson's porch be *my* safe haven.

I wanted to go back to having Mr. Caan as the vice

principal and Mr. Vince in a classroom that I didn't have to go into.

And I wanted to go back to having Casey at school.

Back to him calling me.

"What's wrong?" Marissa whispered.

I shook my head and said, "I should probably just go home. I've been putting off stuff I need to do for Officer Borsch's wedding."

She laughs. "I still can't believe he asked you to be in the wedding. Does he secretly *not* want to get married?"

I tell her, "Hey!" but I know exactly what she means. Whenever Officer Borsch and I deal with each other, there seems to be trouble.

Sometimes *big* trouble.

So him including me in his wedding was either really brave or really stupid.

Maybe both.

Which in a weird Borschman way made sense, seeing how I've accused him of *being* both.

"He doesn't have anything to worry about," I tell Marissa. "I'm just in charge of the guest book. What can go wrong?"

She laughs again. "Everything!"

"Hey!"

So she drops the insults and says, "But that's *next* weekend, right? So what do you have to do today?"

"Grams found me a dress for the wedding, but it's too long and she's making me hem it."

"She's making *you* hem it? Why doesn't she just do it? She's really good at that sort of thing, isn't she?"

"Yeah, but she says it's something I should know how to do myself, so she's going to teach me."

Marissa snickers. "Should be fun."

I scowl at her. "A thrill a minute."

So that's the excuse I gave Marissa for not going over to Hudson's, and it was actually a pretty lame one, seeing how I could have worked on the stupid dress anytime. But Marissa bought it, and I was glad. I don't know why—I just kinda wanted to be left alone.

Trouble is, the minute I'm home, Grams says, "Samantha! Sergeant Borsch called. He needs you to call Debra right away."

"Why?"

"He didn't say, but it sounded urgent."

So I go to the kitchen, pick up the phone, and dial the number Grams had jotted on the notepad. And when Debra answers, I say, "Hey. It's Sammy. I'm supposed to call you?"

"Oh, Sams!" she says, and even in those two words I can tell she's totally frazzled. "How'd you like a promotion?"

"Huh?"

"I need you to fill in for Robyn as my third bridesmaid."

"Uh . . . *why?*"

She heaves a sigh. "Honey, sometimes what happens in Vegas doesn't stay in Vegas."

"What?"

"To cut to the chase, she's no longer in the weddin' party, and I'd *really* appreciate it if you could fill in for her."

"But . . . can't you just fire one of the groomsmen?"

There's a moment of silence. "No."

"But . . . don't you have any other friends who could do it? Or relatives? I mean—"

"Sam, look. I wouldn't be asking if I wasn't desperate."

"Uh, gee, thanks."

She heaves another sigh. "I didn't mean it that way. It's just that the weddin's in a week, and everything's goin' wrong! Gil broke his wrist, Robyn dumped a lifetime of garbage all over me, the florist skipped town with my deposit, and the last time we met with the minister, he was drunk."

"He was *drunk?* And he's marrying *cops?*"

"Well, I'm not a cop, technically. I just work reception."

"You're cop enough," I tell her. "And how did Officer Borsch break his wrist?"

She sighs. "He fell off a treadmill."

"He what!?" I mean, let's just say that Officer Borsch could use time on a treadmill—a *lot* of time—but him actually running on one was something I couldn't picture.

She sighs again. "It was goin' too fast, and he stumbled and fell. It's his left wrist, too. So now his tux won't fit right, and all our pictures'll have an ugly white cast in 'em."

"Wow," I tell her, trying to take it all in.

"Sams," she says, and her voice is suddenly all choked up. "I'm forty years old. I've never been married. This is a big deal to me. Will you *please* do me this favor? Honey, you know the big man adores you. You know we both do."

And that's how I wound up saying, "Sure."

I mean, how could I not?

So she tells me her address on Elm Street and says,

"I'm around the corner from the Community Presbyterian Church. Just go down Constance, turn left, and there you are!"

"You're talking about that little white church?"

"Yes!" she says all excited-like. "Isn't it a perfect place for a weddin'?"

I said yeah 'cause I didn't know what else to say, then promised to meet her at her house the next day so she could take Robyn's dress and turn it into mine.

It wasn't until I got off the phone that I started wondering if her wedding luck was about to go from bad to worse.

After all, I was now officially in the wedding party.

THREE

Grams thought my "promotion" was a little odd, but after I told her about the broken wrist and stuff not staying in Vegas and the florist skipping town, she tisked and said, "Poor dear."

So the next morning I headed for Debra's. And it's not like I was in a hurry or anything. For one thing, I'd left the apartment plenty early. For another, I was getting fitted for a *bridesmaid's* dress.

Who's in a hurry for that?

So I decided to cruise by Hudson's, which was *kind* of on the way, thinking that if he was hanging out on the porch reading the paper, I'd stop and say hi, and that if he wasn't, I'd just keep going.

He must've heard my skateboard, because he was watching the sidewalk with the newspaper already lowered as I clickity-clacked up to his walkway.

"Sammy!" he called, and he actually stood up.

I popped up my skateboard and turned onto his walkway. "Hey, Hudson."

"I've missed you, my friend," he said, pouring me a glass of iced tea as I went up the steps.

I plopped into my usual chair and took the tea. "Thanks," I told him, and I meant it for more than just the tea.

"So how's the new school year treating you?"

"Marissa didn't tell you?"

"Just briefly. But I'd like to hear it from you. What's this Mr. Vince fella's problem?"

I laughed. I mean, usually adults try to get you to see the other adult's side of things, but not Hudson. If I'm up against something, he's always on my side, even when being on my side means helping me see how I can handle things better.

Anyway, I took a nice, long drink of tea and then told him all about Mr. Vince's "death threat," and Mr. Foxmore's ninja face, and Billy Pratt's wanting guest speakers, and Heather Acosta's itchy, witchy ways. It came out in one big, convoluted sentence, and when I finally came up for air, I took another nice, long drink of tea and said, "Aaaaah!" then smiled at him. "I've missed you, too."

"Hmm," he said, smoothing back one of his bushy white eyebrows as he grinned at me, "sounds like junior high is back in full swing."

I laughed. "What was I expecting, right?"

He nodded. "Just keep yourself out of the fray where that Mr. Vince is concerned. I know Billy is a friend of yours, but do yourself a favor and steer clear of his antics. Teachers have more power than students, so you'll find yourself at a distinct disadvantage in any altercation."

"You think it was Billy?"

Hudson took a sip of tea. "You don't?"

The funny thing is, I didn't. I didn't know who it was, and the truth is, I didn't really care. The only way Mr. Vince was going to die from that message is if he gave himself a heart attack over it.

Anyway, Hudson and I talked some more, but when he asked me what was on my agenda for the day, I noticed my watch and jumped up. "Oh! I'm late!"

"Late? Where are you off to?"

"Debra's!" I called from his walkway. "She's marrying Officer Borsch! I'm in their wedding next Saturday! I'm a bridesmaid, if you can believe that!"

He laughed. "That *is* a shocker!"

I tore down the sidewalk and waved. "Thanks for the tea! See ya!"

I found Debra's house, no problem. It was creamy yellow with blue and green trim, and really cute. But it was also really . . . small. Like maybe someone got carried away building a little Danish playhouse. I felt kinda like Alice going up to the Mad Hatter's house.

Good thing I'd already had some tea.

Anyway, the arched door swept open, and Debra greeted me with, "I was afraid you'd chickened out."

"Chickened out?" I laughed. "Me?"

Then I saw the dress.

"Yes, you," Debra said when my jaw hit the floor.

I tried to pull myself together, but I kept my distance from the dress, sort of circling around it. It had short, puffy sleeves and a long, puffy skirt and a big, puffy bow at the waist. And if that wasn't bad enough, it was *lavender*.

"Is that your favorite color?" I asked, trying to think of something to say.

She scratched a long nail through the ratty nest of bleached hair on top of her head. "I was thinkin' princess dresses. You know, a real storybook weddin'?" She looked at me. "You hate it that much?"

I tried to laugh and say "No, of course not!" but it sounded more like I was choking. So I cleared my throat and said, "Hey, I'm into jeans and high-tops, you know that." I stepped closer to the dress, trying to figure a way to be polite about this mountain of lacy lavender. "I can't believe you *made* this," I tell her, holding out one side of the skirt. "It must've been a lot of work."

She nods. "I've been a bridesmaid five separate times where we girls had to buy our own dresses. It cost an arm and a leg! I didn't want to do that to my friends." She sighs. "Besides, my mother made the dresses for the seven attendants at her weddin', and their marriage is still goin' strong forty-three years later. Mom says that the more you invest in somethin', the less inclined you'll be to give up on it." She shakes her head at the dress. "After makin' three of these, plus the men's bow ties and cummerbunds, I guess you'd say I'm invested."

I take a deep breath. "Okay, so what do I do?"

"Let's get you in the dress and see how much I have to take it in."

So she leaves while I switch into the dress. It's got three separate zippers at the waist, but I don't even need to unzip them to get inside it. And when she comes back into the room and sees me drowning in a sea of lavender, she bursts into tears. "I don't have *time* to start all over."

"Are you sure you don't have somebody, you know, *bigger* that you could ask?"

"No!" she says, flinging away a tear. She takes a deep breath, then zooms in and buzzes around me like an angry bee, jabbing pins into the dress as she cinches it up around me. And when she's finally done telling me "Hold still! . . . Arms out! . . . Hold still! . . . Arms down! Hold *still*!" I feel like a porcupine, afraid of its own quills.

"That's it," she mutters as she takes a last walk around me. "We'll worry about the hem after we get your shoes."

"Shoes?" I ask.

She stops moving and looks right at me. "It's just for a few hours, okay?"

"Meaning . . . ?"

"Meaning you've got to go over to KC Shoes in the mall tomorrow and get fit for a pair of shoes. I'll give you a swatch of the dress material."

"Wait, what?"

"They dye the shoes to match the dress?" she says, like she can't believe I've never heard of such a wonderful service. "I'd have you go today, but Kenny's not working today, and he's the only one I trust to get 'em done on time. He'll be there from two to six tomorrow. Is that okay?"

I just blink at her, wondering, Is *what* okay? The shoes? Or the time?

"It's easy, Sams. You just tell him it's for Debra's weddin', and he'll know what to do."

"S-sure," I tell her, then get out of the dress and out of *there* as fast as I can.

Now, as I'm tearing along on my skateboard with a stupid swatch of lavender in my pocket, I'm feeling very pent up. Very claustrophobic. Very, I don't know, *sweaty*. And I'm thinking how I've *never* been the princess-wedding type. Way before this little bridesmaid fitting, the whole fairy-tale-wedding thing was something I just didn't *get*.

Maybe something's missing in my brain.

Or maybe I have no wish-I-was-a-princess gene.

Or maybe my mom just didn't read me enough fairy tales.

Come to think of it, I can't remember Lady Lana reading me *any* of those fairy tales where the girl gets swept up by a handsome prince and they live happily ever after.

No *Cinderella*.

Or *Snow White*.

No *Sleeping Beauty* . . .

And as I'm riding along, it hits me that maybe that's because *her* fairy tale didn't exactly come true. Not that I even know what her fairy tale *was*, but I do know that whoever my prince of a dad is, he didn't exactly ride off into the sunset with her.

He more just left her in the dark, scary woods with me.

Which was probably even harder on her than I know because my mom *is* the princess type. She's beautiful and acts like she's regal and faints at the sight of blood.

There's a reason I call her Lady Lana.

Anyway, there I am, riding along, having a rare moment of sympathy for my mother, when all of a sudden I realize that I'm almost at the house where Heather Acosta and her mother live. And *that's* when I notice that there are two people going up the walkway to the house.

Two people who *are* Acostas, but definitely not the ones who live there.

It's Casey and his dad.

I almost flip a U-ie and beat it out of there. I mean, the last few times I spoke with Casey, he acted strange—distant and sort of uncomfortable—and the last twenty times I called his cell, it rolled over to voice mail and he still hadn't called me back.

Like I can't take a hint?

But I don't flip a U-ie. I can't seem to make myself. Oh, I slow waaaaay down, but I'm like a stupid moth to the flame, moving in closer and closer. And I know I'm going to get singed. I know it's going to hurt. But I can't seem to turn away.

Plus, I can't quite wrap my head around what he and his dad are doing.

They're carrying a bulky black dresser *toward* the house.

And there's a bunch of stuff in the back of a pickup truck in the driveway.

Stuff like a bookcase.

And a bed.

Big stuff.

And it's not new stuff, either.

There's no plastic covering.

Or cardboard boxes.

It sure *looks* like moving day. Only what I can't figure out is . . .

Who's moving in?

FOUR

First, I have another real pang of sympathy for my mother. All I can think is that Candi and Warren Acosta have gotten back together and that my mom has gotten burned.

Again.

Sure the Acostas have been divorced for years, and yeah, who could have seen this coming? But maybe something happened that made them realize that they belong together. Maybe Candi found out Warren was interested in my mom and turned on the ol' charm. To me she seems like some kind of a firecracker cigarette—something I wouldn't let anywhere *near* my lips—but obviously at some point whatever "charm" she had had worked on him.

Anyway, Casey sees me coming, and since he's saddled down with a big ol' dresser, I guess waving is kinda out of the question. But he doesn't even call out "Hey!" or nod hello. He just stops moving and stares at me.

"What's the holdup?" his dad asks, looking at him from around his side of the dresser.

Casey cocks his head in my direction, and even from fifty feet away, I can see Mr. Acosta's face morph into an uncomfortable Uh-oh . . . !

The sections of sidewalk count off slowly under the wheels of my skateboard, clickity . . . *clack,* clickity . . . *clack.* . . . And the sound mixes with this light-headed feeling I'm having, which makes the whole scene seem like something out of a dream. Like I'm desperately trying to get away from a monster, only I'm moving *toward* it.

Casey and his dad have some frantic exchange, and Casey practically drops his end of the dresser, forcing Mr. Acosta to lower his, too.

"Hello there, Samantha," Casey's dad says, like, Isn't it a lovely day, and oh, hey, do you hear the chirping birds? "What brings you out to this neck of the woods?"

I totally avoid looking at Casey but lock eyes with Mr. Acosta. "A bridesmaid's dress fitting. What about you? You and the missus have a reconciliation?"

The minute it's out of my mouth, my brain screams, *The missus?* Who says "the missus"? But it's out there in the air, and I can't exactly take it back, so I just stand there like I've got all the right in the world to go around saying things like "the missus" and quizzing him about his ex.

He looks totally confused. "What?"

I nod out at the truck. "Looks like you're moving in."

"Uh . . ."

I'm still not looking at Casey, but Warren sure is.

"Tell her!" Casey hisses at his dad.

Mr. Acosta looks back at me. "You, uh . . . When's the last time you spoke with your mother?"

"It's been a while," I tell him, and for some reason his question sort of rattles the mortar of my fortress wall, if you know what I mean. "Why? Does *she* know what's going on?"

He hesitates, then says, "She and I . . ." He shifts uncomfortably. "She's been meaning to talk to you. . . ."

I can feel the wall start to crumble. All of a sudden I'm shaky all over, because I just know—Lady Lana is at it again, keeping secrets that seriously affect *me*.

"Yeah?" I snap. "I'm sure she's also been meaning to be involved in my life and bake me cookies and attend my softball games."

He cringes. "Look, Sammy, I'm sorry. I know this is awkward. She said she wanted to be the one to tell you."

"Tell me *what*?"

Casey cuts in. "That my dad got a part on her soap."

Mr. Acosta flashes a look at Casey.

"What?" Casey snaps at him. "I've told you for *weeks* that she'd better tell her or I would, and you didn't do a thing about it. And here I had to tell her, anyway!"

"You didn't *have* to," his dad snaps back.

"Are you nuts?" He turns to face me. "I'm sorry, Sammy. It's why I haven't called you back. They kept saying they were going to tell you and that I couldn't." He shakes his head. "The whole setup stinks."

I blink at him. "You've known about this for *weeks*?" My head wobbles back and forth. "And what, exactly, is the setup?"

Mr. Acosta turns his back on me and drops his voice, but I can still hear him when he says to Casey, "Lana needs to tell her."

"Get real!" Casey snaps, then steps around him and

blurts out, "He's moving to L.A., which leaves me stuck living here."

Now, maybe this should have been obvious from the beginning, but it wasn't. My brain had painted a completely different picture. So even though the actual situation was probably a lot more realistic than my little reconciliation scenario, the news really knocks the wind out of me. "Y-you're moving in with my mom?" I ask Mr. Acosta, and it sounds like I'm gasping for air.

Mr. Acosta hurries to say, "No, no. I have my own place," but he's looking pretty shifty-eyed.

"Sure you do," I say with a snort, doing my best to take cover behind what's left of my disintegrated wall.

"I *do*," he insists.

"Whatever." I push off on my skateboard. "Tell my mom I hope you two live happily ever after."

"Sammy, wait!" Casey calls after me, but I pump the sidewalk hard with my foot and tear past their truck of furniture.

I'm hurt that he knew.

I'm hurt that other people's feelings are more important to him than mine.

And it's killing me that he's been keeping this secret from me. I mean, Lady Lana keeping secrets is one thing. I'm used to that. But Casey? I've trusted him with life-and-death secrets! How could he *not* have told me about this?

Still, half a block later I look over my shoulder, hoping to see Casey, but he's not chasing after me.

He's not even on the sidewalk, watching me go.

It took me a long time to go back home. I was really just trying to find someplace to be alone so I could think, but everywhere I went reminded me of something I didn't really want to think *about*.

Mostly, Casey.

The mall, the little park outside the mall, the dugout at the baseball field . . . they all brought back memories of Casey. And then other places reminded me of *Heather*, which of course made me think about Casey.

It's really hard to forget about someone when everything reminds you of them.

So I finally gave up and went home.

Besides, there was one burning question that I could only get an answer to at home, and the more I thought about that question, the madder I got because I was pretty sure I already knew the answer.

So the minute I'd snuck through the door, I asked Grams, "Did you know about Warren the Wonderful moving in with Lady Lana?"

She was wiping down a kitchen counter and froze in midswipe. "What?" she asked, blinking at me through her glasses.

"You heard me. And I want the truth. Because you know what? I'm tired of you and her having secrets from me. I'm tired of you protecting her and saying you're just protecting *me*. You're always telling me to be honest with you, but you know what? You and stupid ol' Lady Lana *always* keep secrets from me. If you expect me not to hide stuff from you, you better quit hiding stuff from me!" I

33

punch my hands onto my hips. "Did you know that Warren Acosta got a part on *The Lords of Willow Heights*?"

"No!"

Right off, I know that she's telling the truth, but her answer throws me because it's not the one I was expecting. My fists come down. "You didn't?"

She shakes her head. "Are you sure? When did all this happen?"

I snarl, "Who knows?" and plop into a kitchen chair.

Now I'm acting mad at the world, but I actually feel a lot better than I did when I came through the door. At least for once Grams isn't in cahoots with Lady Lana. At least for once I'm not the only one trying to piece things together in the dark.

At least for once I don't feel so *alone*.

"He's moving in with her?" Grams gasps, and sort of dissolves into the chair across from me.

I snort again. "He denied it, but I could tell he was lying."

Grams puts both her hands flat on the table. Like she's steadying it. Or herself. Or maybe the situation. "Samantha, please. From the beginning. And don't embellish."

So I give her just-the-facts-ma'am, and when I'm all done, she takes a long, deep breath and says, "Your mother and I need to have a conversation."

"Good luck there," I grumble, but then Grams gives me the sweetest, most sympathetic look ever and says, "I feel so sorry for you and Casey."

Suddenly my eyes are welling with tears, and my chin is quivering. It's like she totally understands how horrible and complicated this has made everything. As much as my mother's tried to hide it, she's obviously been seeing Casey's dad, and if they're an item, what does that make Casey and me?

Almost siblings?

In-law—no, wait—*outlaw* siblings?

How awkward is that?

And, yeah, at least there was a *reason* Casey hadn't returned my calls, but his dad being with my mom made Casey and me feel so . . . impossible.

I mean, having Heather as a psycho "sister" would be bad enough, but Casey as a stepbrother? My brain can't figure out what to do with that. And, yeah, maybe there's no blood involved, but even before this—even when my mom and his dad had just gone on one date—the thought of them being together totally weirded both Casey and me out. And now that it looked like it was becoming a reality, I just didn't know what to *do*.

Grams holds my hand across the table and forces a little smile. "We'll get through this together, all right?"

I nod and choke out, "Thanks." And even though I know how lucky I am to have her in my life, even though she's the most wonderful, loving person, she's my grandmother.

The person I wish I could get through this with is Casey.

FIVE

Casey didn't call.

Not that night.

Not the next day.

I tried his cell phone a couple of times, but it rolled over to voice mail again, so I just hung up.

Our phone did ring, but it was always Marissa, in a tizzy about her parents. "She's *throwing* stuff at him!" she said the first time. "Can you *hear* that?"

I could.

"Uh-oh, gotta go!" she whispered, and hung up.

The second time it was, "He gambled the house!"

"What do you mean, he gambled the house? How do you gamble a house?"

"I don't know!"

"Were you eavesdropping? Maybe you heard wrong."

"Maybe . . . but I don't think so. Mom is freaking out."

Something crashed in the background.

"Uh-oh, gotta go!" she whispered, and left me hanging again.

The third time it was, "Mikey and I ran away to Hudson's. Can you come over?"

"You ran away?"

"Well, my mom knows where we are."

I rolled my eyes, because until recently Marissa's family had a nanny, a maid, a gardener, and a grocery service, and running away would have involved a limo. "Did she drive you?"

"No! I just called her when we got here so she wouldn't worry." She hesitated, then said, "Are you making fun of me? Because we're in crisis mode over here, in case you haven't noticed!"

I mumble, "Sorry," then say, "Look, we're kind of in crisis mode over here, too, and it's almost nine. I doubt Grams is going to let me come over." I glance at Grams, and sure enough she shakes her head. She also gives me the cut-it-short signal, so I tell Marissa, "Actually, I've got to get off the phone now. We're waiting for a callback from Lady Lana."

"What's going on?"

"I can't get into it now. I'll come by Hudson's tomorrow and we'll catch up, okay?"

She says, "Sure," and I get off the phone.

Trouble is, my wonderful mother doesn't call back.

Not that night.

Not the next day.

I wasn't exactly hanging around, holding my breath that Her Royal Flakiness would return one of Grams' twenty phone messages, but by noon I was sick to death of hoping Casey would call, so I finally grabbed my skateboard and told Grams, "I'm going over to Hudson's and then to the mall for shoes."

"Shoes?" she asks, all hopeful-like.

I laugh because I know she's thinking that maybe I'm sick of my torn-up high-tops and ready for a pair of "decent" shoes. "Yeah, Grams, shoes." I pull the swatch of fabric from my jeans. "Lavender ones."

Her face crinkles. "To match the bridesmaid's dress?"

This totally surprises me because with the whole Lady Lana thing, I hadn't even told her about the Mountain of Lavender or having to get shoes dyed. "Uh . . . yeah."

Her face crinkles harder. "Are the men wearing lavender cummerbunds?"

I tilt my head a little. "How do you *know* these things?"

She swipes some invisible sweat from her forehead. "I cannot see Gil Borsch carrying off lavender."

I laugh. "Me neither."

"Debra's sewing everything herself?"

I nod. "Yup."

"Poor dear," she says with a sad little shake of her head. "Poor, poor dear."

Grams has our door open and is checking the outside hallway to make sure the coast is clear, seeing how it's against the rules for me to be living with her and all. When she's sure it is, she whispers, "Run along. And call me if you're going to be later than six."

So I sneak down the hallway to the fire escape door, go outside and down the five flights of steps to the ground, then make my way along some bushes and across the grass to the sidewalk and jaywalk across the street over to the outskirts of the mall.

It feels good to tear around the mall on my skateboard.

The walkway doesn't get walked on very much because everyone drives to get to where they want to go, but it's a winding path that's like a strip of parkway—it's narrow, but there are lots of little sections. Shrubs. Grass. Pine trees. More shrubs, more grass, more pine trees. I like the parts where the trees are big and touch across the walkway because I feel like I'm skateboarding through the forest.

Anyway, I had a nice ride over to Hudson's, and then a nice time *at* Hudson's. Mikey was there, and it's not like I didn't recognize him, but I did notice a change in him. He'd lost weight, for one thing. Not tons, but some. I noticed it most in his face because I could actually see his eyes. Before they were pretty much just dark slits in folds of fat, but now I could actually *see* them.

"Looking good, Mikey!"

"Thanks," he said back.

"How's fourth grade going?"

"Pretty good," he said with a little nod.

And that's when I started noticing the other change in him.

He wasn't bratty or whiny or belligerent, he didn't argue or call names or try to pull stupid pranks.

He was just . . . quiet.

"Wow," I said after I'd been there awhile and Marissa and I finally had some alone time on the porch. "Mikey's changed."

Marissa nodded, but she frowned, too. "I'm actually kind of worried about him. He's taking this whole thing with Mom and Dad really hard. I tried to explain that they're just in a fight like he and I are always getting into, and that they'll figure things out, but I think he's scared. Shoot, I'm scared. It's like we're in the middle of some big explosion, and family parts are flying everywhere."

"It's because your dad's still gambling?"

She looks over her shoulder and drops her voice even further. "Hudson says you can gamble away your house by taking out a loan or a *second* loan on it and gambling away the money."

"But . . . did your dad really do that?"

"I don't know! Mikey and I were banished to our rooms yesterday, so I had to sneak out and listen through walls. I'm pretty sure that's what I heard, though."

I thought about this a minute. "So your dad would have to pay the bank back, and if he doesn't . . . ?"

"Hudson says the bank seizes the house."

"Like, kicks you out?"

"Exactly."

"Wow."

So we talk some more about her mom and dad and all the things that were shattering inside the McKenze mansion, and when she's finally talked out, she asks, "So what's going on with Lady Lana this time?"

I roll my eyes. "Compared to what you're going through, I feel stupid even talking about it." But when I give her a rundown on Loopy Lana's latest greatest, she gasps and says, "Unbelievable!"

"Yeah, but it's not like she's home throwing things and shouting insults, or has a gambling problem."

"Maybe it's like my dad," Marissa says after a minute.

"Maybe your mom knows what she's doing is messing everyone up but can't stop."

"Oh, please. There's no such thing as Selfish Divas Anonymous. She doesn't *have* a problem, she *is* a problem. She just doesn't care about anyone but herself."

Anyway, I did feel better talking it all out, and after we had some snacks with Hudson and Mikey, I invited Marissa to come along with me to get the bridesmaid shoes. I pulled the swatch from my pocket and said, "Can you picture me in a big, puffy lavender dress with matching shoes?"

Marissa's eyes bugged. "Are you serious?"

I nodded and wagged the swatch in front of Mikey. "Can you believe it? Me. In lavender shoes."

It was the first smile I'd seen on him since I'd gotten there.

"Not high-tops, either," I told him, trying to keep the smile going. "Let me tell you—it's gonna be *weird*."

"Can I come?" he asked.

"To see me get lavender shoes? Are you serious? That seems like the boringest thing ever!"

He looked down. "I'll be good."

We all fell quiet. Then Hudson said to him, "Probably not a good adventure for you, m'man. How about another game of foosball?"

My eyebrows went flying. "When did you get foosball?" I turned to Mikey. "How about *you* go get the shoes and I'll stay here and whip Hudson in foosball."

But I could tell—Mikey still wanted to tag along.

Then Marissa gives me the wiggly eye—you know,

trying to tell me something without letting Mikey know she's spilling a secret. And the funny thing is, I understand right away what she's saying.

Mikey doesn't want Marissa to leave.

"Hey," I tell Mikey, "if you want to tag along and witness the incredible sight of me in sissy feet, come on."

He smiles again, so I point at him and say, "But no blackmailing me, you got it?"

He nods, then turns to Hudson and says, "Foosball after, okay?"

Hudson's fine with that, so I leave my skateboard on his porch and off we go to the mall.

Now, the last time Mikey, Marissa, and I walked to the mall together, Mikey complained the whole way about how tired and thirsty and hungry and *tortured* he was. He even lay down on the sidewalk a few times to throw tantrums. Marissa had to drag him along with a *dog* leash, if you can believe that.

But as we're walking along now, he's quiet. Oh, he's huffing and puffing and even kind of grunting, but he's trucking along behind us in a really *determined* way. Everything's pumping—his legs, his chubby little fists, his puffy red cheeks . . . they're all chugging together like he's some Little Engine That Could going up a steep, steep hill. The sidewalk's totally flat, but apparently for Mikey it's like a twenty percent grade.

"Wow," I whisper to Marissa as we're cutting through a mall parking lot, "that's unbelievable."

She nods. "Hudson's like magic. His boot camp over

the summer really helped. And the kids at school noticed, which helped, too."

"Noticed that he's lost weight?"

She nods.

"Hey!" Mikey calls, hurrying to catch up with us. "Can't we take a shortcut through Cheezers?"

"It's longer to the shoe store that way," Marissa says.

"But it's faster to the mall," Mikey says back.

Marissa and I exchange looks, and then Marissa asks him, "Plus, are you sure you're cool with going through a pizza place?"

"I'm cool with going anywhere that's cool," he grumbles, wiping his brow. "And it's a lot *cooler* going *that* way."

I stand there looking at him a second. "You remember the last time we went on a walk?"

"Yeah," he says, kinda glowering. "Don't bug me about it."

"I'm not gonna bug you about it. I just want to say you did a great job keeping up this time."

"Yeah?" he says, wiping his brow again. "Well, you're not even sweating."

I turn to Marissa. "You know what? His shortcut may be longer, but I think this boy has earned some air-conditioning, don't you?"

"Yes, I do!"

"Thank you," he says, heaving a sigh, and off we go to the back door of Cheezers.

Now, every time I go to Cheezers, I swear I'm not going back. It's one of those pizza places that specialize in cardboard crusts and seem to attract bikers. Plus, I don't like going through it as a shortcut to air-conditioning because you've got to go right past the counter, where some grumpy-looking guy gives you the evil eye as you walk by. There are about five of them who work the counter at different shifts, but I think they're all brothers or cousins or something because they've all got dark hair and a moustache and that same don't-push-it-kid way of looking at you.

Anyway, just before we get to the walkway that leaves the parking structure and crosses over to Cheezers, we pass by three gleaming, custom-painted Harley-Davidson motorcycles. One's dark orange with flames painted across the gas tank, one's blackish purple with laughing skulls, and one's royal blue with screaming eagles across it.

"Those are amazing," Marissa says as we stop and gawk. "My dad almost got a Harley, but Mom wouldn't let him."

"When? Recently?"

She shakes her head and eyes Mikey. "Before the Mess."

"Can we *please* go inside?" Mikey asks. He's trying hard not to whine, but he's obviously not happy with us for stopping.

So we scoot along to the back door of Cheezers, and when we get inside, Mikey lets loose a giant "Aaaaah!" and just stands there for a minute with his eyes closed, soaking in the coolness.

"Come on, Mikey!" Marissa calls, because we're already by the counter trying to ignore the Evil-Eye Guy, who's got us pegged as shortcutters.

Now, there's a half wall that divides the order counter and the soda machine area from the picnic table dining room. And because Mikey's now sniffing the air like he's about to have a major junk food relapse, and because we have to go back for him and I'm trying to avoid the Evil-Eye Guy behind the counter on the right, I turn to the left and get a full-on view over the half wall.

The dining room's pretty empty. There's one couple just starting their pizza, and one table of four bikers wearing do-rags who are down to crumbs and beer. And normally, I would just kind of take all that in and keep on walking, but now I do a double take at the do-rag guys because I *know* one of them.

I'd know him anywhere.

And he's the last person on earth I'd expect to see wearing a do-rag.

SIX

I grab Marissa by the arm and do a sly point into the dining area. "Check it out!"

She gasps, then whispers, "That's Mr. *Vince?*" as we both duck behind the half wall and crack up.

Mikey's figured out that something more interesting than cool air and the aroma of pizza is happening by us, so he hurries over. "What's so funny?"

I stand up and shake my head, keeping my back to the dining room. "Never mind."

Marissa stands up, too, and takes another quick look across the divider before following me toward the main door. And we're both still laughing because . . . well . . . even though there's *always* something weird about seeing your teachers outside of school, seeing them drinking beer in a do-rag? That's beyond weird. That's . . . delicious.

"Why don't you guys ever tell me what's going on?" Mikey asks, and he's definitely in whine mode now.

We're out of Cheezers and on the main walk of the mall, so I stop and tell him, "Well . . . you have a history of blackmail, extortion, and tattling, that's why. I don't know if I can *trust* you with secrets."

"You can so!" he says, and he looks kind of hurt.

"Really?" I eye Marissa like, What do you think?

She shrugs. "He's been pretty great on this walk. I think maybe we should test him with one."

So I nod and say to Mikey, "You up for that?"

His eyes get big—well, as big as they can, anyway—and his head bobs like crazy while his whole roly-poly body seems to bounce in place.

"Okay." I lean in and whisper, "You heard Marissa and me talking about my history teacher, right?"

"The Die Dude guy who hates you?"

I shrug. "Yeah, that pretty much sums it up. Anyway, he's in Cheezers with some friends drinking beer and wearing a do-rag!"

"What's a do-rag?"

"One of those head bandannas that motorcycle guys wear? Mr. Vince is the one in a T-shirt. The other guys have on leather jackets. Go check it out."

Mikey starts to scurry back into Cheezers, and Marissa calls, "Be sly, okay?"

He bobbles his head, then disappears inside Cheezers. A minute later he's coming back out, moving like he's part of a top-secret mission. "I can't believe that's your *teacher*."

"Yup," I tell him. "Neither can I." Then I drop my voice like I'm trusting him with something really, really big. "If you ever see him around town, you let me know, okay?"

"Why?" Mikey whispers back. "Is your teacher a *bad* guy?"

Now, when Mikey asks that, I swear his ears stretch up and out and *quiver*. Like they're just twitching to scoop in some classified information. So I drop my voice even further, look from side to side, then say, "His code name is Captain Evil."

"*Really?*" Mikey asks, and his voice is barely a whisper.

So I nod and put my finger in front of my lips. "Top-secret, okay?"

His head bounces up and down like it's dribbling on his shoulders.

I laugh and say, "All right," and give him a chummy slap on the arm. "Now let's go. I've got foo-foo shoes to try on!"

There are very few stores in the mall where I haven't gone in before, but KC Shoes is one of them. For one thing, I get my shoes at the thrift store. But even if I didn't, I wouldn't go to KC's. The mall's other shoe stores have stacks of boxes and you can just serve yourself, but KC's is like an old-time store where you have to ask to see a shoe in a certain size.

Anyway, we go inside, and right away I'm uncomfortable. There are mirrors everywhere and Plexiglas podiums that have shoes displayed like fine art. I'm afraid to touch anything, and I'm worried that Mikey might have a relapse and become Bratty Mikey.

Or Whiny Mikey.

Or Bull-in-a-Shoe-Shop Mikey.

And then I meet Kenny, which doesn't help matters. He's got slicked-back blond hair, a pencil-line moustache that sits right above his lip and comes nowhere *near* his nose, and three gold rings on his right hand and none on his left. He's also wearing the shiniest shoes I've ever seen, and they're blood-red, with thin black laces.

He looks like he probably has a side job selling snake oil.

I pull out the swatch and show it to him. "I'm here to get shoes for a wedding?"

His beady eyes light up, and he gives me a very snaky smile. "You must be Sams!" he says. "Debra told me you'd be coming in today." And in a flash, he's maneuvered me to a seat and is unlacing my right shoe.

Now, let me tell you, this is a weird sensation. For one thing, I always untie my own shoes. For another, he's down on one knee in front of me and has my worn-out high-top resting against his professionally creased pants. Plus, he's holding my foot, and the only other time someone has held my foot like this was on a camping trip when I had the worst blisters in the whole wide world, and that person was Casey.

So I'm sitting there with my foot on his leg, freaking out a little. And I'm trying to get the thought of Casey out of my mind, but it's like being in the doctor's office and knowing that you're about to get a shot. You can't stop thinking about it until it's over.

At least ol' Kenny was fast on the draw. He had my shoe off quick and tried not to seem too grossed out when he took off my sock.

Hey, it was clean when I left the house, but I'd walked clear from Hudson's, so it was a bit steamy, okay?

Anyway, he had me stand my naked foot on a measuring ruler, then zipped into a back room and returned a minute later with two shoe boxes.

"Here we are," he says, sitting on a stool in front of me. He hands me a nylon sock, whips a shoehorn out of his pocket, flips open a shoe box, and produces an all-white, closed-toe stiletto.

I've only got the nylon half on when my eyes bug out at the shoe. "I can't wear those!"

"Wow," Marissa gasps. "Those are high."

Kenny has the shoe at the ready near my foot. "Of course you can," he says. "You'll be smashing in them."

I finish pulling on the nylon. "Yeah, I'll be smashing onto the floor in them!"

"You'll be fine," he tells me with an oily smile. "It's what the other girls are wearing."

"I can't get flats?"

He looks at me like I've just passed gas. "Heavens no!"

"Just do it," Marissa says. "It's only for an hour, right? You can take them off after the ceremony."

So I stick out my foot, and he does this smooth maneuver with the shoehorn that somehow gets my foot inside the shoe. "How's that feel?" he asks.

I stand up and take a few awkward steps. "Freaky," I grumble.

"Tight in the toe?"

"Yes!"

He checks it out, making me wiggle my big toe. "No, it's perfect. The next size will be too big."

So he slips the other shoe on, and I stilt-walk around the store for all of ten ridiculous seconds, then plop back down in my chair. "Whatever," I say, yanking them off.

He boxes them up, tapes the swatch to the lid, and

says, "I'll have them ready Friday after three. Debra's pre-paid them, so I believe we're all set."

"Thanks," I tell him, and we get out of there as fast as my high-tops can take me.

Now, Mikey had been almost invisible inside the shoe store, so I turn to him and say, "That has to be the worst store in the mall, and you were the best you've ever been!"

Marissa nods. "You were great, Mikey."

He smiles at us. "It wasn't easy."

We laugh, and then Marissa asks him, "So, do you want to go to the pet store?" because watching fish swim is Mikey's favorite pastime.

"Is that okay?" he asks.

Marissa looks at me, so I shrug and say, "Sure."

Trouble is, on our way over to the pet store, we go by the food court, and who do we run into?

The Queen of Mean.

The Ear-to-Ear Sneer.

The one and only Heather Acosta.

She's not alone, either. She's hanging out with her friends Monet and Tenille and a few guys from school. There's Lars Teppler, who I've got in a couple of classes, and David Olsen from Mr. Vince's class, and then there's Billy Pratt.

"Oooh, baby!" Heather calls over to me. "Rebounding hard, huh?"

I give her a look like, *What?*

She points to Mikey. "But you and Blubber Boy look so right together!"

It's been a long time since I've flattened Heather. Oh,

I've had the *urge*—I've just managed to control it. But now I had the urge, and believe me, it was overwhelming. And it wasn't because of some ridiculous insult Heather Acosta was throwing at me—she's always throwing insults at me.

It was Mikey.

She'd called him Blubber Boy like he wasn't even there.

Before I know what I'm doing, I yank her out of her seat and shove her about five feet across the food court. "He's got feelings, you know."

She laughs, but it's a nervous laugh because Heather Acosta's been on the receiving end of my fist before. "Yeah?" she says, trying to act all cocky. "Sorry I didn't see them. Probably because they're buried under all that *fat*."

I stop and just stare at her. Then I look over my shoulder at her group of friends. "Why do you guys want to hang out with a person who makes fun of little kids?"

I've got to hand it to her—even when she's shaking in her shoes, Heather's got nerve. "Hey," she says, "he's not *little*, and I was making fun of *you*."

I stare at her a minute, then shake my head. "You're unbelievable."

And at that moment I knew that flattening her wasn't worth it.

It wouldn't change anything.

So I just turned my back on all of them and said to Marissa and Mikey, "Come on. Let's go check out some fish."

"Wow," Mikey whispered as we started to walk away. "Who was that?"

And then he did something really sweet.

And totally embarrassing.

He slipped his pudgy little hand into mine.

I could tell it was just a reflex. Something he'd done with his mom and dad and sister over the years. And part of me wanted to hold on tight and protect him, but part of me wanted to shake him off.

Like Heather needed any more ammunition?

But I held on, and I looked at him and said, "Her name's Heather and she's spiteful and wicked and you should ignore everything she said. You're doing amazing on your diet, and I'm very proud of you."

"Really?" he asked, looking up at me.

"Really," I told him, and Marissa put her arm across his shoulders and agreed. "Really, Mikey. You are."

Mikey took a long look back at Heather, and we wound up having to kind of drag him along. "Fish, Mikey. Remember?" Marissa said. "We're going to look at fish."

I actually hate the mall's pet store. It's got no dogs or cats or even hamsters anymore. Just fish and snakes and turtles. Oh, they sell *accessories* for dogs and cats, but not the actual pet.

Plus, the place smells. I don't know why, seeing how there's nothing to clean up after, but it still smells like someone ought to be cleaning up after something, if you know what I mean.

So, anyway, I have a pretty low tolerance for the place to begin with, but now it was even worse because I was still all steamed about Heather. And Billy. Maybe Billy *more* than Heather. I mean, he's supposedly my friend. He knows how evil Heather is. What's he doing hanging out with her?

But on top of stewing about them and hating the smell, there's some guy running the self-service pet tag machine and the sound is driving me up a wall. No matter where I go in the store, I can hear it eeking and screeching. And after the guy's made, like, *six* tags, I start wondering if there's something *wrong* with him. I mean, yeah, the first time I saw the machine work, I was pretty entertained, but c'mon. This guy's standing there with his inch-thick glasses, making tag after tag after tag. Why does he need so many tags? Does he keep messing up? Did someone dump a litter of puppies on his doorstep? Is he a tag-making weirdo? I even hang out behind him for a few minutes trying to see what he's doing, but I finally can't take it anymore and just ask Marissa, "Can we get out of here?"

So we grab Mikey and leave. And since we're really near Cheezers and it's an actual shortcut to go out that way, that's the way we go.

Funny thing is, Mr. Vince is still there, still drinking beer. Only he's no longer wearing the do-rag, and now it's just him and one other guy. The guy's big. And his face is blocky and kind of *gray*. Like a big piece of chiseled granite.

Mr. Vince, on the other hand, is definitely red around the edges. He's the one talking, and he's jabbing his finger onto the table like he's pretty upset about something.

"I'm glad he's not my teacher," Mikey whispers.

Marissa nods. "Maybe he's telling his friend about Die Dude!"

I grumble, "He oughta get over it already!" and head for the side door.

And really, as we walked through the parking lot and passed by the laughing-skulls motorcycle that was still there, I wasn't thinking about Mr. Vince. I was too upset about Heather, and Billy, and Heather's stupid comment. Because as much as I hated to admit it, Heather's jab made me think about Casey. She'd said he'd moved on, and from what evidence I had, it looked like she was right.

So, no. I didn't care about Mr. Vince.

Didn't give him another thought.

Not until Monday morning rolled around.

SEVEN

Monday morning, it was obvious that Mr. Vince was still not over it. The only thing he said throughout homeroom was, "That was the tardy bell, people. Sit down!" He had Cole Glenns lead the Pledge and Ellie Statum read the announcements, and after that he just sat at the back of the classroom sort of hunched into the time-out chair.

All of us were a little nervous about the way he was acting. Teachers can freak you out because you never know what they're *really* thinking. And when they act like Mr. Vince was acting, well, it can definitely unravel your nerves. You start wondering, Is he mad at the class? Does he have a headache?

Has he got Montezuma's revenge?

Is he hung over?

About to hurl?

With teachers, you can never really tell.

Anyway, when the dismissal bell finally rang, I got out of there fast and ran right into Billy Pratt.

"Sammy-keyesta!" he says. "Lookin' *muy bonita*."

"Don't kiss up to me," I tell him. "I'm mad at you."

"Hey!" he says, and all of a sudden he's serious. "I just happened to run into her when I was at the mall, okay?"

"No. Not okay."

"I can't even stand in the same place as her?"

"No."

"Look, she's Casey's sister. And he's one of my best buds—what am I supposed to do?"

I frown at him. "After what she said about Marissa's little brother, you should have left. Maybe even followed us. You know—as a sign of solidarity or something?" I shake my head. "It's bad enough that kids at Mikey's school pick on him for being fat. He doesn't need Heather piling on! And he sure doesn't need other people acting like it's okay!"

"I'm sorry," he says, which sort of throws me because he sounds so serious, and it's not like Billy to be serious about anything.

He shrugs. "And you're right, I should have left." He wraps his arms around me. "Don't be mad, Sammy-keyesta."

I tell him, "Thanks," and give him a quick slap-pat on the back.

He hugs me harder.

"Okay, Billy. Let go. That's enough," I say into his shirt.

"I'm an anaconda from Rwanda. Hug me back or I attack."

"Oh, good grief, Billy, stop."

"Hug me," he says, squeezing the life out of me.

I don't know what it is about Billy, but instead of being

mad or annoyed, I hug him back and laugh. "Okay, okay. We're good." Then I break away and head for class, calling, "Vince is acting like the Psycho Barfer today."

"The Psycho Barfer?" He grins. "Can't wait!"

So, once again, Billy's managed to put me in a pretty good mood, which helped me focus in my math and language classes. And after break I'm on my way to Mr. Vince's class when Billy catches up to me and keeps the good mood going. "Beware the Psycho Barfer!" he hacks out, and then starts spazzing, making like he's hurling his cookies over everyone and everything in the vicinity, including Cisco.

"Easy, man!" Cisco tells him, but when Billy doesn't let up, Cisco pulls a mop out of his cleaning cart and plays along, pretending to clean up after him.

So it turns into a real comedy act, and a bunch of us are laughing so hard watching it that we wind up having to race through the sound of the tardy bell to make it to class on time.

My good mood totally crashes, though, when I get into class. Heather gives me the evil eye as I slide into my chair, and Mr. Vince is up at his podium looking grumpy as ever. He passes back our homework papers and couldn't care less that mine's nowhere to be found.

"But I know I turned it in!" I tell him. I point to the in-basket on the counter at the side of the room. "I put it right there!"

"Then why don't I have it?" he says with a frown.

Lars Teppler interrupts our wonderful conversation by shoving his paper in front of Vince. "Why'd you give me an F on this?" He points to some scribbles in the margin of his paper. "What does this say?"

Lars is tall and gangly, and has feathery brown hair that sort of swooshes around his head from right to left. It's like his hair is in its own little universe of powerful centrifugal forces. And from the rapid whooshing of his head, I can tell that Lars is *totally* ticked off, so I back up.

Ol' Scratch 'n' Spit squints at his own writing. "It says, 'I can't read your writing.' "

Lars swooshes his head. "What?! I can't read *your* writing!"

"That was my point," Mr. Vince says like he's oh-so-clever, even though his scribbles are *never* legible.

"But last time you gave me an F for not using complete sentences, and my writing was just like this!"

Mr. Vince shrugs. "So maybe next time you'll get it right." Then he walks away.

Lars just stands there for a minute, stock-still, until finally his head does a slow-motion swoosh and he goes back to his seat.

The class gets completely quiet, and we all just sit there staring at Mr. Vince as he messes with stuff on his desk and then pulls open one of the drawers.

And that's when it happens.

Mr. Vince makes a horrified face and lets out a sound that no teacher in the history of teaching has made in any classroom anywhere *ever*. He stares inside the drawer with his eyes peeled back and his jaw dangling down, and what comes out of his mouth is a gasp and a choke and a cry and a strangled scream and a cough and a barfing sound all wrapped into one.

His eyes roll back in his head and he wobbles for a minute, and then he does something I never in a million years thought I'd see ol' Scratch 'n' Spit do.

He faints.

First we all jump. Then we just sit in our seats with our eyes bugged out and our jaws dangling. And then half of us rush up to him, but nobody seems to want to take charge, so we just stand there looking down at him lying on his side on the floor.

I can hear Sasha Stamos at the back of the room using the classroom phone to dial the office, and all at once people around me start jabbering.

"Do you think he had a heart attack?"

"Somebody take his pulse!"

"Who knows CPR?"

"No way I'm giving him mouth-to-mouth!"

Still, nobody actually *does* anything, so *I'm* finally the one to drop down and poke around on the side of his neck for a pulse. "His heart's beating."

"His heart's beating!" Tracy Arnold relays back to Sasha.

"His heart's beating!" Sasha says into the phone.

"Is he breathing?" someone asks. And then, like this was some magic key to respiration, Mr. Vince's mouth snaps open and he takes in a giant, scary gasp of air.

Well, there I am, hovering right over him, so what's the first thing he sees when he opens his eyes?

Me.

And between his scary gasp and his eyes flying open, I'm sure I look like I just put my finger in a light socket.

"Ah!" he cries when he sees me, and for a split second I think he's going to faint all over again. Instead, he points at me and says, "You! *You* put that rat in my drawer!"

"Rat? What rat?"

"You think I didn't see you laughing at me yesterday?" he rasps.

"Wait . . . What?"

But of course now everyone remembers that Mr. Vince had been freaking out about something inside his drawer, so they all zoom over to his desk. Tracy Arnold squeals, "Eeeew!" and it's not the spit cup she's eeeewing at.

It's a rat.

A hunchy-backed, matted monster of a dead rat with eyes frozen open and lips curled up and away from its long, sharp yellow teeth.

Jake Meers has it by the tail for everyone to see. I swear the thing's a foot and a half long from tail to nose, and dangling from around the rat's mangy neck is a little chain with a metal tag on it.

A bone-shaped *dog* tag.

"What's the tag say?" Heather asks.

Jake holds the rat higher and turns the tag, and his face morphs into a great big *Uh-oh*.

"Read it," David Olsen demands.

Jake pulls a face. "It says, 'Die Dude'!"

Suddenly Mr. Foxmore is standing beside us. "What happened?" he asks Mr. Vince as he helps him off the floor. "Are you all right?"

"No!" Mr. Vince snaps. "And this time you can't just tell me to erase it. You need to *do* something about it!"

"About what?" Mr. Foxmore asks, because apparently he's been so focused on Mr. Vince on the floor that he's somehow missed the monster rat dangling in the air.

Jake Meers steps forward. "Uh, he passed out when he found this in his desk drawer," he says, holding out the rat and showing him the tag.

Mr. Vince staggers toward his roll-around chair. "I'm not feeling so well."

"Did you hit your head?" Mr. Foxmore asks.

Mr. Vince feels around for bruises and bumps, but Angie Johnson, who had a front-row view, says, "He didn't go down *wham*. He more like crumpled and lay down."

Mr. Foxmore turns back to Mr. Vince. "Do you have a history of fainting?"

Mr. Vince glowers at him. "Yeah, right. I'm just a little pansy fainter."

Mr. Foxmore stares at him.

"No!" Mr. Vince snaps. "I don't have a history of fainting." Then he looks straight at me and says, "Someone's threatening to kill me."

"Oh, good grief," I mutter, and excuse myself through the crowd so I can sit down in my seat and be done with his ridiculous implications.

But as I push through the semicircle of students, I notice Heather Acosta off to the side, talking to Billy Pratt.

Right away, Billy pulls a face like, Sorry! and puts some distance between him and Heather.

Still, it bugs me.

What am I, his watchdog?

Does he act one way when I'm around and another when I'm not?

Or . . . is there something he's *hiding* from me?

And then I remember what Hudson had said about Billy, and for the first time I wonder—*Is* Billy the prankster?

Now, it's not that I think a gross dead rat in a drawer is worth fainting over. Actually, seeing a grown man faint over a rat, no matter how big or ugly it is, is a little shocking. Especially since Mr. Vince has always been blustery and gruff and totally gross himself. I mean, if he's gonna faint over the sight of an ugly rat, he ought to pass out every morning when he looks in the mirror.

But that aside, I didn't think the rat-in-the-drawer thing was very funny.

I thought it was kinda *mean.*

Which put me in sort of an odd place in my head. Part of me's thinking how stupid Mr. Vince is, how embarrassing it is that he fainted over a rat, and what a jerk he is for implying it was *me,* but part of me's feeling almost sorry for him.

I mean, who puts a disgusting dead rat in somebody's drawer?

Not somebody who loves ya, that's for sure.

Anyway, Mr. Foxmore's on his walkie-talkie, arranging for someone to take Mr. Vince to a doctor to get checked over, and Mr. Vince isn't saying, No, no, that's okay. I'll be fine.

Nope.

He just sits and waits.

And then when *Cisco* arrives to roll him out of the building in an old *desk* chair, Mr. Vince grumbles, "This is the best they could do? Send a janitor? What am I, the garbage?"

Like, du-uh.

Anyway, when he's gone, Mr. Foxmore turns to us and says, "In your seats."

Everyone sits.

And fast.

Then he walks to the back of the classroom, picks up the phone, punches in a number, and says, "This is Blaine Foxmore, vice principal at William Rose Junior High School. We've had a death threat incident here at the school that requires a police report. . . . Uh-huh . . . Uh-huh . . . That is correct. . . . I appreciate it. Thank you." He hangs up and silences us with one of his ninja looks. "Find something constructive to do and ignore the bells. No one leaves until I say so."

EIGHT

When we finally hear footsteps coming up the classroom ramp, I look over my shoulder and who do I see walk through the door with his forearm in a cast?

The Treadmill Tumbler.

The Lavender Lover.

The one and only Officer Borsch.

Now, maybe I should have been happy to see Officer Borsch, but I wasn't. I was embarrassed. For one thing, it had taken him almost a year to figure out that I was not a problem child.

Or a juvenile delinquent.

Or a serial jaywalker.

Well, okay, maybe I *am* a serial jaywalker, but it had taken him a year to learn to look the other way.

Anyway, Officer Borsch had been at our school on official business several times last year because of something that somehow involved me, and I was afraid he would take one look at me and backslide into thinking that I was at the bottom of this Die Dude business.

The *other* thing was that I'd somehow gone from

being someone he thought was a problem child to someone who was in his wedding party.

Talk about feeling awkward.

Especially since from the minute he walked through Mr. Vince's door, I couldn't stop picturing him in a lavender bow tie and cummerbund.

And sure enough, when Officer Borsch spots me, his face goes all, Oh no, Sammy, *now* what? Then he sees *Heather,* and he looks at me like, Not this again! But *then* his expression goes totally blank, and he acts like he doesn't even know me.

First he has a little hush-hush conversation with Mr. Foxmore.

Then he gets a little tour of the crime scene.

Then he places the rat in a big plastic bag.

And finally he clears his throat and says to the class, "Death threats, no matter how funny you think they are, are still death threats. So here's what we're going to do. Mr. Foxmore will release you from class one at a time. I will be outside waiting, and you will stop and answer a few questions. What you say will be kept confidential, and since aiding and abetting can have the same punishment as the crime itself, be smart and come clean about what you know." He takes a deep breath through his nose, then says, "Holding out always backfires. We can do this the easy way or the hard way. It's up to you."

Now, I *know* Officer Borsch. I actually kinda *understand* Officer Borsch. And part of what I understand about him is, he doesn't get kids.

Especially not teens.

I mean, if he thinks his little speech is going to get a peep out of any of us, he's living in Loony Land. Maybe his intimidation techniques work with some people, but eighth graders?

Please.

Every single person in class is thinking, What a dope! You expect me to squeal about the rat? That'll make *me* a rat!

And even though he's in uniform, he just looks like a big, blustery cop who couldn't chase you down if his life depended on it.

Especially since his forearm is in a cast.

Now, during all this, Mr. Foxmore has been on and off his walkie-talkie half a dozen times. He's also been in and out the door a bunch because the bell to change classes had rung and some of Mr. Vince's fourth-period students hadn't heard their "Report to the media center" announcement.

But now he's focusing on getting us moving. And since they're using roll sheets to release us in alphabetical order, Heather is the first one out the door.

The rest of us are not allowed to look out the window.

We're not allowed to talk to each other.

And we're sure not allowed to text.

Now, it's not like they're *flying* through the list of names, but they're not really dragging it out, either. And while we're all waiting for our names to be called, we're trying to be quiet, but everyone's jittery. Angie Johnson is biting her nails, Sasha Stamos' foot is wagging like crazy under her desk, Lars Teppler keeps pushing buttons on his watch, Jake Meers is spit-washing his rat-hoisting fingers and wiping them on his socks, David Olsen is doodling on his binder . . . everyone's moving something.

Everyone except Billy Pratt.

He's just sitting there, hunched over and quiet.

And then all of a sudden Mr. Foxmore snaps, "That's mine," from over by the door, and in an instant he's at Billy's desk and has snatched Billy's phone right out of his hands.

"Huh, what?" Billy says, because it happened so quick.

"You and I met in my office last Thursday," Mr. Foxmore says, scrolling through Billy's phone. He eyes him. "Do you recall that, Mr. Pratt?"

Billy gulps and nods.

"Hmm," he says, studying the phone. "I'll have to invite Heather to expand on this message."

"She's just goofin' around," Billy says with a laugh.

Mr. Foxmore gives him a sharp look. "And you're just stayin' after school." He pockets the phone. "I'm sure you remember where my office is, don't you, Mr. Pratt?"

"Yes, sir," Billy says.

Mr. Foxmore moves across the room and looks out the window, then checks the roll sheet and scans the room until his gaze stops on me. "Samantha, you're next."

And that's when it finally hits me that I'm in a bad position.

For one thing, he knows who I am.

Why?

Because I really, really, *really* tried to get out of Mr. Vince's class.

Why?

Because I hate the guy.

Plus, after what Mr. Vince said when he woke up from his little nap on the floor, I'm obviously his number one suspect!

I grab my stuff and head for the door, and at the bottom of the ramp I go right up to Officer Borsch and tell him, "I *promise* you, I had nothing to do with this."

"Good enough for me," he says.

I hesitate. "Really . . . ?"

He shrugs. "Go to your next class."

I let out a puffy-cheeked breath. "Thank you."

So I hurry over to the locker room, change for PE, and get out to the fields in time to do a few soccer drills before we're sent back in. Then I race over to the tables where our group hangs out during lunch and find Marissa already huddled up with Holly and Dot.

"Hey!" she says. "We heard about the rat!"

"Yeah!" Dot says, sipping from her can of root beer. "People are saying Billy did it."

"Billy?" At first I'm relieved to hear this, but then I'm not. "That's Heather's fault. She sent him a text, and Mr. Foxmore intercepted it."

"Intercepted it?" Holly asks. "How'd that happen?"

So I explain about the whole interrogation process and about Billy getting his phone confiscated and all that. And then I tell them what Mr. Vince said when he woke up and how Mr. Foxmore knew my name and how I was worried that they thought *I* was the one who'd put the rat in his desk. "Officer Borsch was the cop taking the report, though, and he just let me go."

Holly laughs. "Wow. Six months ago he would have locked you up!"

Dot laughs, too. "And thrown away the key!"

Which makes Marissa totally switch subjects by launching into the story about me being in Officer Borsch's wedding and having to wear spiky lavender shoes. And while Holly's and Dot's jaws are hitting the ground about that, I happen to notice Billy over by the side of the cafeteria.

And who's standing next to him, practically chewing off his ear?

Heather Acosta.

They're alone, too.

"What is going *on* with them?" I mutter.

"Who?" Marissa asks, interrupting herself.

I nod over Holly's shoulder. "Heather and Billy." I watch them a minute, then say, "Wow. I wonder if he really *did* do it."

Now, even though he's clear across the way, Billy sees us looking at him, and all of a sudden he's hurrying away from Heather. "You're right," Marissa says. "He's acting really guilty."

But later, on my way into science, Billy scoots up next to me and whispers, "She's stalking me, okay? And I didn't leave that rat!"

Then Heather appears.

"Talk later," he whispers, and ditches me quick.

All through science, and then all through drama, things were kinda weird. Billy didn't joke around or make any kind of comments at all, actually, which I think was a first. He was just . . . quiet.

Maybe he was worried about having to see Mr. Foxmore after school.

Maybe things hadn't gone so well with Officer Borsch and he had to see Mr. Foxmore about more than just his phone.

Maybe he really *had* put the Die Dude Rat in Mr. Vince's drawer.

Still, as much as I was trying not to be duped by Billy, I didn't *want* it to be him. So my brain scrambled around for another answer, and it kept coming back to Heather.

Maybe she was trying to get Billy involved in one of her stupid little schemes.

But . . . if that was the case, why didn't Billy just tell her to get lost?

Then I remembered—he hadn't told her to get lost when she'd been so rude to Mikey and me at the mall, either, and that had happened before any of this dead rat stuff.

But after a while my brain felt fried from going in circles, so I told myself that I was probably making things too complicated. Maybe it was just simple.

Maybe Billy Pratt wasn't such a great friend after all.

But on my way home after school, I was cruising along the mall's winding walkway when a thought came flying at me so hard and so fast that I stumbled off my skateboard and almost fell over.

"That must be it!" I gasped.

It was the perfect explanation.

NINE

The next morning I cornered Billy before school and said, "She's blackmailing you, isn't she?"

He blinks at me. "No!"

"Aha!" I cry. "You didn't even ask who 'she' was!"

That flustered him. And even though he tried to cover up by saying, "I didn't have to!" I knew I was onto something.

"What's she got on you, Billy?"

"Stop it!" He dodges around me. "You're making me all claustrophobic!"

I chase after him and try to be a little, you know, *gentler*. "Come on, Billy. You don't want to get in deeper than you already are."

He stops. "Deeper in what?"

I look up at the sky. "Ummm. Let's see . . . How'd it go after school yesterday?"

He just stares at me.

"You know, with Mr. Foxmore? Did he grill you? Did you get your phone back? What did Heather's text say?"

"Yes, he grilled me, and *yes*, I got my phone back."

He switches to a chipper British accent. "It was my first infraction with a telly, after all. Henceforth, I'm to be a jolly good chap and keep it off and away during class. It is not to reside on my personage!"

"Boy, you got off easy. Especially since he'd seen you about, you know, séancing dead people?"

He switches back to Billyspeak. "Hey, if you're making the leap to dead *rats,* like everybody else seems to be, I didn't do it." He frowns, and it's like *poof,* a heavy, dark cloud forms over his head. "I swear," he says, "I had nothing to do with that rat."

In all the times I'd seen Billy scolded for clowning around in class, and in all the times I'd seen him sent to the office, I'd never seen him look this serious. So I soften up a bit and say, "Billy, I know something's going on. So if it's not the rat, what is it?" Then I shrug and say, "*Or* if you've decided to align yourself with that evil witch, just say so and quit pretending to be my friend."

He looks at me.

Looks away.

Looks at me.

Looks away.

"Billy, it's *me.* Just tell me."

He looks all around, then breaks down. "Maaaan, I am in so much trouble."

I let out a big, puffy-faced breath. "Okay. Thank you. Now let me help you."

"I'm going to be in boiling hot water if people find out!" He shakes his head. "They'll probably expel me, and then my life will be over."

"Billy," I say, gripping him by the shoulders, "just tell me."

He pinches his eyes closed for a second, then blurts out, "I did that Die Dude on the board, okay? It was actually Heather's idea. I was dressed like a soldier and just goofing around, going, 'Die, dude! Die, dude!' She said it would be a crack-up if I wrote it on the board and pulled down the screen so when Vince rolled it up, *bam*, there it'd be. But while I was writing it, she took a picture of me with her phone!"

"Wait. Without you knowing?"

He nods. "And after she showed it to me, she started making me do stuff like get her lunch and tie her shoe. . . . She was acting like it was a joke, so I just played along, but now that that *rat* showed up, she's like, Do my homework and Give me twenty bucks."

"Or she'll tell?"

"Yeah! And she's serious! She says Foxmore'll never believe I did one and not the other!"

"That evil snake." I think about it a minute, then say, "Just tell Foxmore the truth."

"I can't! Heather's right—he'll never believe me!" Billy wipes sweat away from under his mop of hair. "Man, I should never have told you! If you—"

"Don't worry! I'm not going to tell anyone. I promise."

He heaves a sigh of relief.

I grab his arm. "Look, we'll figure something out, okay?"

He nods, and when the tardy bell rings, he puts on his

class clown smile and hurries away, calling, "See ya, Sammy-keyesta!" like he doesn't have a care in the world.

So there I am, watching him go, trying to figure out what I can do to help him, when a voice next to me asks, "Hey, wassup?"

I jump a little, and there's Lars Teppler standing right beside me. I blink at him a bunch because I may have him in homeroom and in Mr. Vince's class, but I only *sort* of know him, and he's never said "Hey, wassup?" to me before. "Sorry," he says with a laugh. "Didn't mean to spook you."

I laugh, too. "And I didn't mean to spaz."

He flips his head around to the left, whooshing his hair out of his eyes as we start toward homeroom. "Freaky class yesterday, huh?"

"No kidding."

"I don't know why *we* were automatically the criminals. That rat could have been planted way before any of us got there." He whooshes his hair again. "You think that cop got anything out of anyone?"

I snort. "No."

"He sure let *you* off easy," he says, smiling at me.

It's a strange smile. Like only half his mouth is trying. And it makes a little tingle creep up my neck because I remember how I'd noticed him pushing buttons on his watch.

He'd been *timing* us?

All of a sudden it hits me that maybe I should have hung out and chatted with the Borschman a little instead of jetting out of there. All of a sudden I'm thinking that maybe getting off easy was going to turn around and make things *hard* for me.

"Yeah?" I ask, looking at him all surprised. "Didn't feel like it to me."

We're at Vince's class now, so we go inside, only we're not greeted by the sunny attitude of the Spit Collector telling us to sit down and shut up. No, it's Mr. Foxmore at the podium, and apparently he doesn't need the words *sit down* or *shut up* in his vocabulary because everyone does it automatically.

He doesn't explain why he's there or say anything about Mr. Vince. He just leads us in the Pledge, then reads the announcements. It's actually the first time all year that I've been able to *hear* the announcements because no one else is talking. Plus, he's reading them like they matter. He says stuff like, "Here's one that concerns most of you," and then launches into the announcement. Or he reads one and adds, "You kids really ought to try that club— sounds like something that would get you involved in doing good things for your community."

Anyway, when he's done with homeroom business, he says, "I'm sure you're wondering about Mr. Vince. I'm pleased to report that he's fine, and he'll be back tomorrow. For those of you who have a class with him later in the day, be assured a real substitute will be arriving shortly." He smiles at us. "I guess you'd say I'm the substitute's substitute." Then he adds, "I certainly appreciate how well behaved you've been this morning. I've already taken roll, so go ahead and get yourselves ready for first period."

Now, the funny thing is, for all the grumbling and complaining and yelling Mr. Vince does to get us to mind him, homeroom has never been this civilized. It's like Mr. Vince has told us how horrible we are so many times that we don't even care about being good.

I mean, why bother?

Anyway, I spend a couple of minutes getting my binder in order and reviewing my planner, and then I decide to sharpen my pencil for math, which I have right after homeroom. And I would have just gone up, sharpened, and gone back to my seat like a good little girl, only while I'm cranking away, I happen to notice that Mr. Foxmore is clicking away at Mr. Vince's computer.

Something about the way he's doing it feels really intense to me. He's sort of hunched forward, and he's moving the mouse around fast. So I keep that pencil sharpener going, and I see that what he's doing is checking the history list.

Not one that has anything to do with the classes Mr. Vince teaches.

No, the one that shows what Internet sites Mr. Vince has been to recently.

Mr. Foxmore clicks on the next link in the list, and up pops a picture of a set of golf clubs.

He closes that window and clicks on the next link, and up pops a road map to who knows where.

Next comes a video of a dog riding a skateboard.

Then a gleaming cherry red motorcycle.

Then another video that's just starting to play when Mr. Foxmore catches me watching him.

Real quick, he shrinks the window and ninjas me a look that sends me back to my seat. Then when the dismissal bell rings about a minute later, he says, "Have a productive day," in a kind of chummy way as he ushers us out. He even smiles at me, like, See ya.

Now, the teachers' computers belong to the school, so I guess the vice principal ought to be able to use them. But something about Mr. Foxmore nosing around on Mr. Vince's computer felt a little . . . sneaky.

Like he was digging through Mr. Vince's desk drawers.

And really, I shouldn't have cared. I mean, in the few weeks we've been in school, Mr. Vince has probably already given us eight in-class worksheets, and while we sweat to find answers in the textbook, he's up at his desk "working" at his computer.

The monitor faces away from the class, so it's not like we can see what Mr. Vince is doing, but anytime someone comes near his desk, he always shrinks the page and gives them an annoyed look. Like he's in the middle of something really, really important, and how can we be so dumb as to not know how to do a simple worksheet ourselves?

So knowing that ol' Vincy-poo's been surfing the Web really ought to tick me off at *him,* but it's weird—it's like Mr. Foxmore is the one who's being sneaky.

Sneakier, even, than Mr. Vince.

Anyway, I head over to math and try to forget about the whole Mr. Vince stupidity, then go to language, where

Ms. Needer spends the class period instructing us on the differences between similes, metaphors, and analogies. I try to concentrate, but my mind keeps wandering, and boy, am I glad to bust out of there when the bell for break finally rings.

Marissa's already waiting for me at the tables, eating a breakfast bar and swigging water. Marissa used to buy her snack and her lunch at school, but since her family's gone into crisis mode, she's been packing food from home, just like me.

Anyway, besides eating, she's also standing there doing the McKenze Fidget. I used to call it the McKenze Dance because when she got nervous Marissa would bite her thumbnail and squirm around like she had to use the bathroom. It's a lot more subtle now—she just sort of twitches at the knees—but I still know what it means.

"Hey," I say, plopping down my backpack. "What's wrong?"

She doesn't even try to pretend it's nothing. "I think my parents are going to split up."

"Aw, don't doom-and-gloom. They're just fighting over money. They'll figure it out."

She shakes her head. "Mikey and I moved into Hudson's last night."

"Wait a minute—you're *living* there?"

She nods, then bursts into tears. "My dad got totally drunk and was talking crazy stuff. Mom called Hudson, and he came and picked us up."

"But . . . if they're splitting up, why didn't she leave *with* you guys?"

"She doesn't trust Dad to be alone in the house! She's afraid of what he'll do."

"You mean like hurt himself?"

"Like hurt the *house*." She drops her voice to barely a whisper. "He was talking about torching it!"

I blink at her. "He was talking about burning down your house?"

"Shhhh! Yes! That way they could get the insurance money for it and all their artwork and stuff. It would be, like, three million dollars!"

I blink at her harder. "He would never get away with it!"

"No kidding!" She crumples onto the bench as she says, "Everything's gone all crazy!"

I sit next to her and give her a hug. "Look. It's like a really fierce storm, okay? But it will pass and the sun will come out and everything will settle down. For now, you just have to hold on tight and not get pitched overboard."

She wipes away her tears and snorts, "You just got out of Needer's class, huh? Nice simile."

It takes me a second to switch gears, but when I catch up to her, I laugh. "You sure it's not an analogy? Or a metaphor?"

Holly and Dot join us just as the bell rings, and Holly asks, "What happened?" because it's pretty obvious that Marissa has been crying.

"Oh, nothing," Marissa says. "Just stupid ol' Danny again."

Dot frowns. "I thought you dumped him!"

Now, it's probably on account of Mr. McKenze being

in some kind of success competition with his brother—who's Santa Martina's very own "celebrity" eye surgeon—that Marissa hardly ever lets on that things at home are less than perfect. Oh, she does to me, but to the rest of the world? She tries to keep that under wraps. It's, like, drilled into her brain by her dad not to talk about their problems. So I'm not surprised to hear her make up a story, even to Holly and Dot. I'm also not surprised that the story has something to do with Danny Urbanski. For one thing, it's easy—he's in high school now, just like Casey, and he's not around to contradict her. For another, it's totally believable—Danny's nothing but a smooth-talking liar who is really good at making Marissa cry.

Holly obviously agrees with Dot. "He's probably hitting on every new girl he meets at the high school."

I look at Marissa and play along. "You've got to get over him, Marissa. Even Casey's not friends with him anymore."

And just like that, Marissa's off the hook and I'm *on* it. "Hey," Holly says, turning to me. "What's going on with you and Casey, anyway? I saw him at your building yesterday. He went up to the second floor, stopped, just stood there forever, then turned around."

I look over both shoulders and drop my voice when I say, "You saw him on the *fire escape?*" because that part of the Senior Highrise is right across Broadway from where she lives.

She nods. "I tried to call you, but your phone was busy for, like, an *hour.*"

"What time was it?"

She thinks back. "About seven?"

"Shoot. Grams was on the phone a *lot* yesterday trying to get ahold of my mom."

"We're going to be late," Dot says, heading for class. "The bell rang ages ago!"

Holly follows her because they have the same third period, and Marissa and I chase after them, even though our classes aren't in that direction. "Are you sure it was him?"

Holly nods. "Positive." She laughs. "You're not the only one with binoculars, you know."

I have to break away from her or I'll be late, too, so I call, "But what was he *doing*?"

"I have no idea!" she calls back. "I'll see you at lunch!"

"See you at lunch!" we all shout at each other, then scatter to our separate corners of school.

TEN

The substitute in Mr. Vince's class was really nice but
didn't know much about history. "I'm a Spanish teacher,"
she told us, "and I received no real lesson plans, so I'm
afraid I'm going to have to ask you to just read quietly at
your desks."

Sasha Stamos whips out her history book and starts
pawing through it. "We just finished chapter two. Should
we start chapter three?"

Everyone glares at Sasha as the substitute smiles and
says, "Thank you. Yes. Please start reading chapter three."
And while she's looking through Mr. Vince's copy of our
textbook for page numbers to write on the board, I notice
Heather giving Sasha the extreme evil eye.

I guess Sasha picked up on the vibe, because she turns
to me and whispers, "What's *her* problem?"

I shrug. "You just turned free day into assignment day,
and she will never forget it."

"Free day?" She blinks at me. "What?"

"Never mind."

And then she gets it. "Oooooh!" She looks around at
the rest of the class and mouths, "Sorry!"

I lean forward. "Don't expect Heather to accept your apology."

"But . . . you do?"

"Hey, it's no big deal." She still seems to be worried about it, though, so I whisper, "Look, you're right, and the rest of us are wrong. It's just, this is *Vince's* class, you know?"

She whispers, "So why do we even have to come to it?" I give her a beats-me shrug and she faces forward, but a minute later she's talking to me again. "And pointing out that Heather is texting right now would be . . . ?"

"Oooh, very bad," I whisper back. "Suicidal, in fact. Everyone would think you're a rat, and Heather would find some big-time way to pay you back."

"This is stupid," she says, and turns around again.

Heather *is* texting. She's doing a good job of hiding it because her book is open in front of her and it looks like she's reading from it, but both her hands are under her desk and her thumbs are definitely moving.

I check over my shoulder to see if Billy's breaking his little phone probation, but both of his hands are visible and he's actually reading.

Well, there's probably a comic book on top of his history book, but still. He's reading.

And then I notice that Sasha is totally glaring at Heather.

I lean forward and whisper, "You might not want to get in a war with her. Take it from me—it's not worth it."

She glances at me and says, "She doesn't scare me."

I pull back with a little snort. "She should."

This time when Sasha faces forward, she stays that way. So I open my history book and get started on the language worksheet Ms. Needer gave us in second period. Trouble is, the worksheet has us identify metaphors, similes, and analogies, and it makes me think about Marissa, which makes me think about our conversation at break, which makes me think about Holly seeing Casey on the fire escape of the Senior Highrise.

What was he *doing* there?

He won't call me but now he's going up the fire escape?

Or maybe he *had* tried to call but the line was busy. Grams had been on the phone a *lot*.

Anyway, by the time class lets out, I've forgotten all about Sasha Stamos and her little evil-eye exchange with Heather, but Sasha sure hasn't. She's watching Heather very carefully.

Heather's oblivious—mostly because she's texting as she walks, but also because she's multitasking, snarling, "Move, loser," as she elbows past me.

Sasha's right behind me and says in my ear, "I can't believe you put up with that!"

I shrug. "Every time I snap at her bait, *I'm* the one who gets caught." Then I add, "She'll eventually self-destruct. She always does."

Sasha just frowns and passes me by.

So, okay. I have to admit—it made me feel pretty wimpy. I mean, there was a time when I *wouldn't* have put up with Heather's catty remarks. And I shouldn't *have* to put up with them. But after a full year of *trying* to control my fist and *trying* to control my tongue, I've actually gotten pretty good at it.

Well, except for my little relapse at the mall. But I didn't actually *punch* her, so considering what I'm dealing with, I've been a model of self-control.

But now instead of being proud of myself, I'm feeling embarrassed.

You know, *weak*.

Now, there's always a crowd of people going down the ramp when the dismissal bell rings. And even though it's a mini-stampede, there's usually no shoving or jockeying for position. Everyone wants out, and you just make yourself go with the flow.

So I was walking down the ramp minding my own business when all of a sudden Heather cries, "Heyyyyy!" and crashes to the ground with a *thud*, her hands sprawled out in front of her.

Everyone behind her comes log-jamming to a halt except Sasha, who tries to dance around her but takes a little tumble, too.

"You tripped me!" Heather screeches, pointing at me while she peels herself up from her pathetic spot on the ramp. "You hooked your foot around my ankle!"

"Oh, good grief," I say to the sky, and step around her.

Sasha's already back on her feet and going down the ramp, but Heather stays put. "You can run, but you can't hide, loser!" she yells after me. "I'm reporting you!"

But then from behind me I hear, "Sammy wasn't anywhere near you."

It's a guy's voice.

Low, and very calm.

And when I turn around, who do I see has come to my rescue?

The Tricky Timer himself—Lars Teppler.

"Thanks!" I call up the ramp. "But you'll never convince her of that. She'd blame me for her hair being red if she could!" I keep on walking. "Not that there's anything wrong with red hair!"

Lars is helping Heather up, but Heather's more interested in what's *down*. "Where's my phone?" she says, searching around. And after two whole seconds of looking, she says, "Who's got my phone?"

I show my hands. "Not me!"

A lot of people have already stepped around her, but a couple of girls stop and ask, "What's it look like?"

Heather's almost frantic. "It's got pink crystals. And a butterfly charm. It has to be around here somewhere!"

And *that's* when it finally hits me that if I *did* have Heather's phone, I could erase the picture and save Billy from his blackmail nightmare.

So I go back and start scouting around, too. I check the side of the ramp, down the space between the building and the ramp, in the weeds off to the side of the ramp. . . .

"Where's my phone?" Heather shouts. "Who's got my phone?" And she's acting like such a psycho that the few people who are still helping her look for it just bail on her and head off to class, including me.

Now, as I'm running to make it to PE in time, I'm thinking how it would be a miracle for Billy if Heather's phone was broken or lost forever. But it could also be a *disaster* for Billy if someone actually snagged it and saw the Die Dude picture.

So, okay. Maybe I'm slow. Or maybe I just wasn't expecting something so tricky from her, but it wasn't until I bumped into Sasha in the girls' locker room that I thought, Hey, wait a minute . . . !

Sasha seemed to be out of breath and was flying through her clothes change, so I dressed out in record time, too, then ran to catch up to her. Part of me still couldn't quite believe it, but I replayed the whole ramp scene in my head, and it was the only thing that made sense.

So after roll's taken and we're on our way down to the soccer fields, I jog alongside Sasha and ask real matter-of-fact-like, "So . . . what are you going to do with it?"

She just eyes me.

I laugh and say, "You were *smooth*. 'Course Heather thought it was me, but I didn't tell her any different. And Lars stuck up for me, so don't worry—I'm in the clear."

She jogs along without saying anything for a minute but then asks, "Does Lars know?"

My heart starts slamming around because now I *know* it was her, but I try to sound real cool and collected when I say, "He might, but I don't think so. I mean, he didn't say, Hey! It was Sasha!" I make a little X with my fingers over my heart. "And I'm sure not telling. After everything she's put me through?" I do a little sputter with my lips and laugh, "No way!"

She studies me with a sideways look but doesn't say a

thing. And, really, I need more than I've got—I need to know where she's put the phone and if she's already scrolled through the pictures or what.

But I can't ask her because it'll make her all curious and then she *will* scroll through the pictures and, knowing Sasha, the first thing she'll do is turn it over to Mr. Foxmore.

So when we're lined up to run through some cone drills, I whisper, "Where'd you learn that little tripping maneuver? That was amazing. And nobody could tell!"

She hesitates, then gives me a sly grin. "I've got six brothers. You learn to survive."

"Six brothers? Wow."

"Yeah. And I'm right in the middle."

We take our turns through the dribbling drill, and when we've looped around to the end of the line, I ask her again, "So what are you going to do with it? You sure don't want to get caught with it."

"Not a problem," she says over her shoulder.

Now, she's being kind of cagey with her answers, and I'm worried that I'm coming across like I'm grilling her. Still, I've got to find out what happened to the phone so I can tell Billy if he's off the hook. But before I can think of some smooth way to interrogate her without *sounding* like I'm interrogating her, she starts laughing like she's totally *demented*.

I jump back a little and look at her like, Whoa! and then suddenly she stops laughing and blushes. "Sorry," she says, like, Oops! Didn't mean for *that* to slip out!

"You okay?" I ask.

She giggles, then whispers, "That thing has definitely made its last transmission."

"So you . . . broke it? Got rid of it?"

She nods, then pops out her little finger and says, "Pinky swear you won't tell."

I'm thinking, *Pinky* swear? The last time I did a pinky swear was, like, third grade.

But what can I do?

I lock my little finger with hers and tell her, "Pinky swear."

Now, even though part of me is ecstatic and can't wait to tell Billy that he's free, part of me is feeling uneasy. I mean, sure it was just a silly little pinky swear, but Sasha's obviously dead serious about it, and I feel like I've just locked myself inside a cage with some unknown exotic animal.

One that looks cute and fuzzy on the outside, but that has some serious fangs and is not afraid to use them.

ELEVEN

It took me most of lunch to track down Billy. I checked the tables, the cafeteria, the whole outside area in between. . . . He was nowhere.

Then I started asking people if they'd seen him and went from one "I think I saw him over here" to "Did you check over there?" until I finally found him holed up in the drama room.

Now, the drama room's really about three rooms run together as one, with a wannabe stage in the middle. Everything's donated or mom-made, so it has that wish-we-were-more-professional look to it—something you tend to forget when you're in the middle of dropping your lines.

Besides being big, the room's packed with junk. Boxes, costumes, props, sound equipment . . . plus big tubs of lost-and-found clothes. So it's a small miracle that I even noticed Billy sitting on the floor near the lost-and-found, all by himself.

"Hey," I said, scooting in beside him. "You are off the hook."

He cocked his head. "What do you mean?"

"The wicked witch is fresh out of blackmail."

"What?" He perks up. "How?"

I grin at him. "Let's just say her phone's gone missing."

His eyes get huge. "Like, permanently?"

"Like, yeah."

He throws his arms around me and squeezes tight, then plants a great big smackeroo on my cheek. "I love you! You're amazing!"

I laugh. "Too bad I can't take credit for it. It wasn't me."

He lets go. "It wasn't?"

I shake my head. "And here's the deal. You can't talk about it. Not at all. If you tell anyone, it'll come back and bite me, 'cause I told you, so I must know something, right?"

"But . . . so who got it? And where is it?"

"I promised I wouldn't say anything, okay? But the person who got ahold of it destroyed it without even looking at what was on it."

"But . . . why?"

I laugh. "Because I'm not the only one who'd like to land a house on Heather."

I can see the wheels whirring in his head. "You're *sure*?"

I nod like I'm positive, but in the back of my brain there's a little tickly feather of doubt.

I mean, I didn't actually *see* her get rid of it.

And as my conversation with Sasha flashes through my head, it hits me that she never actually said, YES I stole Heather's phone and YES I destroyed it and NO I didn't check it out first.

A quick nod and a pinky swear didn't exactly add up to a sworn confession.

Still. I didn't want to pass the doubt along. I mean, why worry Billy when I was ninety-nine percent sure?

So I stood up and said, "Now get back to being Billy, would ya? No more hiding in the lost-and-found!" Then I head for the door, saying, "Give me a few minutes and go out a different way, okay?"

He gets right away that I don't want Heather or her wannabes to happen to see us and put two and two together. "I owe you big-time!" he says with a great big Billy Pratt smile.

"Nah," I tell him. Then I laugh and say, "It wasn't me!"

So I leave there feeling pretty good, and on my way over to the lunch tables, it hits me that it was actually *nice* to be so caught up in Billy's mess because I'd completely forgotten about my own.

But now I'm remembering about Casey being on our fire escape, and that I have no idea what he was doing there. I mean, he doesn't even know what apartment I'm in or what *floor* we're on. And even though I'd really felt like I could trust Casey with the secret that I was living illegally with my grandmother, now I was worried.

So the instant I found Holly, I plopped my backpack on the lunch table and said, "Okay. I want to know every detail about Casey being on the fire escape."

"Wait a minute," Marissa said. "Where have you been? Lunch is almost over, and *Heather* was looking for you."

My eyebrows go flying. "*Heather* came over here?"

"Yeah, and she was, like, *nice* to us. She said she'd give us a hundred dollars if we could get her phone back. No questions asked."

I laughed. "Oh, really. Well, that's because she thinks *I* have it, which I don't."

"Can you imagine getting your hands on that thing?" Dot whispers. "You could check out all the texts she's gotten and sent. You could probably totally blackmail her!"

I blink at her.

Marissa blinks at her.

Holly blinks at her.

"What?" Dot asks. "There's gotta be a *ton* of juicy stuff on her phone. Way more than a hundred dollars' worth."

Now, the funny thing is, she's right, but giving Heather some blackmail of her own had never even crossed my mind. "So true!" I tell her. "And I wish I had it, but I don't."

And, yeah, I'm *dying* to tell them about Sasha tripping Heather and all that, but I stop myself. It feels weird keeping it from them, but I really don't want to get Sasha in trouble. I mean, she may not know that she saved Billy from blackmail, but I do. Plus, if word slips out that I know *anything* about it, I'm dead. Heather won't rest until she finds a way to destroy me.

So I switch the subject back to the one we're *supposed* to be on in the first place. I turn to Holly and say, "Details, remember? Tell me about Casey."

Her answer's not exactly what I was hoping for. "I think I've told you everything."

"No, you haven't! What was he wearing? Did he, like, stand there for a while thinking or just go up and turn around? Was anyone with him?"

"Of course no one was with him! And what does it matter what he was wearing?"

I look down and shrug. And I'm suddenly feeling really stupid, because for some reason what he was wearing when he was sneaking up the fire escape mattered to me.

So I frown and say, "Was he in shorts? Jeans? A T-shirt? A flannel?"

She rolls her eyes. "Jeans and a flannel."

"So nothing flashy?"

"Definitely nothing flashy. And he was moving cautiously, okay? I don't think he really knew what he was doing. And, yeah, it took a minute for him to turn around."

All this helped.

I don't know why, but it did.

"Look," she says gently, "you should call him."

"But I *have* called him! A bunch of times! He hasn't called me back for *weeks*."

"Well, that was because he was supposed to be keeping the secret about your mom and his dad, right? Have you tried calling him since then?"

"Yes!"

"Did you leave a message?"

I just look down.

"Sammy, it's obviously killing you. Stop being so stubborn and call him."

"Yeah," Dot says. "Call him."

Marissa nods. "It's a no-brainer, Sammy. Call him. Like, *now.*"

Dot slides her cell phone over, and when I finally pick it up and punch in Casey's number, they all hunch forward like a flock of love vultures.

I wait through four rings.

Five.

"It's gonna roll over to voice mail."

They vulture in closer. "Don't you dare hang up!" Marissa says.

"Leave a message!" Holly tells me.

"But—"

Dot says, "Just do it."

So I take *another* deep breath, and after my stupid heart goes wacky over Casey's "Leave a message" message, I say, "Holly says she saw you going up my building. Would you please call me back?"

Then I snap the phone closed and slide it over to Dot.

The three of them look at each other for a minute, and finally Holly asks Marissa and Dot, "Would *you* call her back?"

Dot shakes her head. "Not me."

"She's calling from someone else's phone," Marissa mutters, "and she doesn't even say who she is."

"Or that she misses him," Dot throws in.

"Or even hi," Holly says.

"Nah," Marissa says, "I wouldn't call her back."

"Stop it!" I snap. "I've called him a *bunch,* and he hasn't called me back. What am I supposed to do, beg?"

They all look at each other like, Not a bad idea.

"Stop it!"

"Aw, come on, Sammy," Marissa says. "You could've tried a little harder."

Dot nods. "Been a little friendlier . . ."

"Maybe not jumped in like you were accusing him of something," Holly says.

I plop my head into my hands, and it feels like it weighs a ton. I want to cry, I want to scream, I want to take it all back and try again. I feel so stupid and pathetic.

"Aw, Sammy," Dot says, wrapping her arm around me. "It's easy to fix. Just—" But she's interrupted by her phone vibrating in her hand. "This is probably him now!"

Only it's not a call, it's a text.

And as she reads it, her face goes white.

"What?" I ask. "Is it from Casey?"

She tries to hide her phone from me, but when I wrestle it away from her, what I see makes my heart drop through the floor.

TWELVE

The text is from Casey all right.

It's short and to the point.

Stop calling. We're done.

I just hand the phone back to Dot and tear out of there. And even though Marissa chases after me, nothing she can say will fix this.

It's over.

Officially over.

Making it through the rest of the day was not easy. I mean, as if getting the text wasn't bad enough, having Heather in both classes after lunch was brutal. Not that she harassed me. She actually didn't say boo to me, which was scary in its own way. But just her being there was hard. It was a constant reminder that she'd been right—Casey had moved on, which is exactly what she'd wanted.

And something about Casey and me being "done" before we actually had the chance to start felt really . . . unfair. *Cruel.* Like someone had wrapped barbed wire around my heart and was twisting it tight.

Marissa tried to talk about it again during drama, but it just made things worse. I didn't *want* to talk about it or *think* about it or try to figure out some strategy to win him back.

We're done didn't leave much room for strategizing.

And even though it was nice to see Billy in such a good mood during drama—especially while Heather was obviously in a bad one—the lump in my throat kept getting bigger and bigger, and I was dying to get home so I could finally just let go and cry.

So after school was over, I tore out of there as fast as I could. I did all right while I was pumping like mad on my skateboard, hopping curbs and dodging cars, but once I was off my board and going up the fire escape, I couldn't help it—my eyes just overflowed. Casey had walked these very steps the night before. Had he been hoping to run into me on the fire escape?

But why?

So he could tell me we were done in person?

By the time I'm sneaking down our hallway, I'm a soggy-faced mess. And I'm dying to just flop onto the couch and flood a pillow, only I can't.

Someone else is already on the couch.

Someone *I* sure didn't invite.

"Oh, *great*," I moan. And before my mother can finish her sarcastic little "Why, thank you," I dump my stuff, charge into Grams' bedroom, and slam the door.

The apartment's a one-bedroom, with a tiny bathroom, kitchen, and a one-couch "family" room where I sleep. There really is no place to escape to. But whenever someone unexpected or troublesome or *scary* is at the door, my go-to hiding place is Grams' closet. And since my mother kinda covers all those bases, I find myself diving into the closet and closing the door.

How sad is that?

My cat, Dorito, is already there because he likes my mother about as much as I do.

Smart cat.

Anyway, there I am, surrounded by shoes and dangling clothes, hugging my cat, when my mother opens the closet door and sighs. "Honestly, Samantha."

I pull the door closed.

She pulls it back open. "Please. Show me you're more mature than this."

I pull the door closed, and this time I hold on tight.

"Samantha!" she snaps when she can't open the door. "Get out of that closet this instant!"

I can hear Grams' voice. It's quiet and calm, and it sounds like she's trying to convince my mother to leave me alone for a little while.

"This is ridiculous!" my mother says. "Are you telling me you let her get away with this kind of behavior?"

Grams' voice is louder now. "Give her a few minutes, Lana. Didn't you see she was already upset when she came through the door?"

Things get quiet out there. And after maybe half a minute of silence, I'm starting to feel a little foolish for hiding in the middle of a bunch of shoes with my cat. But then my mother starts up again. "This is completely unacceptable!"

She tries to open the door, but I'm still holding on.

"*You're* what's unacceptable!" I yell at her. "Just go away and stay away! You have totally ruined my life!"

"Samantha," she says with that oh-you-are-*so*-trying-my-patience tone that she loves, "you are thirteen years old—"

"Nice of you to admit it!" I shout, because there was a time when she lied about my age to the rest of the world and to *me*.

And, really, I didn't care that I was running our little through-the-door conversation into the mud. I didn't care that I was acting immature. I just wanted her to disappear, because the bottom line is, things were going great with Casey and me until she stepped into the picture and messed it all up.

"What I'm *trying* to say," she calls through the door, "is that everyone has crushes at thirteen. They don't last. You get over them."

I open the door and shout, "Oh, so it's okay to go around *destroying* them because, what? They're not going to last, anyway?" Then I yank the door closed and hold it hard.

I can feel her trying to open it and then give up. "Samantha, you get out here this instant! My dating Warren should have no effect on your little crush on his son!"

I open the door again. "But it does! We're totally messed up because of you!"

This time I'm too slow closing the door. She wedges herself in the opening with all her movie-star might and says, "Well! Blame me if you like, but you're obviously not mature enough to be in a relationship, anyway!" She turns to Grams. "*Now* do you see why I don't tell her things?"

This makes me furious. She'd pulled so many stupid stunts on me, and I'd *never* had a meltdown like this. Not when she'd left me with Grams so she could run off to Hollywood. Not the gazillion times she'd refused to tell me who my father is. Not when she'd let Dorito get out and he almost got killed and she "didn't have the time" to help me find him. Not even when she broke it to me that I was turning thirteen, not fourteen like I'd thought, because she'd wanted me to start kindergarten a year early so she could have free day care. And I'd flunked kindergarten!

So, yeah, I'd been really mad at her before, but I'd never acted like this. And now that I had, I knew she would use it against me for *years*. Anything she wasn't comfortable explaining, *this* would be the reason she'd give for not telling me. And she'd make it all my fault.

"Please," I said, sobbing into Dorito's fur, "just leave."

"Samantha, really. You should be happy for me. It's not like my life's been easy, you know. And how could I have predicted I'd fall in love with Warren? It just happened."

So there.

She said it.

She was in love.

"Please," I beg her, gulping for air, "just leave."

Grams is pulling her away now, and she's keeping her voice low, but I can hear her tell my mother, "Why are *your* feelings the only ones that matter? Don't you remember what it was like to be thirteen?"

"Having a crush on a boy is *not* the same as mature

love!" my mother hisses. "And I shouldn't have to give up true love for the capricious crushes of a teenager!"

"That teenager happens to be your daughter!" Grams snaps. "And the capricious one in this family is *you*."

"Fine," my mother says with a huff. "Take her side. You always do."

A door slam later, she's gone.

When I finally got tired of crying in the closet, I went into the kitchen and found Grams stirring a kettle of soup. Without a word, she put down the wooden spoon and wrapped her arms around me.

She didn't try telling me that everything would be okay, or that there were lots of fish in the sea, or that tomorrow would be a better day.

She just hugged me.

"I'm sorry I'm such a mess," I sniffed. "I'm sorry I was such a baby. It's been a really, really bad day."

She walks me over to our little kitchen table and sits me down, then brings me a steaming bowl of chicken noodle soup and saltines.

I look at her, wondering why she made me chicken noodle soup, and how come it feels like the only thing in the whole wide world that I would eat right now.

"Thanks," I tell her, and it comes out all choked up.

She sits across from me and fidgets with a napkin as she watches me sip down some broth. I peek up at her, and finally I sigh and say, "Casey told me to quit calling him."

She nods and says, "I'm so sorry," and I can tell from the tears welling in her eyes that she really is.

Then slowly it all comes out. I just give her little bits between sips of soup, and by the time the bowl is empty, I've told her way more than I had intended.

"Well, I completely understand why you couldn't handle finding your mother here."

I pinch my eyes closed. "If she marries Casey's dad, I'm just going to *die*. What if they expected us all to live together? What if Warren wants us to be one big, happy family? Them and Casey and Heather and me?"

Grams laughs. "Your mother as a stepmother? She can't even handle being a mother!" She shakes her head. "Can you imagine her in the same house as that wicked Heather? There'd be no survivors!" She reaches over and holds my hand. "I can't see that scenario ever coming true, Samantha. Besides, your mother is not about to give up her television career, and it sounds like Warren is just starting his." She lets go of my hand and adds, "I sure don't see them wanting to be the Brady Bunch, now or ever."

"The Brady Bunch?"

She shakes her head and chuckles. "Never mind. It was an old TV show. It used to be synonymous with a happy melded family, but I guess time marches on."

We're quiet for a minute, and then I ask, "What was she even doing here today? It's *Tuesday*. Isn't she supposed to be on the set or whatever?"

"Well," Grams says, taking off her glasses and inspecting them for spots, "if you'd keep up with the story, you'd know that Jewel has gone missing and Sir Melville is frantically searching for her because he knows she's found the ruby amulet and he's afraid she'll—"

"Wait—what's the ruby amulet?"

She huffs on a lens and buffs it with the hem of her blouse for the longest time. Finally she says, "Your mother has a point, you know."

"About *what*?"

"That you don't bother to watch her show."

"Grams! It's a *soap*. It's overdone and embarrassing."

"But it's your mother's work, and even if you don't appreciate the art form, you could show more interest than you do. Besides, she's quite good at it."

"At being overdone and embarrassing? Yeah, I agree."

Grams eyes me as she cleans the other lens of her glasses.

"Sorry," I grumble. "That was mean."

She nods, then pops her glasses back on her nose and says, "Have you ever considered that if you showed more interest in your mother's life, she might do the same with yours?"

I just stare at her as she gives me a minute to let that sink in.

Then very gently she adds, "You know I've recorded all her episodes for you. You had time this summer, but you wouldn't even consider it." She leans forward a little. "Samantha, think about what a nice gesture it would have been. Plus, it would have given you something to talk to her about." She sits back again. "You might even have gotten hooked."

"Oh, so you want me hooked on a soap?"

She gives a little shrug and says, "I want you to know what the ruby amulet contains and why Sir Melville is desperate to save Jewel from herself."

"So tell me."

She gives me a sly smile. "Oh no. You need to watch the show." She gets serious and adds, "You understand I was using the ruby amulet as a metaphor, right? I really want you to know what's going on with *her*. And, yes, your mother should take some initiative, too, but you both need to show more interest in each other."

I was quiet a minute, trying hard to battle against the feeling in my gut that she was right. And because I wasn't about to admit it—at least not while I was still so ticked off at my stupid mother—what popped out of my mouth was, "Are you sure that wasn't an analogy? Or maybe a simile?"

She thought about it a second, then grinned. "No, I'm not."

I don't know why the conversation made me feel better, but it did. So after I finished my soup, I took a shower and got on my homework. And after we had some real dinner, I actually read ahead on my assigned book until bedtime.

I tried not to think about Casey.

Tried not to think about my mother.

Tried not to think about being the Brady Bunch.

And when Grams caught me dozing off on the couch, she pulled the book out of my hands and kissed me on the forehead. "Tomorrow's another day," she whispered.

And oh boy, was it ever.

THIRTEEN

The next morning Bad Mood Bob was back. And although he's never Mr. Chatty, he actually didn't say one word to us in homeroom. Oh, he grunted at Cole Glenns, which translated to Get up here and read the announcements, and he snorted and rolled his eyes at Crystal Agnew when she asked if he was doing okay, but that was it.

Well, except for a disgusting belch after he downed half a can of Coke, but what else is new?

And I guess his bad mood didn't get any better during first or second periods, because at break Marissa and I saw him ripping into Cisco outside his classroom. We couldn't hear what he was saying, but he was definitely red in the face and jabbing his finger at Cisco.

"Wow," Marissa whispered when the Vincenator had finished his tirade and was storming into his classroom. "I wonder what that was about."

We waited for Cisco to move away from the classroom, then ran up to him.

"What bee flew up his butt?" I asked.

Cisco just kept on walking.

"Hey!" I called, hurrying to keep up with him. "What happened?"

He shakes his head. "A window in his room was left open last night."

We wait for more, but no more comes. "Was something stolen?" I finally ask, 'cause the windows in Mr. Vince's room are low enough for someone to climb through.

He shakes his head.

"So that's it? He was all bent out of shape over an open window?"

Cisco snorts. "Nothing new. He finds something to explode over a couple of times every year." Then he mumbles, "I'm just tired of him calling me Nacho."

"He calls you *Nacho*?"

"Like I said, nothing new."

"But . . . have you reported him?"

He shakes his head. "I'm not interested in another one of his fake apologies, man."

The tardy bell's about to ring, so we tell him to hang in there, and then Marissa runs off one way and I do a U-turn back to Vince's classroom.

Now, the stuff with Cisco made me plenty mad, but it was during third period that things got *really* interesting, and that started with Billy Pratt.

He came in wearing a chicken hat on his head.

You know, the kind with the wings over the ears and the neck sticking out over the forehead?

Anyway, Billy comes clucking into class, jutting his chicken head forward like he's pecking at air, then sits down at the tardy bell and clasps his hands on top of his desk like he's a good little boy.

Now, I'd had Ms. Needer's class right before break, so I might have tried to figure out if there was any symbolism to the chicken hat. After all, Billy had basically said that anyone who wouldn't say that Mr. Vince's class needed guest speakers was a chicken.

But Billy isn't into symbolism.

He's into fun.

And he was obviously back to being the Billy we all knew and loved.

"Mr. Pratt," Mr. Vince sighed after a long eye pinch. "The hat."

"Yes, sir; thank you, sir; you like it, sir? It's my thinking cap."

Mr. Vince gives him a hard look. "Obviously, it's not working." He jabs a finger against the top of his desk. "Up here with it. Now."

So Billy delivers the hat. And the funny thing is, he doesn't make any goofy faces or cute remarks, he just puts the hat on Mr. Vince's desk and goes back to his seat.

Mr. Vince studies him for a moment. "Mr. Foxmore briefed me on your infraction yesterday. Where's your cell phone?"

Billy hoists his backpack and pats the front pocket. "Zip-a-dee-doo-dah'd away, sir!" he says with a salute.

Mr. Vince scratches an elbow and says, "Well, I think it'd be a good idea if it was up here, too."

Billy blinks at him. "But—"

"*Now*, Mr. Pratt," the Nasty Scratcher demands.

So Billy shuffles up to his desk again and puts his cell phone next to his chicken hat.

Mr. Vince snorts at him, then says, "Now maybe we can get some work done in here," as he hands out a cross-word puzzle. "This is due by the end of class. No talking."

When our stack gets passed down our row, Sasha immediately raises her hand. And when Mr. Vince finally gives her the go-ahead grunt, she says, "This says chapter two, and we've already been tested on chapter two."

"It's good review for the final exam."

She turns to me and whispers, "Final exam? That's not until December!"

"Can you say busywork?" I whisper back.

She blinks at me and shakes her head. "Why do we have to put up with this?"

"Because he's the teacher . . . ?"

"This is so stupid. Someone should *do* something about him. There's no way he should be getting *paid* for this!" Then she faces forward with a huff.

And she's right—the assignment's a colossal waste of time. Still, I get to work on it, because what choice do I have? But after a few minutes Sasha slips me a note.

> Don't put your name on your paper.
> You do the downs, and I'll do across.
> Then we'll swap.

It's actually a very tempting idea, especially since the assignment is so ridiculous and the clues are really vague.

But it's definitely cheating, and if we get caught, Mr. Vince will nail me.

Maybe even find a way to suspend me.

Plus, a pinky swear with Sasha was weird enough. I sure didn't want to start *cheating* with her. So when she gives me a quick you-in? look, I just shake my head.

She squints at me like she can't believe it, then does a sniff of disgust and turns around.

So, fine. She thinks I'm a wimp.

Again.

Whatever. I get busy on the puzzle, but my heart's not in it, and I keep getting distracted. First by Heather, who seems to be studying everybody in class, one at a time. That, of course, includes me, so I give her a closed smile and the peace sign, which somehow makes her think she should flip me off.

Then Jake Meers can't seem to quit digging through his backpack.

And Lars Teppler whooshes his hair every time he writes down an answer.

And David Olsen's foot won't stop wagging. It's like a hyper little foot fan. Wag-wag-wag-wag-wag!

Then Heather uses her sweet-as-pie voice to ask, "Mr. Vince? Could we maybe open some windows? It's really stuffy in here, don't you think?"

And it is, which is funny, considering Cisco had gotten reamed because there'd been a window open all night.

Mr. Vince grunts an okay, and Heather moves through the classroom like a combination of Miss Congeniality and Biggest Flirt, saying, "I'm sorry. . . . Can I get by? . . .

111

Thank you! . . . Excuse me!" as she pushes open windows and props open the door.

She finally sits down in her seat with a little squiggle and an "Ah, much better!" and everyone gets back to the puzzle. But after a while I look up and notice that Mr. Vince is sitting at his desk like he always does when he gives us busywork, but he's not clicking around on his computer. He's pushed away from the desk a little and is kind of hunched over.

Now, at first I think he's having a moment of, you know, *reflection*. But then he sits up, and his right arm pulls back and then moves forward. Like he's just slipped something into the pocket of his slacks.

Something that seemed to be about the size of a phone.

Right away, I check for Billy's phone.

It's still there, by the chicken hat.

So then I'm thinking, Wow—did Mr. Vince have *his* phone out in class? Was he checking messages? Was he *texting*?

How hypocritical would *that* be?

But I couldn't remember ever seeing Mr. Vince use a cell phone, so maybe it wasn't a phone. Or wait . . . wow . . . maybe he had gotten ahold of *Heather's* phone?

But how would he have gotten Heather's phone? He wasn't even at school when it got lost!

And Sasha sure wouldn't give it to him. . . .

Would she?

No, of course not!

But . . . what if Sasha never really had it in the first place and she was just playing games with me? She *was* a little odd.

A little *extreme*.

So, yeah, I was spiraling into Doubtsville fast. And I knew I was being irrational, but something about Heather's phone kept nagging at me. It was like I needed to *see* the dead body to believe there *was* a dead body.

Now, I've been told more times than I can count that I have an "overly active imagination." So I was actually in the middle of trying to rein it in, telling myself that I was being stupid and that the Vincenator was either putting his own phone away or doing another one of his disgusting scratch maneuvers, when all of a sudden the fire alarm goes off.

"Aaaagh!" I cry, and jump about six feet in the air.

Heather totally busts up. "Dork," she sneers across the aisles.

"Fire drill, people!" Mr. Vince bellows from his desk.

I tell you. The guy's a regular brain surgeon.

But then Mr. Foxmore's voice comes over the PA. "This is not a drill. File out to your assigned evacuation sites immediately."

"Not a drill?" everyone says, looking around at everyone else.

"You heard the man!" Mr. Vince snaps. "Get moving!"

So we all hurry to file out, leaving everything behind like we're supposed to—which feels weird, but those are the rules.

Only apparently Sasha doesn't know the rules.

"That stays here," Mr. Vince says, pointing to her backpack.

"But—"

"They lock up," Angie Johnson tells her. "It's the rules."

So Sasha leaves her backpack, but you can tell she really doesn't want to.

"Our evacuation site is the track!" Mr. Vince calls. He's standing outside the door now, kind of flagging us along as we all file out. "And don't think you can ditch this!" he shouts as he locks up. "Roll will be taken!"

So we head for the track. We can hear sirens in the distance, and there's a lot of scurrying of adults. Mr. Foxmore is touching base with teachers as they file by, Cisco's giving instructions to the lunch ladies, and even our phantom principal, Dr. Morlock, is out waving students along, telling them to keep moving.

After our class is assembled on the track, Mr. Vince barks through the roll sheet. But I notice he starts with Tracy Arnold, not Heather Acosta, and when I look around, I don't see Heather anywhere.

So I snicker, "Figures," and just kind of shake my head, because if I know Heather, she kissed up to him for a bathroom pass so she could suck down a cigarette. And come on. I mean, how pathetic is it when you're Scratch 'n' Spit's pet?

Anyway, when Mr. Vince is done with roll, he hands the sheet over to the teacher next to us and tells us, "Mrs.

Ambler's in charge. Don't cause her any trouble! I've got assigned duties to get to!"

Mrs. Ambler's a pretty cool teacher, so right away the whole class relaxes and breaks away into little groups. And since some of us were in her class last year, she starts asking us how the new year is going and what we did over the summer and all that stuff. But after a while everyone looks around like, What's taking so long? I mean, usually the all-clear bell rings almost right after we've reached the evacuation site. So finally I ask Mrs. Ambler, "Is there really a fire?"

"I heard there was a call from off-site. Someone spotted smoke." She shakes her head. "It might be a false alarm, but they still have to clear all the rooms and bathrooms . . . everything."

We're already way into fourth period, and apparently the wait's a little too long for some people, because only a really desperate person would ever use the Porta-Potty by the track. It's not even an option as far as I'm concerned. I stepped inside it once, and boy! I got out of there quick. It wasn't just the smell, either. It was the, uh, *level.* It was flat-out revolting.

But Rudy Folksmeir—who's obsessed with dirt biking and not exactly worried about personal hygiene—comes blasting out of it, only he's not choking or dying or gasping for air.

He's jumping for joy like he's just won the lottery.

"Heather!" he shouts. "Where's Heather Acosta?"

I'm tempted to shout back, "Holed up with the

Marlboro Man!" but it's a good thing I didn't because just then Heather emerges from the far end of our group. "Right here," she calls with one hand up. But then when she realizes who's asking, she shouts, "What do *you* want?" across the track at him.

"A hundred bucks!" Rudy shouts. "I found your phone!"

"Really?" she asks, but then immediately goes pale. "Wait. You found it in *there*?"

"Yeah! And you are *not* gonna want it back!" he calls. "But I found it, so pay up!"

I look right at Sasha, but she gives me a totally cold stare. Like she is done with me, and she's going to deny anything I think I know.

So much for complimenting her on the brilliance of her disposal. Instead, I focus on Heather, who's just standing there not believing what she's hearing. And you can tell—she does *not* want to go in and see for herself what Rudy's talking about. "Well . . . get it out of there!" she yells at him.

He laughs. "*You* get it out of there!"

"Are you sure it's mine?"

He shrugs. "Pink sparkle, right?" He starts back toward the outhouse. "Come on, check it out!"

Heather's not the first one to brave the Hunny Hut, though.

Billy is.

It only takes him a minute, but when he emerges, he's got a great big grin on his face. He holds the door open for Heather and makes a grand, sweeping motion with his hand. "Your phone awaits!"

Well, Heather *does* look inside, but it's quick, and she starts squealing and flapping her hands through the air, going, "Eew! Eew! Eew!" as she escapes. And on her way back to the track, she tells Rudy, "I'm not paying you! It was a reward for *recovering* it, not just finding it!"

"Hey, you said it was a hundred bucks for *finding* it!"

"No, for recovering it!"

Rudy is ticked off. "Yeah? You want it recovered? Okay, I'll recover it!"

"You wouldn't!" she shouts as he heads back to the outhouse.

"For a hundred bucks? Sure I would!"

Everyone around me goes, "Eeeew!" and Heather yells, "You're gross! And there's no way I'm paying you a hundred bucks for that!"

Right then the all-clear bell sounds, and Mrs. Ambler shouts, "Back to class! Everybody, report to your *third*-period class and stay there! Rudy, get to class! And make it quick. We only have ten minutes before lunch!"

So we scatter back to class, and we don't do any of this follow-the-teacher stuff, either. I break away from my group and race around all over the place until I finally find Marissa, who is with Dot and Holly, coming off the soccer fields. "Guess what?" I gasp. "Rudy Folksmeir found Heather's phone in the Porta-Potty by the track!"

"Like, down the john?" Marissa asks.

I nod and actually *giggle*.

Their eyes pop wide, and they all cry, "No!" and totally crack up.

"Gotta get back to Vince's," I call, and take off running, because his classroom is clear across school and I do *not* want to get in trouble for being the last one back.

Turns out I'm *not* the last one back.

Mr. Vince is.

"Where *is* he?" Tracy finally asks, because there's now only a couple of minutes left in class, and we have no idea if we're supposed to stay or check into fourth period or just head to lunch. "And why was the room open if he wasn't in it?"

Nobody seems to have an answer for that, either.

And then Billy says, "Hey! Where's my phone?" He's got his chicken hat, but the phone's nowhere to be found.

Heather snorts. "Now you know what it's like, stupid. Go check the outhouse!"

All of a sudden Sasha's digging through her backpack, checking to make sure everything's still there. And since there's no teacher around, Heather acts like *she's* in charge. "Which one of you put my phone in the outhouse, huh?" she demands. "Whoever did it, you're a disgusting pervert!"

Lars swishes his hair and grumbles, "You sound like Vince."

She squints at him. "What?"

"You do," he says with another swish. "You have no idea who did it. Maybe somebody after school found it. Maybe the janitor did."

"*And threw it in a Porta-Potty?*" she screeches.

Before he can answer, Mr. Vince walks in.

"Was there a fire?" Jake Meers asks him.

"False alarm," he says. "Complete waste of time."

"Hey, Mr. Vince?" Billy asks, going up to him. "Do you have my phone?"

Mr. Vince frowns at him. "No."

"Well, it's not on your desk. Someone took it!"

But Mr. Vince doesn't care. He just shouts, "Finish the puzzle at home, people!" over the lunch bell and kicks Billy out of the room.

FOURTEEN

When I met up with Marissa, Holly, and Dot at the lunch tables, they were having a little gloatfest about Heather's phone. "You guys!" I whispered, because they were really getting carried away. "Be cool. I do not want her thinking I had anything to do with it, okay? Besides, Billy's phone's disappeared, and I think she might have it."

They all snapped to face me. "What? How?"

So I'm in the middle of telling them what happened before the fire alarm went off when Billy joins us.

"Did you find it?" I ask.

He shakes his head. "I bet Heather's got it."

I scowl. "I bet she does."

"Why would Heather take it?" Marissa asks, looking at Billy. "I thought you guys were 'friends'?"

He cocks his chicken head at me and says, "You didn't tell them?"

Marissa, Holly, and Dot turn to me. "Tell us what?"

I throw my hands in the air. "Oh, good grief."

"Sorry," Billy says, pulling a face.

"I can't believe you're holding out!" Marissa says. "On *us*."

"He made me swear I wouldn't say anything, okay?" I give Billy a fierce look. "And you're an idiot if you're telling people!"

"I'm not!" Billy says. "But I thought for sure you'd tell *them*." And even though he doesn't say it, what's implied is that of course I told them because they're trustworthy and reliable and know how to keep a secret.

"Yeah," Marissa says, and she's obviously miffed. "Of course you'd tell *us*."

I stare at Billy and shake my head. "Remind me why I swore I wouldn't tell? Something about you being in boiling hot water if anyone found out? Something about your life being over if anyone found out? Something about getting expelled from school if anyone found out? Something about—"

"Found out *what*?" Holly says. "Just tell us already!"

So I eye Billy, then lean in and whisper, "Smart boy here let Heather talk him into writing 'Die Dude' on Vince's whiteboard. Then she takes a picture of him in the act and blackmails him with it. And *then* when somebody *else* leaves the rat in Vince's drawer, she really puts the screws to him."

Dot looks at Billy. "So you put the message on the board but didn't leave the rat?"

"Who's ever going to believe *that*?" Holly asks.

"Exactly!" I tell them. "And since the rat is kinda . . . *sick*—"

Marissa cringes. "Totally nasty."

I nod. "—and since the little dog tag detail was so *Billy* . . ."

"He gave in to her blackmail," Dot says.

"What if she's got a copy of the picture on her computer or sent it to someone else?" Holly asks.

Billy shakes his head. "I don't think she did."

Marissa gives Billy a suspicious look. "You swear you didn't leave the rat?"

Billy crosses his little chicken-headed heart. "I swear it wasn't me!"

Marissa frowns at me. "I can't believe you didn't trust us."

"I *trust* you," I tell her, then I glare at Billy. "I just swore I'd keep it a secret."

Billy gives me sad little puppy dog eyes. "I'm sorry, Sammy-keyesta."

Just then we hear a sound.

A jazzy, jumpy, *happy* sound.

"My phone!" Billy cries, checking his backpack, his pockets, his chicken hat. . . .

But the ringing doesn't sound like it's coming from his backpack.

It sounds like it's coming from *mine*.

I mutter, "What the heck . . . ?" And when I unzip my front pouch, what do I see?

A phone buzzing around inside.

I take it out, and everyone's looking at me like, Huh . . . ? and then Marissa says, "Answer it!"

So I open the phone and say, "Hello . . . ?"

There's a moment of hesitation, and then, "Who's this?"

It's a guy's voice.

Kinda gruff.

I snort and snap back, "Well, who's this?"

After a second of silence the voice asks, *"Sammy?"* and all of a sudden I recognize who it is. "Officer *Borsch?*"

Everyone at our table leans back a little and looks at me with big eyes, and mine are cranked pretty wide, too, believe me. I feel like I'm in some sort of weird dream.

But I'm *not* dreaming, and it *is* Officer Borsch. He heaves a big sigh and says, "I didn't think you had a cell phone."

"I don't!" And since my head feels like one big scramble of confusion, I ask, "So how'd you get my number? I mean, who are you calling? I mean, *why* are you calling? I mean . . . I don't know what I mean!"

He makes a little sucking noise. Like he's cleaning some leftover pastrami out of his teeth. "Where are you?"

"At school."

He heaves another sigh. "You need to come up to the office. Now. And bring the phone."

He clicks off, and I'm left staring at the phone. I blink at Billy. "How did *your* phone get in *my* backpack? And why are the police calling it?"

Holly pulls a face. "This does not sound good."

I shoulder my backpack and grab Billy by his chicken-wing earflap. "You're coming with me."

"Wait! Where are we going?"

"Officer Borsch says I have to go up to the office. With the phone. Now."

"Is he the cop who came the day of the sumo rat?"

"Yeah, that's him. Now come on."

"Do you want us to go with you?" Dot asks.

I shake my head. "We'll be fine."

Marissa calls, "You might want to take off that hat, Billy!"

So I swipe it off his head and jam it inside his backpack. And when we get up to the office, there's Officer Borsch, waiting for us.

With Mr. Foxmore.

And Mr. Vince.

"Uh-oh," Billy says under his breath.

"What have you gotten us into?" I ask between my teeth.

"Nothing!" Then he gives me his stupid puppy dog eyes and does his little cross-my-heart thing again, and starts to run away.

I grab him by the sleeve and bungee him back. "So what's up?" I ask Officer Borsch as I drag Billy along.

Mr. Foxmore ninjas a look at Billy and me and says, "What's *up* is a meeting in the conference room." He puts out his hand. "The phone?"

I hand it over, and we all file into a room that has a big oval table with a conference phone in the middle of it. "Sit," Mr. Foxmore commands Billy and me, so we do. And since they're all still standing and sort of glowering at us, I ask, "What happened?" and believe me, my voice is not sounding too steady.

"There was a message left on Mr. Vince's phone," Mr. Foxmore says. "On his school extension." Then he cocks an eyebrow at Mr. Vince and gives him a little ninja nod that apparently means Activate the conference phone, because Mr. Vince leans forward and punches the keypad until a mechanical voice says, "You have . . . *no* new messages and . . . *one* saved message. To listen to your messages, press one. To—"

Mr. Vince presses one on the keypad, and suddenly the room is filled with a deep, dark, angry voice. "You're gonna DIE, dude!"

When the machine is quiet, I just kind of stare at it and then at Mr. Foxmore and then at Officer Borsch.

"The call came from your cell phone," Mr. Foxmore says to me.

"It isn't my cell phone!" I cry.

"We know that," he says, like Vice Principal Smarty-Pants. He zooms in on Billy. "It belongs to Mr. Pratt."

Billy jumps up. "I *swear* I didn't leave that message! I *swear.*"

"Sit down, Mr. Pratt," Mr. Foxmore snaps, then looks at me. "Why did you have the phone?"

"Somebody put it in my backpack! We were sitting around eating lunch, and all of a sudden it started ringing. I had no idea it was there!"

They turn to Billy, whose mouth moves up and down while his hands go jerking around in front of him, but no sound comes out, until *finally* he says, "Mr. Vince asked me to put my phone on his desk. It got taken during the fire alarm, and someone put it in Sammy's backpack!"

Mr. Foxmore eyes him. "Why shouldn't I think that someone was you?"

"What?" Billy cries. "Why would I do that?"

Mr. Foxmore just scratches an ear.

So I say to Mr. Vince, "Look, *everybody* knew Billy's phone was on your desk. And we all left our backpacks in the classroom for the fire drill. And even though you locked it, the room was *un*locked when the fire drill was over! So *anybody* could have used Billy's phone to make that call and then put the phone in my backpack."

Mr. Foxmore's mouth pulls way off to one side. He looks like a fish on the line, but he makes it clear that *I'm* the one on the hook. "Someone like, say, *you*."

"No!"

"Well, let's see," he says, producing a small notebook from inside his rumply suit coat. "According to the phone's time stamp, the message was left about one minute after the all-clear bell rang." He looks at me. "According to Mrs. Ambler, you dashed away from your assigned safety area, and according to, uh, *others* in your class, you were the last one to arrive back at Mr. Vince's room."

"I was trying to find my friends! Ask Marissa McKenze! I went to the soccer fields!"

Mr. Foxmore whips a ninja look at me. "You were told to go directly to class."

"But—"

"So why was seeing your friends such a priority for you?"

"Because . . . because they're my friends!"

Then Billy pipes up with, "Are you saying *Sammy* left that message? The voice on the recording isn't a girl's. It's a guy's!"

Mr. Foxmore looks at him. "And you, Mr. Pratt, are a guy."

"But I don't sound anything *like* that."

"I'm familiar with voice changers, Mr. Pratt. They're probably already in the stores for Halloween."

Then, *finally*, Officer Borsch says something. "It is possible, isn't it, that these two have been set up? Who would use their own phone to leave a death threat?"

"It seems like a pretty elaborate setup," Mr. Foxmore says. "And who would do *that*?"

Billy and I look at each other, then blurt, "Heather Acosta!"

Mr. Vince snorts. "I knew you'd say that. And I did give her a bathroom pass, but that was at the start of the drill." He leans in and snarls, "But there's also the mysterious destruction of *her* phone—something she seems to think the two of you *also* know something about."

Well, okay. At that point I want to jump up and demand a lawyer. I mean, come on! If Mr. Vince is on my jury, just shoot me now. So I push back in my chair and say, "I feel like I'm being railroaded here. I had nothing, *nothing* to do with any of this Die Dude stuff, and I had nothing to do with Heather's phone winding up in the outhouse. I also have no idea how Billy's phone wound up in my backpack!"

Officer Borsch steps forward and says to Billy, "The whole class knew your phone was on Mr. Vince's desk?"

"That's right, sir. And when we came in from the fire drill, it was missing."

"And you've got people who know where you were during the time the phone call was made?"

Billy nods. "I came straight back to class."

He turns to me. "And you were with your friends? Can an objective third party corroborate your whereabouts during the time in question?"

"I'm sure someone saw me. But I was with three of my friends—Marissa McKenze, Dot DeVrees, and Holly Janquell. Call them in here one at a time—they'll all say the same thing."

Officer Borsch turns to Mr. Vince. "You locked the door on the way out to your evacuation site?"

"That's right."

"Were you surprised to see your students inside your classroom after the all clear was given?"

"Very."

"So who unlocked the door?" Officer Borsch looks at Mr. Foxmore. "Who else has a key?"

Mr. Foxmore pulls out a chair and sits down across from Billy and me. "All the administrators have master keys. So does the custodial staff. And some of the teachers . . ."

"And you have an assigned routine to check each building during a fire alarm?"

"That's right."

"So, as part of your all-clear routine, somebody went in and checked Mr. Vince's room, correct?"

"That's correct. But are you implying—"

"I'm just collecting information. Could you get me a list?"

"Of?"

"Of anyone with a master key. And I'd like to know who's assigned to clear Mr. Vince's room during drills and alerts."

Now, I'd never seen Officer Borsch act so calm and professional.

Ever.

So I'm thinking, Go Borschman! but Mr. Foxmore seems kind of annoyed, and Mr. Vince is shaking his head like he thinks Officer Borsch is an idiot. Especially after Officer Borsch says, "I'll want to question anyone who had access to the room."

Mr. Foxmore stands and says to him, "And I'll want a meeting with the parents," like Billy and I are not even there.

Billy closes his eyes and sort of sinks into his chair, and I take a deep breath and try hard to look like I've got no problem with them calling home.

The fact is, though, I've got a huge problem with it.

I look at Officer Borsch, and he knows what I'm thinking.

This has just gone from really, really bad.

To even worse.

FIFTEEN

Billy and I were put in different holding cells while Mr. Foxmore brought in our "parents." Billy got put in the Box, and I got put in a supply room across the hall from the faculty lounge that was full *of* boxes.

Now, the Box is not called the Box by people who work in the office. It's called the Reflection Room. But anyone who's spent any time reflecting in it knows—it's a box. It's got nothing on the walls but paint, it's got one light overhead and one chair to sit in, and I swear it's smaller than Grams' closet.

I should know—I've spent plenty of time in both.

But since there were two of us and there was no way Mr. Foxmore wanted Billy and me "reflecting" together, he put Billy in the Box and stuck me in the supply room. "Stay here," he told me, like I was a naughty little puppy.

The supply room was actually worse than the Box because it was hot and stuffy inside, and I had to sit on a stack of copy paper boxes. I sat there for what seemed like an eternity, too, looking around at other boxes and a cubby-holed wall of colored paper. After I was bored blind from that, I made a fleet of paper airplanes and flew them around. They couldn't go very far, though, and kept crashing behind boxes where I couldn't reach them.

Anyway, I got so hot and sweaty and claustrophobic that I finally couldn't take it anymore, so I opened the door a crack and peeked outside.

Across the hallway, the faculty room door was wide open. I couldn't see any teachers in it, but I *could* see a big pink donut box in the middle of a table.

Now, Foxy Foxmore had confiscated our backpacks, and since I hadn't exactly had a chance to eat my smashed PB&J during lunch, I was starving. That box of donuts was only about twenty-five feet away, and it was calling my name.

Loud.

So I opened the supply room door a little more and checked up and down the hallway. The coast *seemed* clear, so I snuck over and stuck my head inside the faculty room.

Nobody home!

Well, unless someone was in the faculty room bathroom . . . but I decided to take my chances. I zipped over to that donut box and flipped open the lid, and what was waiting for me inside?

Half a sorry-looking chocolate cake donut.

Still. It *was* better than nothing, so I snagged it. Trouble is, as I'm heading for the door with it, I hear voices coming down the hallway. It doesn't sound like Mr. Foxmore—it sounds like two women, but I can't be sure he's not, you know, walking with them.

Now, students are not allowed in the faculty lounge. Everyone knows that. And I can't exactly jet out of there clutching a stolen donut—I'll run right into whoever's in the hallway! And I can't just *stand* there, because whoever it is will see me and think I'm a crummy donut thief.

Which I am!

Besides, Mr. Foxmore had told me to stay put.

Which I didn't!

So I panic. My head goes whipping around, looking for someplace to hide, and since there *is* no place, I dive behind the door and pull the big trash can in to *make* myself a little wedge of a hiding place.

So there I am, crouching behind a door and a trash can, holding my breath—and half a stale donut—when the voices enter the room.

". . . and it's terrible to be treated that way, but there's a reason the kids hate him. He never has a nice thing to say about them, he's rude and crude and condescending to them, and from what I understand, he assigns a *lot* of busywork."

"He didn't used to be that way," the other, sorta warbly voice says. "When he first started, he was so young and enthused. . . ."

"Weren't we all? And we're all overburdened. But if he doesn't like *kids*, he shouldn't be teaching!"

I can hear the clink of a coffee cup against the counter, and then the Warbler says, "I think Suzanne leaving him had a profound effect on him."

"Well, that's true. And I did feel very sorry for him when it happened, but it's been over two years! And regardless, it's not professional to be such a pill at work."

Now, I just know they're talking about Mr. Vince, and

I'm pretty sure the stronger voice belongs to Mrs. Ambler, but I have no idea who the Warbler is. So I inch over and peek through the space between the edge of the door and the side of the trash can. Sure enough it's Mrs. Ambler, and she's with a teacher named Mrs. Sanford. I've never had Mrs. Sanford, but everyone says she's nice, even though she looks like she's been teaching for about eighty years.

Mrs. Ambler's fixing herself a cup of coffee, and Mrs. Sanford is opening the donut box, saying, "Personally, I think Suzanne leaving him sparked a midlife crisis. It happens to a lot of men, you know. Especially if they're dumped for a younger, more attractive man, and that's what happened to Bob."

Mrs. Ambler shakes her head. "Times sure have changed, haven't they?"

"*Kids* sure have changed, I'll give you that." Mrs. Sanford closes the donut box. "Can you imagine threatening a teacher? Good Lord. It's unbelievable."

"Well, you're right about that," Mrs. Ambler says, stirring some sugar into her mug of coffee. "I just hope it's not the two they suspect."

"Samantha and Billy?" she asks, like I'm somebody she actually knows.

Mrs. Ambler nods. "Sammy's had a rough go of it here. And she and Bob had a rocky year last year, but I can't imagine her resorting to that sort of tactic." She taps the spoon against the rim of her mug and sighs. "Maybe she got caught up in Billy's antics. I hope not."

Now, I'm so wrapped up in what they're saying that it takes me a minute to realize that Mrs. Sanford is coming toward the garbage can with the donut box. "I don't know why it's so hard for people to throw away their trash," she mutters.

Mrs. Ambler laughs. "Usually, there's half a donut left so that they don't feel they have to!"

Now, for somebody who's got to be closing in on a hundred, Mrs. Sanford is moving quick! So I cram back inside my little wedge and hold my breath while my heart does its best to slam an escape hole right through my chest. And I know it doesn't make sense, and I know it's a stupid thing to do, but I duck my head between my knees and cover my head with my arms. Maybe there's no science behind it, but I think eyes are like magnets for each other, and that looking at someone you're hiding from somehow makes them look at you.

So there I am, feeling like a stupid ostrich, hiding my head in my knees, when I hear Mr. Foxmore's voice. "Have either of you seen Samantha Keyes?" And let me tell you, he is not sounding happy.

I bury my head even deeper.

All I can think is, I'm dead.

I am so dead.

Then all of a sudden there's a loud crushing noise right next to me, which makes my skin about fly off my body, and Mrs. Sanford is saying, "Samantha?"

So, yeah, I'm totally busted.

Only then Mrs. Sanford says, "She's certainly not in *here*."

I almost can't believe my ears. And when I dare to turn

my head and look, there's a donut box sticking out over the rim of the trash can and Mrs. Sanford is gone.

They start filing out, talking at the same time about where I might be and where I'm *supposed* to be and where I'm gonna wind up if I've ditched school. And since I can't exactly materialize inside the supply room and pretend I've fallen asleep behind some boxes or something, I do the only thing I can think to do.

I dump the donut in the trash and beeline for the faculty lounge bathroom.

Once I'm inside, I start making noise like I'm having a humdinger of a time using the facility. I flush the toilet, I run the faucet, I bang down on the towel dispenser lever, and I come out whistling and pretending to dry my hands.

Mr. Foxmore's head pops into the faculty room just as I'm coming out of the bathroom. "What are you doing?" he demands.

"Sorry!" I tell him, tossing the paper towel beside the donut box in the trash can. "Nobody was around to ask permission, and I really had to go!" Then I turn it back on him. "I can't believe you left me in there so long! Especially since I haven't even done anything wrong!" I put my hands on my hips and say, "Do you know how hot it is in there? I could have passed out and you would never have known. Isn't there some kind of law against locking students in a closet?"

"It's not a closet, and obviously you weren't locked in!"

"Could have fooled me," I grumble. "And I'll bet there's a law."

He gives me a look *and* a head wag—a double ninja strike meaning, Watch your mouth and, Follow me.

So I follow him, but it's really helping my nerves to be on the offensive, so I *don't* watch my mouth. "I'm not the bad guy, Mr. Foxmore, and I don't like being accused. Just because you don't know who's been doing this Die Dude stuff doesn't mean you can lock me in a hundred-degree closet with no food and no bathroom. I didn't get a chance to eat lunch because of all of this, and I'm—"

And then we walk into the conference room, and who do I see?

My mother.

Not my grandmother, making up stories about why my mother can't be there.

My *mother.*

And she's chumming it up with Officer Borsch like he is the most interesting man on the planet.

My mother is always beautiful. Makeup or no makeup, first thing in the morning or late at night, she's always beautiful, and she knows it.

Worse, she knows how to *use* it.

Now, she's not wearing jeans and some sort of random top. She's wearing the movie-star version of a power suit. It's a few shades shy of tomato red, and *soft*-looking. Like the material is just happy to be wrapped around something so beautiful. The skirt hits about three inches above the knee, and the blouse under the blazer is a silky white. Her lipstick matches her suit, and so do her high-heeled pumps, which are pointy and have little brass buckles across the tips. I guess so her toes aren't tempted to pop out and run away.

Anyway, she looks amazing. Her hair is perfect, her makeup is perfect . . . she looks powdery and clean and, well, like she belongs in the movies—something that is obviously not lost on our new vice principal.

"You must be Mr. Foxmore," she says, gliding over to him with her hand out as he tries to pull his jaw off the floor. "I'm Lana Keyes. Samantha's mother?" She takes his hand and gives it a gentle shake as she coos, "I understand that my daughter might be in some sort of trouble?" She gives me one of her movie-star smiles. "Hello, darling."

Well, even though this is the first time in the year-plus that I've been going to William Rose that my mother's stepped foot on this campus, she's obviously here to audition for the Perfect Mother Show.

Which I guess is better than her playing her usual role in How I Ruined My Daughter's Life.

So I say hi back and plop my tattered jeans into a conference chair. "I've done nothing wrong," I tell her. "I have an alibi, and I'm being railroaded. Plus, they locked me inside a hundred-degree closet for an hour without lunch or a bathroom."

My mother gives her own version of the ninja look. It's not a flying side kick or a roundhouse slam like Mr. Foxmore delivers.

It's gentle.

Open.

Disbelieving.

And I can tell—it knocks him flat.

"Is this true, Mr. Foxmore?" she asks, and it sounds more like a melody than a string of words. "I would think you'd be worried about a lawsuit."

This is not a threat.

It's concern.

Deep, heartfelt concern.

"We're just trying to get to the bottom of this, Ms. Keyes," Mr. Foxmore says. "We didn't mean for it to take this long. And I would like to resolve things quickly. Has Sergeant Borsch told you about the events leading up to this?"

"He has," she says with a dainty nod. "And I must say I'm puzzled that Samantha would be under scrutiny, given the male voice on the recording and the"—she shivers—"nature of the second threat." She looks at Mr. Foxmore with big, innocent eyes. "Honestly, can you imagine Samantha capturing and killing such a beast?"

Before he met my mother, Mr. Foxmore would probably have said, "Oh yeah. I can definitely see that." But now that I'm this delicate beauty's *daughter,* well, that changes everything. "We're worried that her friend got her involved in this," Mr. Foxmore tells her. "That maybe she just went along out of peer pressure."

My mother turns her movie-star eyes on me. "Samantha?"

"I had nothing to do with any of this." I look at Mr. Foxmore. "Unless it's a crime to be Billy Pratt's friend. And if it is, you'd better charge the whole school. I know you're new here, but everyone loves Billy. And that's not just because he's funny—he's also *nice*. He tries to keep the peace between groups. . . . He's like a goodwill ambassador. And, yeah, he does stupid stuff sometimes, but that gross dead rat? That voice on the phone? None of that is Billy's style. He's more just goofy, and I can't believe he had anything to do with it, either."

Mr. Foxmore doesn't seem to know what to say to *that*, so Officer Borsch jumps in with, "It does all seem circumstantial where Sammy's concerned. And it wouldn't be the first time I got called here for pranks that one student tried to blame on another."

There's an awkward silence. Like Mr. Foxmore is not really appreciating the Borschman's comments. But my mother soothes the vibe by making a suggestion. "It seems to me," she says gently, "that there's a considerable amount of reasonable doubt here. Why don't we let Samantha get back to class so she doesn't miss any more valuable learning time, and let Sergeant Borsch continue his investigation?"

Mr. Foxmore scratches his eyebrow, then nods and says, "I really appreciate your coming. It helps to meet the parents and get a bigger picture of a student's situation."

And that's it.

I'm free to go.

And since there's only about twenty minutes left in school, and since I have no idea what to say to my mother, I start for the door. Only then I remember—my backpack.

"I'll be right back with it," Mr. Foxmore says when I ask him about it.

So there I am, stuck with my mom and Officer Borsch, feeling unbelievably awkward.

139

"No 'thank-you,' Samantha?" my mother asks softly.

"Thanks," I grumble. Then I eye her and say, "I guess I'm still in shock to see you here. And just so you know, I really am innocent."

"I'm sure you are," she says, coming toward me with a smile.

Obviously, she's still auditioning.

She turns her smile on Officer Borsch as she wraps an arm around me. "Gil tracked me down."

Officer Borsch nods and tells me, "Your grandmother helped me with that."

My mother lets go of me and fingers a strand of hair away from my face. "I understand you're going to be a bridesmaid in his wedding this weekend."

Trouble is, delivering that one line totally blows her flawless performance, because just as she says it, Mr. Foxmore walks back in the room.

Now, I'm not sure if Mr. Foxmore heard what my mother said, or if it sank in who "his" was, but there's suddenly a really awkward vibe in the room. It could be coming from the Borschman, or it could be coming from Mr. Foxmore. I don't know, but I can only do one thing.

Grab my backpack and go!

SIXTEEN

I was charging over to drama, taking a shortcut behind the cafeteria, when I ran into Billy sitting against the wall.

He was on the ground.

By himself.

"Hey," I said, skidding to a halt. "You okay?" But as I moved in closer, it was easy to see that he was *not* okay. So I swung off my backpack and sat next to him. "What happened?"

He digs a stick into the dirt. "Foxmore doesn't believe me, and neither does my dad." He gives a sort of dejected shrug. "Nothing new."

"Wait. Your *dad* didn't believe you? Why not?"

He snorts. " 'Cause I'm a screwup and a loser and a great big disappointment."

I squint at him. "*What?*" I watch him a minute, then say, "Wow, Billy. Even my mom—who, believe me, is not my biggest fan—stuck up for me."

He digs at the dirt harder. "Yeah, well, like I said—nothing new."

Now, sitting there watching him, it hits me how the whole time I've known Billy, I've never heard him talk about his family. Ever. And maybe it's because I totally avoid talking about mine, but not knowing anything about his never seemed odd to me.

Until now. Now all of a sudden I want to know: Are his parents together? Divorced? Does he have brothers? Sisters? Dogs? Cats? Do they live in an apartment? A house? Is there a gerbil in a cage on his dresser?

I cock my head a little. "So your dad and you . . . don't get along?"

"It's my dad and everybody," he grumbles. "And I don't want to talk about it." Then he stands up and puts his hand out to help me up. "Come on, Sammy-keyesta, we better get to class before they arrest us for something else we didn't do."

He's trying to sound cheerful, but it's really not working. And once I'm standing and we're face to face, he *doesn't* head to class—he just stares at me.

"What?" I ask him.

"Do *you* believe me?"

I look him right in the eye. "I do."

He takes a slow, deep breath. "Thanks." Then, as we start toward the drama room, he asks, "So who do you think's doing this stuff, and why are they trying to frame me?"

"You? How about *me*? They put your phone in my backpack, remember?"

He gives me a halfhearted grin. "Well, *you*, I understand."

I backhand him. "Hey!" Then I ask, "You do believe me, don't you? That I didn't swipe your phone?"

"Are you kidding me, Sammy-keyesta? Of course!" Then he frowns and says, "Heather was really ticked about her phone, but I don't know how she could have pulled off stealing mine."

"She might have snagged it off the desk on her way out to the drill. Anyone could have, but I don't know who else *would* have."

He nods. "She was back in class before me, too."

"She was?"

"Yeah." He shakes his head. "But I still don't think it's her. I can't see her getting anywhere near a rat."

"What do you mean?" I grumble. "She *is* a rat." But I have to admit—he does have a point. Then I have a thought. "What if . . ."

"What if what?"

I drop my voice. "What if she's blackmailing someone else?"

"Like who?"

"Could be anyone, knowing her." I think some more. "Or what if she's just *working* with someone else?" But Monet and Tenille were the only two people I could think of who might go along with one of Heather's schemes, and they weren't smart enough to pull something like this off. I also couldn't see either of them anywhere near that nasty rat, even with Heather cracking a whip.

So I shrug and say, "Or maybe Heather has nothing to do with it. Maybe it's just someone who hates Vince. Or some*ones*." I snap my fingers. "What if *one* person did the rat and *another* took your phone and did the phone message?"

143

He looks at me. "Kinda like I did the board but not the rat?"

"Exactly! Maybe it's like a Die Dude Derby or something, where everyone who thinks Vince is a pain enters the race to leave him a message!"

"A Die Dude Derby?" He pulls a goofy face. "We'll be Die Dudin' all year!"

I laugh. "See what you started?" Then I whisper, "Did you tell your dad or Mr. Foxmore about writing on the board?"

He stops. "Are you kidding me? No!"

"Well, you were being so, you know, *cavalier* about it during lunch."

He starts walking again. "Yeah, well, everyone knows I'm an idiot." He snorts. "Just ask mah daddy."

Now, we're hustling to get to drama before class is completely over, only just before we get there, the door *next* to the drama room opens and Cisco walks out. "Hey," he says, looking around as he's locking the door behind him, "did you get yourselves cleared?"

Billy eyes me, and I can tell he's thinking what I'm thinking: *Man, I hate gossip.*

"How'd you find out?" I ask.

He just shrugs. "I hear things."

"Well, hear this—we're innocent."

He laughs. "Did I say you weren't? You two are good kids. Anyone can see that." He grins at Billy. "You're a clown, but that doesn't make you bad."

"Well, whaddya know," Billy says. "Thank you, Cisco!"

Cisco's still grinning at him. "You wouldn't, for example, have target practice on some little princess's, uh, *muddy* pink phone, would you?"

We both blink at him like, What?

"Hmm," he says, looking up at the sky. "Then again, maybe if it came right down to it, you would. Maybe *I* would." He scratches the back of his neck and does a real relaxed one-shoulder shrug. "Every boy in the last two PE classes couldn't seem to resist."

I start busting up. "Are you saying . . . ?"

He's *still* grinning as he starts to walk away. "I'm saying nothin'. And whatever it is I'm not sayin', you didn't hear it from me, got it?"

"Got it!"

So, yeah, Billy and I are totally cracking up as we jet over to drama, but before we go inside, we try to straighten up and act serious. I mean, how good would it look to come to class laughing after being grilled about "death threats" by the VP?

Turns out I was worrying about nothing because since school's almost out, everyone in the drama room is talking, and it's super loud inside. Still, we act all serious as we check in with Mr. Chester, but the minute we're done with that, Heather corners us and says, "I don't know how you got it, but I know you did. And you are going to pay, you hear me? You're gonna pay!"

Now, she is right in my face spraying hate spatter all over me, and I'm sorry, but I've about had it with her stupid accusations. So I shove her back and say, "No, *you* listen to *me*. I didn't touch your phone, and I'm not the one having target practice on it. So keep your stupid, unfounded, backstabbing accusations to yourself!"

She squints at me. "*Target* practice?" And then she gets it. "Who . . . ?"

"Every boy in the last two PE classes, that's who." I look her in the eye. "It's called karma, Heather. What you do to other people winds up coming back on you."

Then I grab Billy and take off, wondering if what I'd said would ever soak in.

"Wow," Marissa said after school let out. "Were you and Billy in the office that whole time? What happened?" She looks over her shoulder. "And what did Heather say to you in there? I thought you were going to pound her!"

So I start with the juicy stuff—target practice.

"No!" Marissa gasps.

And then I launch into the story about my mother and how she put on the Perfect Mother Show for the Borschman and Mr. Foxmore.

"She's still in town?" Marissa asks.

"Apparently," I tell her, rolling my eyes.

"Well, at least she *helped* you for once."

"I know," I grumble, because it's so much easier to deal with bad when it doesn't dabble in good.

Now, to make a long story short, Marissa used to ride her bike to school, but over the summer her dad totaled it with his car as he was tearing away from the house. So instead of a bike, she now has a skateboard—one that Hudson got for her for two dollars at a garage sale.

Trouble is, she doesn't ride very well. She's wobbly and can't seem to decide which foot to push with. She keeps switching. And fumbling. And picking up the skateboard and walking.

It drives me crazy. Especially when I want to *move*.

Anyway, on the days she "rides" it, she keeps her board in Mr. Tiller's classroom, because she has him for homeroom and he's one of those cool teachers who doesn't mind. And since I had Mr. Tiller for math last year, and since his classroom is pretty close to the Vincenator's, that's usually where I park mine, too.

So *anyway*, we're heading for Mr. Tiller's classroom and I'm catching Marissa up on what happened in the office when I notice Cisco. His arms are out like he's pushing his cart of cleaning stuff, only his body's leaned waaaay back and his head is twisted to the side so he can look around the corner behind him.

I stop talking, and I stop walking. And when Marissa notices that I'm checking out Cisco, she laughs and says, "It looks like he's waterskiing with his cleaning cart."

Now I'm wondering if maybe something new happened in ol' Scratch 'n' Spit's classroom, because it's right around the corner. So we tiptoe up to where Cisco is, and I whisper, "What's going on?"

He jerks forward with a "Huh?"

"Sorry! I didn't mean to spook you."

He puts a finger in front of his lips and waves for us to have a peek around the corner. So Marissa goes high, and I go low. And when I've got my eyeball wrapped around the corner, what do I see?

Mr. Vince arguing with Mr. Foxmore.

"I can't quite hear," Cisco whispers. "Can you?"

So I hold my breath, but I can only barely make out Vince's half of it. ". . . how do you expect me to teach? How do you expect me *not* to freak out? . . . I am *not* overreacting! Don't you watch the news? There are crazy people in this world! . . . No, I don't think it's them! . . . How am I supposed to know who it is? This is an open campus. It doesn't have to be a student—it could be anybody! . . . No, the best thing is for *you* to do *your* job! You're supposed to make this a safe school, and if you can't do *your* job, how do you expect me to do *mine?*"

Mr. Foxmore says something, then starts to move away. So Marissa and I duck back, and when Cisco asks us, "Could you hear?" Marissa nods and gives him a quick rundown of what she'd heard—which pretty much matched what I'd heard. Then she whispers to me, "It sounded like Mr. Vince *doesn't* think it was you and Billy, did you get that?"

I nod. "Miracle of miracles."

"That *is* good!" Cisco says. Then he pushes forward, saying, "I'd better get moving before someone wonders what we're doing."

So he goes one way, and we go back to Mr. Tiller's room to grab our skateboards, only Mr. Tiller kinda corners me and says, "Please tell me it wasn't you."

"It absolutely positively wasn't me!"

He half sits on the edge of a student desk. "So what *is* going on? The rumors have been really flying this afternoon."

"About Heather's phone? Or about Billy and me getting grilled in the office?"

"Both!"

So we wind up hanging out in Mr. Tiller's classroom for a good twenty minutes while I tell him *my* side of things, leaving out the stuff about Billy writing on the board and Sasha picking up Heather's phone and Cisco helping us get inside information. And when I'm all done, he shakes his head and says, "It's been a very strange day. From the fire alarm to all this phone business. . . ." He stands up and laughs. "It's *way* too early in the year for this! Usually, we have meltdowns and crises at the *end* of the year." He starts toward his desk, saying, "Let's just hope they figure it out soon."

So we finally get out of there, and since we're not allowed to ride skateboards on the walkways at school, we shortcut over to the alleyway that delivery trucks use to bring in food or pipes or whatever, and ride out of school that way. And I'm almost to the alleyway gate when Marissa calls, "Hey, wait up!"

I look over my shoulder as I cruise along and see her jumping off her board, running to catch it. So I stop at the gate and wait while she grabs her skateboard and runs toward me crying, "I hate being so bad at this!"

"Look," I tell her, "you need to decide on a foot. Just push with your right foot, okay?"

"But it feels weird."

"So push with your left foot."

"But that feels weird, too!"

"Well, you can't push with both."

"I could if it was a bike!"

I frown at her a minute. "Okay. How about this—close your eyes and pretend it's a scooter. What would you do?"

So she actually closes her eyes and puts her hands up like she's holding the handle of a scooter. "I'd push with my right."

"Yay!"

There's a big gap between the doors of the gate, so I squeeze through it, backpack and all. And after Marissa has done the same, I take her board from her and put it down at her feet. "Okay. You're gonna push with your right, and you're gonna *commit*. No more of this scaredy-cat stuff. You can always jump off, right? So quit worrying about falling off or crashing. Just push like you mean it and enjoy the ride!"

So she gives it a shot. And even though she's pumping more than she's riding, she's actually leaning into it, pushing like she means it. It probably helps that it's not a real public spot, so she doesn't have to feel self-conscious about people watching her. Plus, we're on cement, not asphalt, and there are no dips or curbs or typical sidewalk hazards like, you know, bulging tree roots or dogs or *evidence* of dogs.

The *trouble* is, this kinda unpublic place happens to be the teachers' parking lot, and all of a sudden I notice taillights.

"Marissa!" I call, because she's ahead of me, riding straight for an SUV that's backing up. And it's backing up *fast*. "Marissa! Car! MARISSA! CAR!"

When she finally looks up, she panics and jumps off

her board, sending it flying forward as she staggers and stumbles and then falls to the side. And before I can even finish blinking, the SUV goes MUNCH, CRUNCH, *THWUMP* right over the skateboard.

The brake lights come on, the driver's door flies open, and then who comes scrambling out?

The Kid Detester himself.

"What the hell are you doing back here?" Mr. Vince shouts after he sees the demolished skateboard.

I blink at him a minute, then help Marissa off the ground as I tell him, "Thanks so much for your concern, but I think she'll be fine."

He snarls at me, then walks around the back bumper, which is chalky-looking and already dinged in at least two places, and has three faded oval stickers on it that say STURGIS.

Whatever that is.

And when he finally decides that we haven't done any suable damage to his awesome ride, he kicks what's left of Marissa's skateboard out from under his car and says, "This is the *teachers'* parking lot, not your little skate park. You're lucky nobody got hurt."

Then he gets in his car, slams his dirty blue door, and leaves us in a cloud of burning rubber.

SEVENTEEN

So much for riding skateboards home. After we threw away the scraps of Marissa's board, we wound up hoofing it out of there some back way that Marissa wanted to go. It was an odd route, too, and finally I ask her, "Why are we going this way?"

She just shrugs and says, "Nobody from school goes this way."

I snort. "Well, yeah! Why would they?" But then something hits me. "Are you avoiding someone?"

"No!" She laughs. "I just like the trees, don't you?"

Well, the trees don't look like anything special to me, but I don't tell her that. I just walk along wondering what's really behind our going this way, 'cause I'm getting the feeling it has nothing to do with trees.

She lets out a sigh. "First my dad runs over my bike, then Mr. Vince runs over my skateboard. What's next?"

I eye her. "Got Rollerblades?"

She laughs. "No, but if I did, I'd leave them in the closet!"

Now, while she's talking, she's kinda glancing away from me, looking to the right. And she *keeps* glancing to the right as we walk along, so I do, too. And I'm sorry, but I don't see what's so doggone interesting about a one-story tract house with a sort of patchy lawn.

And then we pass by the mailbox.

"Urbanski?" I ask, my eyes bugging out as I read the faded letters on the side of the mailbox. "This is *Danny's* house?"

"Shhh!" she says frantically. "Be cool! And keep walking!"

I grab her arm. "Marissa, how can you *not* be over him? After everything he's done to you? He's a liar and a sneak . . . and you hated him! Remember during the summer when you saw him kissing *Heather*?"

"I know," she cries, her face crinkling up.

"Oh, good grief." I pull her by the wrist. "I can't believe you're stalking him!"

"I'm not stalking him! He's not even out of school yet!"

Which was true. The high school lets out forty minutes after we do.

So I stop and look at her and ask, "Okaaaaaay . . . so what *are* we doing? Stalking his *house*?"

"No!"

"Then . . . ?"

"I don't know!" she wails. "I just can't help it. He *lives* there. He *walks* here. He . . . he breathes this air!"

I shake my head and yank her along. "You're obsessed, you know that?" I look at her. "How often do you do this?"

She shrugs.

"Like, every time I don't walk home with you?"

She shrugs again, but there's something more to it than just a Yeah.

"Wait . . . you come this way in the morning, too?"

She cringes. "Sometimes."

I stop and turn to face her. "This is crazy, you know that."

She nods.

"You have to stop it!"

"I know."

"Is that why you took me this way? Because you wanted me to catch you stalking his house?"

"I'm not stalking his house! And no!" She marches on, muttering, "I can't believe you even noticed."

"Are you kidding me? An avalanche would have been more subtle!" I frown at her. "And if you *weren't* trying to tell me, then I can't believe you've been keeping this from me."

"Me?" she says, her eyes popping. "What about *you*? I can't believe you didn't tell me Billy was the one who wrote on the whiteboard. *Billy* couldn't believe you didn't tell me!"

So, yeah, I totally bite at her subject-switching bait. I get all defensive and try to explain *again* why I didn't tell her about Billy, but still, no matter what I say, she keeps coming back to how Billy is her friend, too, and how she had the right to know. And before we've even settled *that* argument, she gives me a defiant look and says, "So what other secrets are you keeping from me?"

"I'm not!" I snap, but then I remember.

Sasha.

Sasha and the phone.

"What?" Marissa asks, zooming in on my expression.

I blink. "Uh . . ."

She gives me a little shove. "Tell me!"

"Oh, maaaaan."

"Tell me!"

"I promised I wouldn't!" But this suddenly seems like a really lame excuse. I mean, it's not like Sasha was my friend—she was actually kind of strange. And she'd been all huffy to me. Forget that—she didn't even seem to be *talking* to me. Why should I keep the secret of some strange, huffy girl from my best friend?

Seeing the look on Marissa's face did me in. "All right, all right!" But I'm hot and tired and just don't feel like walking while I'm talking about it. So I diagonal over to the shade of a tree, plop down on the curb, dump my backpack and skateboard, and heave a sigh. "It's about Sasha."

Marissa dumps her backpack, too. "Sasha? That homeschooled girl who lives out in some farmhouse in Sisquane with six brothers and twelve cats?"

"What? How do you know all that?"

Marissa shrugs. "I have her in math. Preston Davis is always quizzing her about random things before class starts. She's really smart." She eyes me. "And a little . . . different."

"Yeah, well, that can be a good thing, right?"

Marissa nods. "So what secret are you keeping for her?"

"I don't know if I'm keeping it *for* her or *about* her. I just pinky swore that I'd keep it, and—"

"You *pinky* swore? With *Sasha*?"

"I know. Weird, huh?"

"How did *that* happen?"

So I tell her the whole thing. From the top. About Sasha sitting in front of me, about me trying to clue her in to the ways of public schooling, about her thinking I was a wimp for not standing up to Heather, and then finally about Heather falling on the ramp and losing her phone. "Heather swore someone tripped her, and of course she thought it was me . . . but it wasn't."

Marissa gasps. "*Sasha* did it?"

So I tell her how it took me a while to figure that out because she'd been so *smooth,* and I just didn't expect that sort of thing from her.

Marissa thinks about this a minute, then says, "If I was surrounded by six brothers in a farmhouse out in Sisquane, I'd probably know some tricky moves, too. Just for survival."

I nod. "True." And for the first time, Sasha being a stealth tripper totally makes sense.

Then Marissa asks, "So when did she admit it? And how come a pinky swear?"

So I tell her about PE and how it had felt like performing some sort of delicate surgery to get anything out of Sasha.

"But she did admit it?"

"Well, sort of. That was weird, too. She didn't actually come out and *say* she did it, but she did this demented laugh and a little nod and then made me pinky swear not to tell."

"Good enough for me!" Marissa laughs. "And anyone who takes Heather on like that is a friend of mine."

"Yeah, well, don't be so sure."

"What do you mean?"

So *then* I tell her about the whole you-do-the-downs-and-I'll-do-across thing and how Sasha's attitude totally changed after I wouldn't go along with it, and how she's basically not talking to me now.

Marissa thinks about this a minute, then says, "You'd think she'd be worried that you'd tell people she's the one who put Heather's phone in the Porta-Potty."

"You'd think," I snort. "But she can just deny it because it's my word against hers. And what if she decides to turn it around on me and say that *I* admitted to *her* that *I* did it?"

"Wow . . . ," Marissa says, blinking at me. "And who would believe you over her, right?"

"Exactly. So I'm just gonna leave it alone and appreciate that she tossed Heather's precious phone in the turd tank." I grin at her and snicker, "Target practice!" and we both totally crack up.

Now, I guess we were kinda comfy sitting on the curb in the shade because we wound up staying parked there while we talked about everything from our teachers to our parents to what Billy had said about his dad to Danny to Casey—a subject I immediately shut down—to softball. "I don't even think I'm going to play this year," I tell her, re-tying the laces of my high-top. "Ms. Rothhammer says she's not coaching, and ol' Scratch 'n' Spit *is*. It's just not worth it."

"I can't believe how much things have changed," Marissa says with a sigh. "Softball used to be so important to me, and I barely even care about it anymore."

"That's because of everything that's going on with your family and living in limbo at Hudson's and—"

She reaches for my wrist. "What time is it?" And when she sees, she bolts off the curb. "Quarter to *five*? How did it get to be quarter to *five*? Mikey's going to be worried!"

I stand up, too. "Mikey is?"

"Oh, you have no idea," she says, dusting off.

So we grab our stuff, and off we go to Hudson's, where I figure I'll call Grams and tell her why I'm late.

It turns out Marissa's right—Mikey is waiting for us. He's doing it by sitting smack-dab in the middle of the sidewalk in front of Hudson's porch, and when he sees us coming, he jumps up and starts running toward us.

Running.

I just stop dead in my tracks, because the idea that Mikey would jump up and run was outside the scope of, you know, Mike-ability.

Only it's not Marissa he's charging toward.

It's me.

"Guess *what*?"

I blink at him a minute, 'cause his eyes are shining and his cheeks are glowing, and he's . . . well, he's just not the same old Mikey.

Or even the same *new* Mikey.

"What?" I finally ask.

"I spied on Captain Evil today!"

I blink at him some more.

"*You* know!" he says, jumping up and down a little. "Your teacher?"

"Of course I know who Captain Evil is." I look over both shoulders and whisper, "Where'd you see him?"

"On my power walk!"

I raise an eyebrow at him. "Your power walk, huh?"

"Yeah. And he dropped this!"

He hands over a flimsy piece of paper.

It's a receipt, crinkled and smudged.

Hudson has joined us now, and he says, "The power walking was Mikey's idea. We started on Monday." He winks at me. "But today we were apparently on a mission."

"So what was"—I look both ways—"Captain Evil doing?" I ask Mikey as I hand him the receipt.

Mikey looks up at me, shocked. "Don't you want that?"

Hudson gives me a look and a bouncy nod, which means YES! You want it!

"Are you sure I can have it?" I ask Mikey.

His head bobs up and down. "I can't figure out what it's for! Neither can Hudson."

So I look at it more closely and try to decipher the faded type. There's the SKU number and then "12x18mgntsn," with a price of $19.95 next to it.

It's the only item on the receipt, and the receipt is from a place called Jiffy Print.

Probably something the Vincenator had to get printed for school.

So, yeah, what I'm holding is garbage. But what I say to Mikey is, "Hmm. I'm going to have to try to crack this code," and then I slip the receipt in my pocket.

He nods, super excited to have handed over this invaluable piece of evidence.

"So where's Jiffy Print?" I ask, but Hudson cuts in with, "We saw Captain Evil at the motorcycle shop on Main Street."

"He was trying on *chaps*," Mikey giggles.

I look at Hudson. "Chaps?"

Hudson holds open the screen door, and as we file in, he says, "Leather overpants. They protect against asphalt scrapes better than jeans."

"They had fringe!" Mikey says. "He tried on a jacket, too. With fringe!"

"Lots of fringe," Hudson says, giving me a secret roll of the eyes. "Michael and I spent our walk home discussing fringe."

"It looks like hairy armpits!" Mikey says. Then he blurts, "Captain Evil has hairy armpits!" and totally busts up.

I laugh and tell him, "It's a good thing you're getting yourself into superhero shape, 'cause I don't know if your sister and I can handle Captain Evil by ourselves. Not if he's gonna start running around with hairy armpits."

"Yes!" he cries, and he actually jumps a few inches off the ground as he pumps his fist in the air.

"Looks like we've got a sidekick," Marissa whispers as I go to use Hudson's phone to call Grams. And as I'm dialing, it hits me that six months ago Marissa would have been desperate to get rid of Mikey, but now she seems happy.

Happy and *grateful.*

So I'm feeling pretty good . . . and then I talk to Grams.

"Where have you been? You don't have softball practice already, do you?"

"Uh . . ."

"Why doesn't anyone call me to let me know what's going on? Did Gil find Lana? Are you still in trouble at school? Why did they think you were making crank calls? *Were* you making crank calls?"

"No! And everything's fine. I'm at Hudson's now, and—"

"Why didn't *he* call me?"

"We just got here!"

"So they held you after school this whole time? Was your mother there?"

I take a deep breath and say, "You know what? I'll be right home. Just stop worrying, okay? I didn't do anything wrong, and I'm not going to jail."

She lets out a big breath and says, "Well, that's a relief."

"Grams!"

"Well, it is! You have no idea where my mind has traveled these past few hours."

"Okay, well, you can dock it in Reality Station now. I'm on my way home."

And I'm just about to hang up when she says, "Oh! Holly called. Apparently, she has news about Casey."

I put the phone back to my ear. "About Casey? Like what?"

"Do you think she'd tell *me*? But she did sound quite keyed up, so when you get home, remember to give her a call."

I hung up and grabbed my stuff, wondering what in the world Holly knew about Casey.

EIGHTEEN

I didn't wait to get home to call Holly.

Actually, I didn't call her at all. I went straight to her house.

Well, it's not a house like you're used to thinking of. She lives in an apartment over the Pup Parlor, which is a dog-grooming business that her adoptive mom and grandma own. And it turns out I didn't even have to go up to the apartment. Holly was downstairs, sweeping up dog hair.

"Hey!" she said when I walked in.

It was after five and she was alone, so I jumped right in with, "Grams told me you had some news about Casey."

She stops sweeping. "He was hanging out by the school. Like, right after school."

"So . . . ?"

"So I think he was looking for you."

I heaved a sigh. "Aw, c'mon."

"I'm serious! He just had that . . . that *look* about him."

"Holly, please." All of a sudden I'm so tired that I just want to collapse. This wasn't "news." This was my stupid little hopes getting dashed, and I felt like a total idiot for

163

letting any hope creep in in the first place. I plopped on a grooming table and sighed again. "I'm sure he was looking for his sister."

"But he wouldn't cut school to—"

"Who says he cut school?"

"They let out forty minutes after we do!"

"So maybe they were on half day or something."

She eyes me. "Yeah, well, I thought the same thing, so after I couldn't find you anywhere, I went by the high school, and guess what? Parking lots all full. PE classes out on the fields. . . ." She starts sweeping again. "He cut school."

I slap aside the hope that's trying to worm its way back inside me. "Yeah, well, if he did, it had nothing to do with me. You saw that text."

"I know. Which is why I didn't go over and talk to him. But now I wish I had." She scowls at me. "Because if he *wasn't* looking for you, I could have reamed him for being such a jerk to you." Then she asks, "So you didn't see him?"

I shake my head. "Long story short, the Vincenator annihilated Marissa's skateboard in the teachers' parking lot—"

"What?"

"He ran over it." I shrug. "Marissa's fault, but he was a total spitwad about it."

Holly laughs as she dumps a pile of dog hair into the trash. Then she grins at me and says, "It's not like she could ride that thing, anyway."

I laugh, too. "Yeah, I know. But afterward she dragged

me some long, stupid back way home because she's been stalking Danny's house."

"She's been *what*?"

So I tell her all about that, and when I'm done, she just shakes her head and says, "She needs to get *over* him already."

I slide off the grooming table and tell her, "Yeah, and I need to get over Casey, so no more Casey sightings, okay?"

She shrugs and says, "Okaaaay."

So we say our see-ya-tomorrows, and I head home, jaywalking Broadway, then crossing over to the Highrise, being careful to look like I'm going somewhere else before cutting through the shadows and up the fire escape. And really, I'm kinda dreading getting home and having to explain everything to Grams. It's not like I have anything to hide from her, but I feel like I've spent so much time explaining stuff to other people that I just don't want to talk about it anymore. Besides, Grams likes to go over the *details* of things. I can't just tell her, Mom showed up and sorta bailed me out, and everything looks like it's gonna be fine.

No way.

I'm going to have to get into every little *breath* that was taken and every little *word* that was spoken and every little *glance* that was given . . . and I'm just not up to the Granny Inquisition.

But I told her I'd be right home, so home I go.

"Samantha!" Grams says when I slip inside, and she's sounding really . . . cheerful. "I just got off the phone with your mother!"

I dump my backpack and skateboard. "And . . . ?"

"She told me what she did for you at school!"

"Yup," I say, forcing half a smile, "Lady Lana to the rescue." I plop into a kitchen chair and ask, "So where is she?"

Grams blinks at me. "Where *is* she?"

"Yeah. Like, where's she staying? Is she still in Santa Martina?"

"I . . . I didn't think to ask."

I scowl. "Yeah, and she didn't volunteer." I eye her. "So how did Officer Borsch find her? You gave him Casey's dad's name?"

She nods.

I shrug. "Well, there you go."

Grams sits across the table from me and very gently says, "Samantha, look at the good. Your mother went to your school and got you out of a very tight spot."

"How hard was that? I didn't do anything wrong."

She frowns at me. "There are people on death row who didn't do anything wrong. But there they sit, on death row."

I shake my head and mutter, "Whatever. Yeah, she showed up. Yeah, she was great. Whatever."

Grams studies me a minute. "Well," she says, standing up, "I think you could be a little more grateful. Give credit where credit is due, that's what I always say."

I knew she was right, but I still felt really . . . disgruntled. I mean, my mother showing up one time doesn't erase all the times she *hasn't* shown up. I'm not just talking about for the times I've been in trouble, either. I'm talking about Back to School Night and Open House and parent conferences and . . . you know, stuff that parents go to because they're *parents*.

This was the first time she'd been to William Rose.

Ever.

And knowing her, it would be the last.

Still. As much as I tried to tell myself that one great performance as a mother did not make her a great mother, all through dinner and all through dishes and all through homework, Grams' words kept spooking around in my head.

Not just the ones about giving my mom credit or about being a little more grateful.

The ones about my not being supportive of *her.*

About how I refused to watch her stupid soap.

Which, according to Grams, wasn't so stupid.

As hard as *that* was to believe.

Anyway, Grams "retired" at seven-thirty, shutting herself in her room with a book and a glass of water. And since I really was wiped out from what seemed like the longest day ever, it was barely nine o'clock when I hit the couch.

Trouble is, as I'm taking off my high-tops, I see the charm that I wear laced to my shoe. It's a little horseshoe that I got from Casey about six months ago, and it's always there making me smile, reminding me of how lucky I am to have him in my life.

But seeing it now and facing the cold, hard fact that he's really *out* of my life is suddenly too much for me to take. I rip the laces out of my shoe, pull off the charm, and throw it across the apartment. And after I've cried my eyes out, I just lie on the couch feeling miserable, thinking about Casey.

I really thought I knew him.

I'd trusted him.

Believed in him.

How could he have given up so easily?

I tried to go to sleep, but I couldn't. All I could think about was Casey. So I finally got up and went to the kitchen, got myself some graham crackers and milk, and went back to the couch.

And then I just sat there, eating and staring straight ahead at the little black screen of our TV, thinking about Casey.

Eventually, my eyes wandered down to the stack of videotapes in the TV stand. They were all labeled: *Lords* 1, *Lords* 2, *Lords* 3 . . .

There was a *Lords* 24.

And I don't know—I guess anything was better than thinking about Casey, so I put in *Lords* 1. I figured if that didn't put me to sleep, nothing would.

And it should have. It was totally lame. The cheesy music between scenes, the overdramatic acting, the phony English accents, the swooshing of dresses, the awkward cliff-hangers . . . it was all so over-the-top and stupid. *The Lords of Willow Heights* is like a retro-vampire soap without the vampires, only there's a *normal* world in the valley below where one of the "lords" works as an emergency room doctor. I don't know *what* it's trying to be.

I started fast-forwarding through all the scenes my

mom wasn't in, only that made it so I didn't understand the story line. So I let the tape run, and eventually it did the trick. When my alarm went off in the morning, the remote was still in my hand, Dorito was sleeping on my head, and the tape had popped out, leaving the TV buzzing static.

"Ohhhh," I groaned, feeling totally wiped out.

It crossed my mind that I should just stay home from school, but then Grams started clanging around in the kitchen, and Holly called to see if I wanted to ride to school together—something we hadn't done all year.

So I took a quick shower, gobbled some oatmeal, and snuck out of the building and across the street to the Pup Parlor, where I met up with Holly.

It would have been a whole lot safer to just stay home.

NINETEEN

Holly *does* know how to ride a skateboard, even though she hasn't had hers all that long. In some ways, she's a lot more like me than Marissa. She's tough. She's had to scrape through life even more than I have and, as Hudson says, she's not afraid to "jump into the fray."

But I've known Marissa since the third grade, and I've only known Holly about a year, and there's something about having history with a person that sort of glues you together.

And it's not *just* that I've known Marissa a long time, it's that we've been sharing secrets and getting in and out of trouble together for as long as I can remember. I mean, there are people that I've known for just as long, but there's no glue between us because we've barely even talked for that whole time. Oh, maybe there's a drop of glue here and a drop of glue there—like we can say to each other, Hey, do you remember that time back in fourth grade when Benny Salizar barfed on the teacher's desk? Or, Hey, do you remember gator taters? 'Cause that was everyone's favorite thing in our elementary school cafeteria. But after that, there's no glue. Your conversation just sort of splits apart, and you go back to being separate people in parallel universes traveling through the same slice of history.

So Marissa and I have some serious glue—long, wide ribbons of it that make us stick together. But what Holly and I have is like little squirts of *superglue*. We've been through some really heavy stuff—stuff that we never talk about anymore but is still always there, holding us close.

And we might have a better bond of, you know, *regular* glue if we rode to school together every day. It would make total sense to do—we live across the street from each other, and we both ride skateboards. But I'm always running late, and it drives Holly crazy. She's, like, punctual and organized and disciplined, where I tend to scramble around, or forget things, or get sidetracked. And we usually don't ride together *after* school 'cause Holly volunteers at the Humane Society, and that's in a different direction.

Anyway, as usual, I got to Holly's late, only this time her solution to that was to say, "Race ya!"

Well, she knew I couldn't turn *that* down. I laughed and said, "You're on!"

She kept up with me along Broadway where the sidewalk segments were long and straight. But when we turned down a side street, there were more alleyways and intersections, and since she doesn't hop curbs yet, I started to get a pretty good lead on her.

Still, every time I checked over my shoulder, there she was, pumping like mad to close the gap.

About a block and a half from school, I let up a little,

171

just to make it fair. And since there was no one in front of me, I was cruising along, watching her over my shoulder, when all of a sudden, THWACK, something rams hard against my shoulder, and I go sprawling across cement.

You know those stars that circle over the heads of cartoon characters when they get clobbered? Well, I saw them. And I swear I heard little birds chirping, and the whole world spun for a few seconds.

And then, through the spinning and the stars and the tweeting birds, I hear a voice.

"You should watch where you're going, loser!"

And suddenly a devil is floating in the little spinning stars above me.

A devil named Heather.

And on either side of her, little devilettes, Tenille and Monet.

"I didn't touch your phone!" I spit out, fighting back the tweeting birds and the swirling stars.

"This isn't about my phone!" she screeches at me. "This is about your mother stealing my father!"

Her leg cocks back to kick me, only all of a sudden *she* goes staggering to the side. "You weasel!" Holly shouts as she shoves her clear of me. "You think you can just hide behind a fence and *tackle* people?"

"Don't touch me, Trash Digger!" Heather shouts at her.

It wasn't the first time Heather had called Holly Trash Digger.

She'd also called her Ugly Orphan.

And Homeless Hag.

And even though Holly had always just walked away before, suddenly she's had enough. She grabs Heather by her shirt, and then *wham*, she buries her fist in Heather's stomach so deep it looks like it might come out the other side.

Then she just lets go.

Heather doubles up and falls to her knees. "Help me!" she gasps at Tenille and Monet.

Now, all of us know that this Help me does not mean Help me get to my feet or Help, I need air or Please, I think I'm going to *die*. It means GET THEM.

And since by now I'm back on my feet, there's no way Tenille and Monet are going to take us on.

"Hey," Tenille says to us, her hands in the air like someone said, Stick 'em up. "I was just walking to school."

"Me too!" Monet eeks out, and they both scurry away.

Holly and I pick up our skateboards, but instead of just walking away, I squat down in front of Heather and say, "You think I *want* my mom with your dad? You think it's *my* fault they got together? Think again, sister." I stand up. "Or should I say *step*sister."

And *then* we walk away.

In a strange way I felt sorry for Heather. I mean, talk about being the last one to know. Obviously, she had *just* found out. And when I'd said "stepsister" to her, I could see the horror in her eyes. Like she hadn't even known long enough to think through what my mom and her dad getting together might mean. And the more I thought about it, the more I had to shake my head over the whole new dimension of this.

For the first time ever, Heather and I *agreed* on something—neither of us wanted her dad with my mom. And I hate to admit it, but it did cross my mind that Heather and I could maybe team up and find some way to break up our parents.

We would be unstoppable.

But I immediately got the creeps and was totally revolted at myself for going there, even if it was only in my mind.

My hands and shoulder were scraped up and bleeding, so in the time we had before the bell rang, Holly helped me clean up in the bathroom. There was blood blotched around on my clothes, and there was a hole in my T-shirt sleeve from where I'd skidded across the sidewalk.

"That *witch*," Holly muttered as she soaked off the blood on my shoulder with a paper towel.

I pulled a face 'cause it felt like she was scraping rocks out of my arm. "It would have been worse if you hadn't stopped her."

Holly quit cleaning. "You okay?"

"Yeah, just do what you have to do."

"We need some Neosporin and Band-Aids."

The bell rang, which meant we had four minutes to get to homeroom. But the gouges in my hands were pretty deep, and I knew she was right. So I said, "I'll go to the office and get some. You go to homeroom. No sense in us both getting detention for being tardy."

"No one's going to give us detention! Not for this. Besides, Mrs. Tweeter will give us a pass."

I snort. "You want to risk it? This may not have happened *at* school, but it was close enough, and it sure qualifies as 'brawling.'"

"You're not going to report Heather?"

"And get you in trouble?"

"Me? I was just stopping her!"

I look at her a minute. "No . . . you were getting even. Which she totally deserved. But I think it's better to just drop it." I push her along. "So get to class!"

Now, I could have gone to class, too, but it was homeroom with the Vincenator, and it wasn't like I was dying to see him. Besides, I was sore all over and probably couldn't even have moved fast enough to make it to class on time. And I *was* hoping I could get a pass from Mrs. Tweeter. She'd slipped them to me before, and even though she would never come out and say it, I could tell she thought I was all right—and that Heather was a pill.

So I dragged myself up to the office and told Mrs. Tweeter I'd had a little accident on my skateboard and needed some Neosporin and maybe a Band-Aid or two, and after she saw my shoulder and hands and scolded me for "riding that thing without a helmet," she got me a first aid kit and let me have at it.

So I'm off in a corner chair next to a big fake potted tree, patching myself up, when Cisco walks into the office and says to Mrs. Tweeter, "Does Bob know about his car?"

"Bob . . . Vince?" she asks, peering at him over the tops of her glasses.

He nods.

Mrs. Tweeter pulls her glasses off her nose and lets them dangle. "What about his car?"

Cisco takes a deep breath. "It's been vandalized."

Mrs. Tweeter snatches up her phone, and before you know it, Mr. Foxmore and Cisco are going out the way Cisco had come in, Mrs. Sanford is in the office warbling, "I'll cover his class for him," Miss Anderson is coming out of her counseling office asking, "What happened?" and Lars Teppler is walking in late with a note. "We had a flat," he tells Mrs. Tweeter, who just scribbles off an admit for him and gets back to the phone.

Now, the whole time it's like I'm invisible. I'm just sitting there watching people scurry around like mice let out of a cage. And part of me's dying to go out and see what happened to Mr. Vince's SUV, but a bigger part of me knows that I shouldn't get anywhere *near* it.

And then Lars spots me.

He does a double take, then looks over his shoulder before coming over to ask, "What are *you* doing here?"

"Uh . . . had another scrape with the law?"

Now, I'm obviously joking, but he doesn't seem to get that. He stares at me like he still can't quite believe I'm just sitting there, then centrifuges his hair and says, "Well, *I'm* going to class," like I'm a derelict and he's some goody-goody swooshy-haired honor-roll boy or something.

"You do that," I call after him.

Then the passing bell rings, and almost immediately the office is a cross-flow of people. So real quick I finish with the first aid kit, slip it back on the front counter, and hurry to first period.

And it's weird. It's like there's a whole world of turmoil going on inside the universe of William Rose Junior High, but the turmoil is in the front office, which is light-years away from the little moons of learning.

All is quiet in the far reaches of the galaxy.

But by break, stealth probes have successfully infiltrated the Quiet Quadrants, and our little universe is once again waging a full-blown war against the Gossip Invaders.

At least I am.

"Who said it was me?" I ask Marissa after she tells me that that's what she'd heard. I plop my backpack onto the lunch table. "I don't even know what I supposedly did!"

"Scratched a huge DIE DUDE into Mr. Vince's car!"

"Like keyed it into the *paint*?"

Marissa nods. "Across the driver's door. It had to be done after he got to school or he would have seen it."

Then Dot and Holly run up saying, "People think it was *you*."

"Why do they think it was *me*?" But then I remember. Lars Teppler.

"Oh, good grief."

"What?" Marissa asks, because she can see the lightbulb over my head. And since she now also sees the state of my shirt and the Band-Aids on my hands, she adds, "And what happened to *you*?"

So Holly and I catch her up on our little before-school

run-in with Heather, and then I tell them all about my crack to Lars when I saw him in the office.

"Another scrape with the law?" Dot asks, looking at me like I've lost my very last marble.

"It was a joke! How was I supposed to know someone had keyed Vince's car!"

"Probably shouldn't go for a career in comedy," Marissa mutters. "You've got lousy timing."

And that's when it starts to sink in just how unfunny this really is. Mr. Vince knew I knew what his car looked like—he'd practically run over my best friend with it the day before.

And obviously I knew where he parked it.

Plus, where was I right before school when Vince's car must've been getting keyed?

Holed up in a bathroom with only a friend as a witness. Not just any friend, either. A friend who'd stick up for me to the point where she'd punch out my archenemy—not exactly someone Mr. Foxmore would think was a "credible witness."

"Oh, maaaaaan," I said, crumpling onto the bench seat of the lunch table. "I can't *believe* this!"

Then I closed my eyes and shook my head, wondering how long it would be before I got called back to the office.

TWENTY

I didn't *even* want to go to third period, but what choice did I have?

Well, I suppose I could have gone to the office and turned myself in for something I didn't do, but I wasn't *that* desperate.

Anyway, who was the first person I saw when I trudged through the door?

Good ol' Swooshy Head.

"Thanks a lot, Lars," I snarled as I pushed past him.

"Hey, what did *I* do?"

"You told the whole world that I was the one who keyed Vince's car!"

"I did not!"

"Yeah?" I turned to face him. "Well, did you tell *any-body?*"

He stared at me, then did a guilty little swoosh of the head.

"Yeah, that's what I thought." I gave him an annoyed squint. " 'Scrape with the law' was a *joke,* you dope. I was in the office for a first aid kit 'cause me and the sidewalk got a little too well acquainted this morning."

"How was I supposed to know that?"

"Oh, gee, let's see. Me, blood, a mutilated shirt, a first aid kit . . ." I pull a face at him. "Yeah, you're right—no clues at all."

The tardy bell rings, so everyone shuffles to their seats, and that's when I notice that some key players are missing.

Mr. Vince, for one, but that's no big surprise.

What *is* a surprise, though, is that Miss Anderson is the substitute. "I'm not here as a counselor," she announces. "We're all filling in for Mr. Vince while this situation gets straightened out." She gives me a keen look but then gets busy taking roll. "I show Heather Acosta, William Pratt, and Sasha Stamos as absent. Is that correct?" she asks.

Angie Johnson confirms that it is, but I can't help wondering *why* they're gone.

I mean, the Ambusher, the original Die Dude Dude, and the Cell Phone Destroyer, all absent?

It seemed like too much of a coincidence.

So my mind kicks into hyper-scramble trying to figure it out. Maybe Heather didn't come to school at all. Maybe Holly popping her little stomach balloon had sent her flying home. *Or* . . . maybe she was in the office now making up another one of her outrageous lies.

Or wait. Maybe Marissa had let it slip about Sasha and the phone. It wouldn't be the first time she spilled a secret. So maybe Sasha was in the office *with* Heather? Maybe the whole Porta-Potty incident was hitting the fan!

But . . . did that mean Sasha was going to sic her twelve

cats and six brothers on me 'cause I'd broken our little pinky swear?

Something about that seemed really scary.

Like there'd be pitchforks involved.

And what about Billy?

Where was he?

This whole Die Dude thing had gotten really vicious. Had Heather ratted on him for Die Duding the whiteboard? Was she pointing out what good friends Billy and I were and how we were obviously a duo of Die Duders?

Actually, I was pretty worried about Billy.

Especially after seeing him so . . . vulnerable yesterday.

So, yeah. I was kinda freaking out. And I knew—just *knew*—that any second the room would become even emptier 'cause *I'd* be summoned to the office, where Foxmore and ol' Scratch 'n' Spit would grill me over the Flames of Injustice until I was shriveled and charred and . . . and . . . and just plain *dead*, dude.

But I didn't get called to the office.

Not that period.

Not during PE.

Not during lunch or science or drama.

And although rumors about Mr. Vince having a nervous breakdown and being hauled off in an ambulance buzzed through the halls like swarms of biting gnats, and even though people said that the police had been there, and that men in suits and sunglasses had been there, at the end of the day, I just walked off campus.

"Maybe they're having me followed," I whispered to Marissa on our way home.

"You are being so paranoid! And quit looking over your shoulder—it makes you seem guilty."

"You know what's so stupid? I *feel* guilty. Why do I feel guilty?"

"Maybe because you've been keeping guilty people's secrets?"

I thought about that a minute. "Wow."

"Tell the truth—do you think it's Billy?"

"Doing the Die Dude stuff? No!"

She shakes her head. "Well, I'm not sure. He was absent all day today. Lacey Knotts is an office aide fourth period, and I heard her telling Hannah Loman that they were sending cops to his house."

"No! Why didn't you tell me this before?"

She shrugs. "Because I don't want to believe it, either." She eyes me. "And because I knew you'd want to go over there and try and fix things."

"I don't even know where 'over there' is! I have no idea where Billy lives, do you?" And that's when I *really* start getting all spun up. "I don't actually know anything about him except he always makes me laugh and I think he's got a really kind heart and his dad thinks he's a screwup and—"

Marissa grabs my arm. "Why are you crying?"

"I don't know! Okay? I don't know!" I fling away a tear. "Billy is not doing this stuff, okay? It *can't* be Billy." I take a deep breath. "I wish I knew where he lived. I *would* go over there. I don't even know his phone number."

She walks beside me a minute, then says, "But we know someone who does."

"Who?" But from the look on her face, I know who. "No way," I tell her. "I can't call him."

She shrugs. "But I can." And as soon as we get to Hudson's, that's exactly what she does.

Trouble is, it rolls over to voice mail. I shake my head at her like, Don't leave a message! but she does anyway. "Hey, Casey, this is Marissa," she says, all business-like. "Sammy and I are trying to track down Billy. It's important. Please call me back at this number as soon as you can." Then she hangs up.

"But you didn't leave the number."

"Hudson's number will show up on his cell."

I tell her, "Oh yeah," but never having had a cell phone, it wasn't something I was really on top of.

We tried calling a few other people, but they were all dead ends or not picking up. So finally I said what I'd been thinking but not wanting to say . . . even though I knew Marissa had been thinking it, too. "You want me to try Danny?"

She hands over the phone and tells me the number, and when I dial it, she stands up and does an *extreme* McKenze Dance, squirming side to side and gnawing on her thumbnail.

One ring.

Two rings.

Four rings.

I cover the receiver and whisper, "It's going over to voice mail. Should I leave a message?"

Her head jackhammers on her neck, so I roll my eyes and wait. And then the recording kicks in. "You've reeeeeeeached Danny! If you're a babe, I'll call you back. If you're not, you're outta luck. Unless you're one of my homies, of course. Here's the beep!"

Well, I'm not about to leave a message after *that*. I hang up quick and squint at Marissa. "Have you heard his message?"

Her lips pinch and her nose wrinkles and her head bobs a little.

"How can you like him? He's such a snake!"

"Yeah, I know," she says, but it's a real *pathetic* Yeah, I know.

Now, while I'd been calling Danny, Hudson had quietly come in and put something on the table in front of me, but I hadn't noticed it was the phonebook until now.

I laugh and flip it open. "Boy, are we dumb."

But it turns out there are twenty-two Pratts in Santa Martina, and hardly any of them have addresses listed.

Marissa shakes her head. "I sure don't want to call all these people, and you're not going to, either." She takes the phonebook from me and closes it. "Everyone stays home from school once in a while. He was probably just not feeling well. Or up too late watching movies."

I didn't really want to give up, but then Mikey came in all excited that I was there and asked if he could do homework with us—not that we were *doing* homework, but I guess with the phonebook out and our backpacks on the table, it looked like it to him.

And since Marissa gave me an awww-that's-so-sweet look, and since I knew homework wasn't exactly something Mikey usually did without being nagged, I said, "Let me call Grams and see what's up."

So I did, and since nothing was up, I stayed at Hudson's. And I did try to tackle my own homework, but Mikey wanted me to help him with his, so I wound up quizzing him on his spelling words and coaching him through his math instead.

Now, while we're working, Hudson delivers snacks. Sliced pears. Almonds. Carrot sticks. Some kind of seedy cracker. It's a lot different from the brownies and cakes he used to serve, but all of us munch away, and it really does taste good. Then when Mikey's homework's all done, Mikey asks, "Do you want to go on my power walk with me?" His face is totally lit up as he says, "Maybe we'll see Captain Evil!"

"Gee, Mikey, I wish I could, but I still have *my* homework to do."

Good ol' Hudson to the rescue. He maneuvers Mikey away from the table, saying, "Why don't you and I go scout around for Captain Evil and let the girls do their homework?"

"Uh, I can wait for them to finish," Mikey says, looking back at us.

"It would be a *long* wait," I tell him.

Marissa nods. "Go on, Mikey. We've got a *lot* of homework."

So Mikey and Hudson take off, and while they're gone,

Marissa and I buckle down and get some serious work done. I write up my lab report for science, finish an English worksheet, and finally face off with my hardest subject—math.

And I'm actually making good progress on the math when Marissa says, "Wow. They've been gone a long time."

I look up at her and say, "Maybe they're hot on the trail of Captain Evil," and that's when I notice something outside move.

Something that was in the window a second ago but disappeared.

Something *hairy*.

Not a cat. Or a rat. Or any other windowsill-walking creature.

This hairy thing had gone straight *down*.

"What?" Marissa asks, looking over her shoulder. "What did you see?"

"I think someone's spying on us."

"Spying on *us*? Who?"

We give each other a quick look, then shove back from the table and charge for the door.

TWENTY-ONE

Marissa and I bolt out the front door, fly down the porch steps, and race across Hudson's lawn to the side of the house where the window is.

And who do we trap in the shady strip that's between the house and the side fence?

Nobody.

The fence divides Hudson's property from his neighbor's, and it cuts away as you get closer to the sidewalk. It's lower. Something you could just jump over.

So I back up to the low section and look behind the neighbor's side of the fencing.

Nobody there.

So I look this way and that, back and forth, all around, and so does Marissa.

"Are you *sure* you saw something?" she finally asks.

And I *am* starting to wonder if my eyes had been playing tricks on me, but when I go back to the window and start checking around, I discover prints.

Not footprints.

Fingerprints.

Well, not the kind you can dust for and then take into

187

the lab to analyze. These were more like finger *marks*. And they were *in* the dust.

"Look!" I say, pointing to the eight smeared lines on the windowsill. "That's where they held on when they were looking through the window."

She thinks a minute, then says, "When you first said someone was spying on us, I thought it might be Mikey, since he's into the whole spying thing now. But there's no way he could move that fast."

"And Hudson would be around here somewhere."

She looks at me with wide eyes. "What if it was Danny?"

"Danny? Why *Danny*?"

"What if he did a reverse lookup?"

"A what?"

"You know. Someone calls you and you don't know who it is? Even if they didn't leave a message, their number's recorded, so you can do a reverse lookup on the computer and find out who called. It shows the address."

I give her a serious squint. "Or you can just call the number back to find out who it was . . . ?"

Marissa pulls a face. "Not if you didn't want them to know you cared."

I slap a hand to my forehead. "The reverse lookup would have shown Hudson Graham! And I didn't leave a message, so he wouldn't know it had anything to do with you!" I drop my hand and just stare at her. "You have *got* to quit obsessing!"

She gives a little pout. "Well, what if it was Casey?"

"Oh, good grief! Stop it!"

She stands there a minute looking really dejected, then

says, "Well, if it wasn't anyone we like, then this is giving me the creeps."

"No kidding."

She edges toward the porch. "I think I want to go back inside."

But I'm not done looking around yet, so I head out to the sidewalk and check up and down Cypress, hoping to see someone running away or hiding behind a tree or being chased by a dog. Something!

What I see instead is a whole lot of nothing.

And then all of a sudden I spot Mikey and Hudson rounding the corner at the end of the block.

"Hey!" I call over to Marissa, who's waiting for me on the porch. "Hudson and Mikey are almost home!"

"Was it them?" she asks, coming toward me.

I shake my head, 'cause the two of them are obviously serious about their power walk. "Geez, look at them go!"

When Mikey spots us, he makes like it's a race to the finish. His arms and legs go into hyper-pump, his red cheeks huff and puff, and he keeps checking over his shoulder to make sure Hudson's not going to pass him.

"Wow," Marissa gasps. "I think you'd call that *running*." Then she hollers, "Go, Mikey!"

So I cup my hands around my mouth and act like I'm an announcer at a horse race. "It's Mikey McKenze out in front, Mikey McKenze holding the lead! Mikey McKenze pulling ahead! Listen to the crowd go wild! Ladies and gentlemen, Mikey McKenze is . . . the . . . winner!"

He doubles over when he reaches us, panting like crazy

as he leans his hands on his knees. "We . . . ," *huff, huff,* ". . . saw . . . ," *huff, huff* . . .

"Captain Evil?" I ask.

He shakes his head and huffs and puffs some more before gulping in air and saying, "That girl you almost beat up at the mall!"

I blink at him. "The one who called you Blubber Boy?"

He nods like crazy, still panting away.

"Where?" And I can feel a lightbulb going on over my head.

He points behind him. "She was running thataway."

Marissa and I look at each other, and at the same time we say, "It was Heather!"

I turn to Mikey. "Someone was spying on us through the window, but they got away before we could catch them."

Marissa asks, "Where was she?" and since Hudson's standing there now, he says, "She was around the corner, almost to Cook Street. And she seemed none too happy to see Michael."

"Bus-ted!" I put my arm across Mikey's shoulders. "Way to go! You just cracked the case!" Then I nod and tell him, "You know what? I think you've earned yourself a code name."

He looks up at me all rosy-cheeked and shiny-eyed. "How about Spy Guy?"

I laugh, 'cause it's like he'd already been thinking he needed a code name. I look at Marissa. "Well?"

She nods and says, "Spy Guy it is!"

"Yeah!" he says, giving the air a little punch.

As we start toward the house, Hudson asks, "Hasn't Heather tried following you home in the past?"

Which was true. Heather's tailed me home quite a few times before, but I've always managed to ditch her. It's been on my way to the Senior Highrise, though, and I'm in a state of hyper-paranoia whenever I go home. I've never actually worried about being followed anywhere else. I mean, what's it matter? A friend's house is just a friend's house, not the place I live illegally. Not the place where Grams could get kicked out if people *found* out.

Still, I couldn't really believe Heather had managed to follow us to Hudson's. Not with the way I'd been looking over my shoulder for the FBI or whatever. But then I *had* been kinda wrapped up in worrying about Billy. So I tell Hudson, "Sorry I let her tail us. If she eggs the place or—"

"*I'll* catch her!" Mikey cries.

We all laugh because it's just so . . . *cute.* But Mikey goes, "Really! I will!" so I get serious and say, "I know you will." I look at Marissa. "I think this boy needs a cape!"

She nods. "Spy Boy to the rescue!"

"It's Spy *Guy,*" he tells her.

"Oooh. Sorry!"

I eye her. "Yeah, Marissa. You don't want to mess with Spy Guy."

Mikey slaps five on me, then says to Hudson, "You got any weights? I need to build some muscles!"

Marissa and I look at each other like, Whoa, this is out of control! I mean, there's no way a nine-year-old boy is going to be *bodybuilding,* but Hudson just gives us a wink and tells Mikey, "I do. But you're going to have to let me teach you proper form."

"Let's go!" Mikey cries, and bounds up the porch steps.

Marissa shakes her head. "Unbelievable." And as we go back to the table to finish our homework, she says, "And what a relief that it was only Heather, huh?"

I laugh. "A relief? If Vince is Captain Evil, she's Commando Evil!"

She thinks about this a minute, then adds, "Why do you think she was spying on us?"

I laugh again. "Getting even?" 'Cause Marissa and I have not only spied on Heather through her window, we've infiltrated her house wearing Halloween costumes.

But then the reason hits me.

And I can't help it—I gasp.

"What?" Marissa asks.

"I'll bet she's looking for my *mom.*"

Marissa's eyes bug out. "Oooooh. Now that's scary."

"No kidding!"

Marissa nods. "First her brother, then her dad . . . ! You and your mom have annihilated her little world."

"It was annihilated way before we showed up. And I'm out of the picture now, remember?"

"Yeah, but now she has someone to *blame.* And you know what? If my dad was moving away because of my archenemy's mom, I might go psycho, too."

All of a sudden I'm worried. "You think she'll go psycho on my mom?"

Marissa pulls a face. "It's *Heather.*" Then she adds,

"And she followed us here, didn't she? She was spying through the window, wasn't she? She was looking for something, and I don't think it was you." She snorts. "She can find you at school anytime."

So that shook me up a little. I mean, my mom may be self-absorbed and inconsiderate and *willful,* but at the same time she's weak. She faints at the sight of blood, she shrieks if she finds a mouse, and she thinks vacuuming is strenuous. And maybe I've gotten used to Heather going psycho on me, but picturing what she might do to my mom?

It was like a horror film flickering through my head.

Marissa got back to her homework, so I tried concentrating on finishing my math, but it was hard. My mind kept slipping to questions about my mom. Was she still in town? How had Heather finally been told? Had my mom and her dad broken the news to her . . . together? Had she found out some other way?

I didn't have any answers, so I made up scenes in my head. Really wild, dramatic scenes. I even pictured my *mom* breaking it to Heather in one of the castle rooms from *The Lords of Willow Heights.* My mom was in a long velvet dress and was gliding across the room toward Heather, who was in an arched doorway wearing jeans and smoking a cigarette. "I have something to tell you," my mom coos.

"Yeah? Well, I have something to *show* you!" Heather snarls. Then she grinds out her cigarette and produces a long, gleaming knife.

There's no blood on the knife, but even the *thought* of blood can do my mother in. And since obviously this long,

193

gleaming knife was going to produce some of the drippy red stuff, my mother's hand flutters to her forehead and she crumples to the ground.

"Sammy?"

I blink and see Marissa waving a hand in front of my face. "Huh?"

"You okay?"

"Um . . . yeah. Yeah, I'm fine."

"I was just saying . . . about Mikey?"

"What about Mikey?"

She kind of squints at me. "Where *were* you?"

I shake my head. "Never mind. What were you saying?"

She drops her voice a little. "I was saying how I think Mikey's finally getting a childhood."

I almost asked her what she meant, but all of a sudden I understood *exactly* what she meant. The McKenzes' house is like a museum. They have glass furniture—if you can believe that—and Mikey grew up being told not to touch, well, *anything*. Plus, they live way up on East Jasmine, where the houses are, like, a mile apart and there are no kids around to play with. Plus, if you knew Mikey McKenze, believe me, you would not invite him over.

At least not the old Mikey.

And it wasn't like his parents ever invited other kids over. With glass furniture and priceless artwork on display?

Please.

Plus, they were gone all the time, and their nanny sure didn't want to deal with any more than she had to.

So, yeah, in a flash, I got it. I got how Mikey was finally someplace where he could go exploring. Someplace he could turn into Spy Guy and people were cool with that. Someplace where people were actually letting him be part of the action.

Marissa tears up. "I hate to say this, but maybe my family falling apart has been a good thing."

"You don't mean that."

"I know I don't," she sniffs. "But maybe if all the money's gone, we can start living like this?"

I give a little shrug. "Your parents would have to *want* it for it to be like this."

She sighs. "I know. And I just can't see them wanting it." She gives me a quivery smile. "You have been the best friend ever, you know that? I can't believe how nice you've been to Mikey."

So we sit around and talk a little more about her brother, but finally I notice what time it is and collect my stuff, saying, "I've got to get home."

"Can't you stay for dinner?" Marissa asks.

I have to laugh 'cause she says it like it's *her* house and *she'll* be the one cooking. "Nah. I've got to get home to Grams." Then I holler, "Bye, Hudson! Bye, Spy Guy!" and after they holler bye back, I jet out of there.

So I'm just cruising along on my skateboard, minding my own business, taking shortcuts when I can, jayriding when it's safe, thinking about what another crazy day it's been, when I turn a corner near the mall and finally notice something:

I'm being followed.

TWENTY-TWO

The car following me is a really generic-looking white sedan. It's clean and seems to be in good shape, but it's an older style. Sort of big, with lines that are sharp instead of rounded. And I'm sure I could have ditched it by cutting through the mall, but I didn't like being spied on or followed, and I wanted to find out who was following me. So instead of ditching it, I flip a U-ie, cruise down a driveway, cut into the street, and ride my skateboard straight for the car's front grille.

The car nose-dives to a halt.

I stop, too, and pop up my board. And when I see the driver through the windshield, my jaw drops. "Officer Borsch?"

He powers down his window. "Are you *nuts?*"

"Why were you tailing me?" I ask, coming around to the driver's side.

"I was trying to catch up to you! Which would have been a lot easier if I ran stop signs and hopped curbs and cut corners!" He looks in his rearview mirror. "Get out of the street already!"

So I zip over to the sidewalk, and when he's pulled up

to the curb, he rolls down the passenger window and leans across the bench seat. "I've been taken off the Vince case."

I bend down. "What? *Why?*"

"I've been told I have a conflict of interest."

"A conflict of—" But then I get it. " 'Cause of me being in your wedding?"

He nods.

"So Foxmore heard my mom talking about it?"

"That's right."

Now, he's looking real uncomfortable, with his cast hand gripping the steering wheel, leaned clear over the way he is. And since he's not exactly parked legally, and since I've got a gazillion more questions and don't want him just taking off, I ask, "Can I get in?"

He hesitates, then pops up the lock. So I jump inside, skateboard, backpack, and all, and as he pulls back into traffic, he says, "If I didn't know better, I'd suspect you were a compulsive liar." He eyes me. "Which is exactly what Blaine Foxmore thinks."

"But you do know better, right?" I cross my heart and tell him, "I *swear* I had nothing to do with any of it."

He nods. "I believe you." Then he raises an eyebrow and adds, "And I would be alone in that, except for Bob Vince."

I hesitate, 'cause I'm pretty sure I heard that wrong. "You're saying Mr. *Vince* believes me?"

He turns onto the road that winds between the mall and the parking structures. "Every time someone suggested it, he brought up other people he thought might be guilty."

"But he *hates* me."

"Well, apparently, you're not the only one who hates him. He thinks these are real death threats."

"So . . . who *does* he think it is?"

"He's all over the map. And he's very testy. He's got no patience for logical analysis. One minute he thinks this, the next that."

"Well, who do *you* think it is?"

"I keep hitting roadblocks." He eyes me. "Although Billy Pratt is hiding something." A heartbeat passes. Maybe two. Then he adds, "And I'm pretty sure you know what it is."

"Officer Borsch, he's *not* the one doing this stuff!"

He comes to a complete stop at an empty mall crosswalk. "You seem pretty sure about that," he says, studying me. "But I questioned him at his house today, and I'm not."

"Wait—you went to Billy's house today? How is he? And where does he live?"

Officer Borsch raises an eyebrow at me. "I wouldn't tell you where he lives any more than I would tell him where you live."

I don't actually *say* Oops, but I know it's written all over my face.

"And if you're so sure he's not the one who's doing this, then tell me what he *is* hiding. Because I know it's something."

I felt like I was standing in the middle of a bridge that was collapsing. On one side was Billy's secret, on the other, Officer Borsch's trust. And the way Officer Borsch was looking at me . . . well, I knew that if his trust in me was broken, I would never get it back.

It was a miracle that he'd given it to me in the first place.

So as he pulled forward, I blurted out the truth. I told him about Billy writing the Die Dude on the board and about Heather blackmailing him, and how Sasha Stamos disposed of Heather's phone and all that. And I probably didn't have to tell him about Sasha, but I was doing a truth dump, and the story felt like it had holes in it without the Sasha part.

Now, while I was talking, Officer Borsch turned into the mall parking structure and stopped the car. I guess listening to me was too distracting, because he didn't exactly pull into a parking *slot* or anything.

He just, you know, stopped.

So when I'm all done running at the mouth, I look around and ask, "Uh . . . should you be stopped here?"

He eyes me. "Roadway concerns from a notorious jaywalker?" But he does pull into a parking slot and cut the motor. He stares straight ahead, and I can tell there are some heavy thoughts duking it out inside his skull, and I'm guessing they have to do with telling me things that maybe he shouldn't.

So I throw a few punches of my own. "Look, the stuff I just told you? That was a big secret between Billy and me. And it was a secret between Sasha and me, too. So whatever you're thinking about not telling me? You need to just spill it. Fair's fair."

199

He sucks at a tooth. It's a long, slow, sputtering sound that migrates from one side of his mouth to the other. Finally he says, "What makes you think I'm not telling you something?"

I shrug. "You're Gil Borsch, aren't you?"

He laughs.

Then I kind of look around and say, "And are you on duty or what?" because I can't quite figure his car out. There's a police scanner mounted under the console that's been staticking and chattering in the background the whole time I've been in the car, and there's one of those portable magnetic lights on the floor by my feet. You know—the kind cops can stick out through their window and slap up on their roof? Plus, Officer Borsch is in uniform, and there's a gun at his hip.

"No, I'm on my way home."

I'm still looking around. There are boxes of stuff and a beat-up old briefcase on the backseat. There's also a big black flashlight, a pair of handcuffs, and about a dozen to-go coffee cups on the floor *behind* the front seat. I look back at him. "So . . . is this an undercover car?"

"No. It's mine."

And that's when it hits me—Officer Borsch is a cop. He's not a guy with a family who dotes on his kids, or likes to watch movies, or follows basketball on TV and *also* reports to his job as a cop. He *is* a cop. From the minute he wakes up to the moment he falls asleep—and probably also *in* his sleep—Gil Borsch is a cop.

And that's when something *else* hits me.

"It bugs you to be taken off a case, doesn't it."

He sucks around his teeth some more, and *finally* he says, "I hate it."

"So stay on it through me!"

"How's that?"

"Tell me whatever it is you're thinking you don't want to tell me."

He frowns. "It's not that I don't want to tell you, it's that it's not professional for me to discuss it with . . . a suspect."

"But you know I didn't do it, and if I really am a suspect, I could use some help getting unsuspected."

He frowns and just sits there, quiet.

"Oh, would you tell me already? I promise to keep it totally to myself."

"Hmm," he says, and I'm thinking he's probably thinking what *I'm* thinking—that I'd promised Billy and Sasha that I'd keep their secrets to myself, too. But then he says, "It's nothing earth-shattering. Just a pile of random facts that don't seem to add up."

"Such as?"

"Such as . . ." He looks at me. "Your vice principal seems to have a certain level of disdain for Bob Vince."

"What do you mean?"

"I don't think he likes him very much."

"Well, who does?"

He shrugs like, Yeah, true. "Vince's ex-wife also seems to have a real beef with him. Apparently, the child-support payments have stopped."

"Wait. Mr. Vince has *kids*?"

"Two girls, ages ten and eleven."

I slide down in my seat a little. "Man, I feel sorry for those kids."

"Yeah, well, he told me he didn't want to get divorced and that he's tired of having to pay while the boyfriend acts like he's their dad. His ex told me she's going to attach his wages."

"What's that mean?"

"She's going to get a court order that will automatically give her part of his paycheck."

"But if *she* left *him* . . ."

"It doesn't matter. They're still his kids, and he owes child support."

I think about this a minute. "But she can't be the person doing the Die Duding. For one thing, no middle-aged lady is going to say 'Die Dude.' And besides, how can anybody think it's a woman or a girl or whatever when that phone recording was a *guy's* voice?"

He eyes me. "Maybe it's the boyfriend."

"Oh, wow."

Officer Borsch sorta shrugs. "That theory's got holes in it, too. And it doesn't do you any good at school. Foxmore thinks that you and Billy are in it together and that you used a Halloween voice changer. And I did some checking. They are in the stores already, and when I had Debra speak into one, she sure didn't sound like herself." Then he says, "And speaking of that phone message, something about that whole day bothers me."

"Yeah?"

"I don't believe in coincidence."

He just sits there staring through the windshield, so finally I ask, "And . . . ?"

"And the timing of the fire alarm and the phone message seems like a strange coincidence to me. Sure, someone could have seized on the fire alarm as an opportunity to leave Vince that phone message, but it's all too tightly choreographed for me. Especially since there was no fire."

That made my eyebrows reach for my bangs. And the thought of the calls being connected and someone trying to frame *me* for it was kinda freaking me out. "So . . . did you figure out who made the call about the fire?"

He gives me a little smile. "Very good. And yes." He does a nose wag out through the windshield toward the mall. "The call was placed from that phone booth right over there."

I let *that* sink in. "No view of the school from here."

"Unless you're on the roof of the mall, and even then, barely."

"So it was a crank call, but . . . how does that connect to someone using Billy's phone to leave a message on Vince's machine?"

He shakes his head. "More random facts that don't seem to want to work together." He eyes me. "But I still don't like the coincidence."

We sit there a minute, and finally I ask, "So what else? What about his car getting keyed. How bad was that, anyway?"

He reaches over and grabs the briefcase off the backseat with his good hand. "You want to see?" Then he clicks open the latches and pulls out a laptop. He boots it up, then jabs in a password with his right hand, and pretty soon I'm looking at the messiest computer desktop I've ever seen. It doesn't slow him down, though. He double-clicks on a folder icon and then opens up a photo file.

Suddenly the screen is filled with a picture of Mr. Vince's SUV's door.

The DIE DUDE looks angry and deep.

And the letters are *big*.

Like, four inches tall.

And they go nearly clear across the driver's door.

I shake my head. "That's brutal."

He nods, then clicks through some other pictures of the door, until he gets to one where the DIE DUDE takes up about half the screen. "Notice anything interesting here?"

I study it but have no idea what he's seeing that I'm not.

He gives me a minute, then says, "I didn't really notice it when we took the report, but I definitely see it here."

I study the picture some more, but I still don't get it.

So he tells me, "Maybe lean back a little," and when I do, I notice that there's a rectangular area around the DIE DUDE that seems darker than the rest of the door. "This right here?" I ask, tracing the area.

He cries, "Yes!" which is weird because I don't think I've ever seen Officer Borsch *excited* before. Then he says, "I've been told I'm imagining things, or that it's just a function of lighting, but once you notice it in one of the

pictures, you start seeing it in all of them. It's very uniform. Maybe a foot by a foot and a half."

"So what do you think it is?"

"That's just it. I have no idea. If the message had been
sprayed on through a stencil, I'd think it would be from
contact with the stencil. Or maybe someone held something up to the door to prevent leaving fingerprints."

"But you wouldn't need to touch the door to scratch
in the letters, would you?"

"That's right," he says with a frown. "So you see what
I mean? The more we know, the less things seem to
add up."

I think about this a minute, then say, "Well, I probably
should get going." And as I grab my stuff and open the
door, he asks, "You don't want a ride?"

"Nah."

"Well, thanks for the talk," he says as I'm getting out.
"I don't know why, but I feel better."

"Me too," I tell him. "Except that now I know Mr.
Foxmore has it in for me."

"Just tell the truth. And *try* to be respectful." He
shakes his head a little. "Do yourself a favor, Sammy, and
curb the attitude."

So I tell him, "Yeah, yeah, whatever," with *plenty* of attitude.

He actually laughs, then all of a sudden stops laughing
and says, "Oh—and watch that kid . . . What's his name?
Lance? Larson?"

"Lars? Lars Teppler?"

He snaps his fingers. "That's him."

"What about him?"

"He seems to have a lot of observations. About you in particular."

"Yeah? Like what?"

"Like he saw you waiting in line to use the pet tag machine at the pet store."

"He what?" But then I remember the Dog Tag Weirdo I'd been watching when we'd been at the mall with Mikey.

"He also says you've got a lot of upper-body strength and that the classroom windows were open during the evacuation."

"So he's saying I pulled myself in through the window? And how would *he* know about my 'upper-body strength'? That's just weird."

"He told me you had the chin-up record in your PE class."

"But he's not even in my PE class! And guess what? *Heather* opened those windows. Right before the alarm!"

"Hmm," he says with a scowl. Then he starts the car and says, "Well, Foxmore was very keen on all Lars' observations. So, like I said, do yourself a favor and curb the attitude at school. This is a lot more serious than you might think."

So I tell him thanks and close the door, and when he takes off one way, I take off another. My head feels like it's swimming, and the only clear thought I seem to have is that Officer Borsch is right.

The more I know, the less things seem to add up.

TWENTY-THREE

I came home to a note from Grams telling me she'd gone out to dinner with my mother. "Nice of them to invite me," I grumbled to Dorito as I leaned on the open refrigerator door, looking for something to eat. Actually, I was glad they hadn't asked me along. Being around my mom always makes me lose my appetite. Why waste a good dinner?

Anyway, there was a whole lot of nothing in the fridge, so I wound up opening a can of tomato soup. And as I sat at the kitchen table eating goldfish crackers and soup, it hit me that I never have dinner alone in the apartment. Even when I come home late and eat by myself, Grams is always around. She could be in her bedroom with the door closed, but I know she's right *there*. I can feel her, right *there*.

Once I had that thought, sitting there eating all alone felt weird.

Really weird.

The crackers seemed loud.

The hum of the refrigerator was buzzy.

The clock on the wall clicked.

Click . . . click . . . click . . .

Had it always clicked?

Why didn't it tick?

What kind of clock clicks instead of ticks?

Now, I'm not supposed to eat in the living room, but I scooped up my soup bowl and the box of crackers and went to the couch, where everything was quiet.

Well, except for the crackers—they were still loud.

I turned on the TV for company, but there was nothing good on, so I figured I'd earn a few brownie points with Grams and put in a *Lords* tape. I was planning to watch for just a little while, but since Grams had recorded the episodes back to back and had cut out the commercials, one episode just sort of ran into the next. And even after the soup and crackers were long gone, I still sat there, stupidly watching. I think I was too beat up to move. I mean, it *had* been another crazy day, and who could blame me for just vegging on the couch, right? But then before I know it, it's after eight o'clock, and Grams' key is sliding in the door lock.

In a flash, I press the OFF button of the remote, scoop up my dishes, and dash for the kitchen. But I guess I didn't press the button long enough, because the TV *doesn't* go off.

Now, given the choice, I'd rather be caught eating in the living room than watching a soap. And even though I was just doing it so Grams couldn't accuse me of not being "involved" in my mother's life, I still felt embarrassed about it. Like I'd been caught doing something I *wasn't* supposed to do instead of something Grams had been *asking* me to do.

"How was dinner?" I ask from the kitchen, hoping she'll come over and talk to me instead of noticing what's on TV.

Well, I guess I was acting a little too cheerful, because right away her granny radar goes up. She zeroes in on me suspiciously, then scans the apartment until she focuses on the television. "Oh!" she says, moving over to the living room. "You're watching *Lords*."

I hurry in there, too, and switch off the TV. "Only so you'll stop saying I'm a terrible daughter."

She blinks at me through her glasses. "I never said that!"

I plop onto the couch and cross my arms. "Well, Lady Lana's a terrible mother, and you said I was just like her."

"Samantha!" she says, but she says it softly. Like she's shocked by my interpretation. And maybe a little hurt by it, too.

And, really, I don't know why I'm acting the way I am. I don't know why I feel so embarrassed. "Sorry," I mutter, grabbing a pillow to hug.

She studies me a moment, then picks up the remote, saying, "Well, where are you in the story? Is Abigail still brain-dead?"

"What do you mean, *still* brain-dead? If you're brain-dead, you're brain-dead!"

Grams gives me a look like, Oooooooh, maybe not! Then she asks, "Well, has Mrs. Porter confessed who Abigail's father really is?"

I snatch the remote from her. "No! And why would I watch a stupid soap where people don't know who their father is when I'm *living that life*?"

Grams covers her mouth, then looks up to the ceiling, her eyes blinking like mad. *Blink-blink-blink. Blink. Blink-blink. Blink!* It's like she's praying in Morse code.

Finally she says, "That was very stupid of me. I'm sorry. And I will have another talk with your mother about this, because I agree with you—the situation's ridiculous." She eyes me. "Especially now that she's head over heels for Warren."

I roll my eyes. "Oh, great."

"She is," she says, shaking her head. "They're like two teenagers in love."

I look at her. "What? Wait—you went out with *both* of them?"

She nods. "It was delightful."

I squint at her. "Anyone else there? Like Heather? Or Casey? Or *Candi?*"

"No, of course not."

"So it was meet-the-mom time?"

Grams shrugs. "I suppose so."

"Great," I say, slouching into the couch. "Just great." I turn my head to look at her. "She barely knows him! And he doesn't know *her* at all!" I sit up a little. "Like, does he know she can't cook and hates to clean? Does he know she freaks out if it's windy 'cause it messes up her hair?" I sit up even straighter. "And, hey—does *he* know who my father is? 'Cause if it's such a big oh-my-God-don't-tell-Samantha secret, shouldn't he know before he marries her?"

"Good heavens! Can you not rush them to the altar?"

"*Me?* I have nothing to do with this! But can't you see?

That *is* where this is going—why else would she want you to meet him? Officially! Over dinner!" I squint at her. "I mean, why is she still even here? She never stays this long!"

Grams eyes pop. "You don't know?"

"Know *what*?" I throw my hands in the air. "And of course not! I'm the last person to know anything!"

"She's going to the wedding."

"What wedding?" But then it hits me. "No! She can't crash Officer Borsch's wedding! And why would she want to?"

"She's not *crashing* it."

"Well, you can't just take her! She barely even knows him!" I flash her a disgruntled look. "But see? Not knowing someone and weddings make total sense to her!"

"Samantha," Grams says with a laugh, "Gil invited her."

"He *what*? Why would he do that?"

She shrugs. "You're in the wedding? She's your mother?"

"But why would she go?"

She gives another shrug, and this time it comes with a little smile. "You're in the wedding? She's your mother?" Then she adds, "She's excited to see you as a bridesmaid."

"Oh, *right*," I grumble. "The only reason she'd go is to steamroll everyone when they toss the bouquet."

She studies me a minute, then says, "That's not fair. She's trying, okay? She helped you out at school, she was very agreeable at dinner, she's staying for the wedding. . . ."

I scowl at her. "There is no *way* she's hanging around all this time just to see me in a stupid poufy dress."

Grams nods. "Well, she is also helping Warren clean and paint the inside of the house he was renting out in Sisquane."

"She's *what*?"

"They want to make sure he gets his security deposit back."

"No, I mean you've got to be kidding me. She doesn't know how to clean. She doesn't know how to paint."

Grams laughs. "It's not hard to figure out."

"But it's hard *work*. She faints at the sight of a dust mop!"

"Oh, she does not," she scoffs, but she grins at me like she knows *exactly* what I'm talking about.

"And you know what? If she's gonna stick around town until Saturday, she'd better watch her back."

Grams frowns at me. "What is *that* supposed to mean?"

So I tell her about Heather spying through Hudson's window and all that, and when I'm done, she says, "Are you sure she wasn't just spying on *you*?" So *then* I have to tell her what Heather said when she ambushed me and all *that*. "See?" I say, showing her my hands and then pulling up the sleeve of my gym shirt, which I'd kept on after PE so people would stop asking me what happened.

"Oh my!" Grams says, and believe me, her eyes are enormous.

"And at this point Heather must know Mom's on *Lords*, right?"

"Yes, I suppose so."

"So what lie has Mom fabricated about where I'm living? I mean, does Warren know I'm living here?"

Grams shakes her head. "I have no idea."

"Well, it *matters*."

"Yes, it does!"

I grab my forehead. "Isn't anybody else worried about this? I mean, maybe Warren won't blow the whistle on us, but if Heather finds out? She is majorly ticked off and would love to make our lives miserable! So, yeah, Mom better watch her back, 'cause if Heather gets a chance, she will go totally psycho on her."

Grams thinks about this a minute, then takes a deep breath. "Heather would probably feel anger toward *any* other woman." She shakes her head a little. "Girls can be very possessive of their fathers."

I scowl at her. "I wouldn't know."

She just ignores that and says, "I'll tell Lana what you said, though." She pats my knee and stands up. "Maybe Warren can smooth things over with Heather."

"Good luck there," I grumble.

She heads for the kitchen, but halfway there she turns and says, "Oh. Your mother had a message for you."

I twist my head to look at her. "Yeah, what?"

She looks up toward the ceiling like she's trying to remember. "She said to tell you: 'The note was unnecessary. There's no reason you both can't be happy.' "

I sit up straighter and twist all the way around. "What?"

So she repeats the message, then says, "She said you'd understand."

I snort and flop back around. "Well, I don't."

"I sensed it had something to do with Casey," she says, moving into the kitchen, "but she refused to elaborate."

"Well, I didn't write him any *note*," I tell Grams. "And I didn't write *her* any note."

And, really, if I'd had a normal mother, I would've just called her up and asked her about it, but I didn't want to think about her, or Casey, or Warren the Wonderful, or anything else, for that matter.

I just wanted to take a shower and go to bed.

Ol' Scratch 'n' Spit was not in homeroom the next morning, and there was something weird about his desk.

It was totally . . . clean.

The substitute also looked very . . . clean. He seemed too young to be a teacher. And he had a really shiny nose. Actually, his whole face was shiny, but his nose looked *polished*.

He also seemed a little too happy to be filling in for Mr. Vince. Like maybe this was the first time he'd been on that side of the podium and he thought it was really *amazing* to be there.

Whatever. All I know is he was nice, and happy, and didn't scratch or spit.

He also had no information about Mr. Vince.

"Can you find out?" Crystal Agnew asked. "We're worried about him."

The rest of us eyed each other like, Oh yeah, *right*—speak for yourself.

Now, after what Officer Borsch had said about Mr. Foxmore thinking I was grand marshal of the Die Dude Parade, I'd actually considered staying home from school. Before, Officer Borsch had had my back, but now I was flying on my own, and I sure didn't want to spend the day trapped in the office.

Besides, I'd woken up tired, and I figured what would one day—one *Friday*—hurt?

Plus, I could sure use a day without Heather Acosta.

It was the thought of Billy that got me moving. I still had a sort of low hum of worry about him. It was like a sound you don't even know is there until you notice it, and then you hear it all the time. And you ask yourself, Where is that sound coming from?

So I dragged myself to school, and at break I was glad I had.

"Sammy-keyesta!"

When I turned around, the low hum vanished. "Billy!" I called back with a wave. I hurried over to him. "I missed you yesterday!"

We gave each other a hug, and then Billy said, "The police did, too. They came by to see me."

"Oh yeah?" I asked, playing dumb. And then I tried to be sly by asking, "How'd that go over with your dad?"

"It was just my mom, so that was cool." Then he gave me a look I've never seen on Billy before. It was soft. Really *sweet*. "He came back last night and told me he had it on good authority that I was not the Die Dude Vandal."

"Your *dad* did?"

"No, goofy. The cop."

Now, I can't help it, I go a little shifty-eyed. "Uh, that's really good news."

"Yeah. At first I thought he was kind of a jerk, but he turned out to be a pretty cool dude." He plants a big, squeaky smooch on my temple. "So thanks, Good Authority."

I give him half a smile, 'cause I still feel like if he knew I'd spilled the beans about his little message on the whiteboard, he wouldn't be planting kisses on me.

But then he says, "He also told me that next time I should keep the markers capped."

My eyes pop, and then I pull a face. "I'm sorry, okay? But he knew you were lying about something, Billy."

"No! It's cool. You have no idea how good I feel today. I'm, like, *free*."

Now, I really hated to break it to him, but I thought he should know. "Uh . . . did he mention he's been pulled off the case? And that Foxmore still thinks that you and I are in this together?"

"*Sí, sí,* Sammy-keyesta. But have you been called into the office today? Have I? No! And I'm in the clear with the police for yesterday, so I'm not going to stress about it."

So just being around Billy has put me in a sunny mood, and then we hear whistling and see Cisco coming around the corner with his cleaning cart. "Good morning!" he says when he sees us. "How are you two this glorious day?"

I laugh. "Glorious?"

"How would you describe it?" he asks, raising his palms up to the sky.

Billy and I kinda look at each other and laugh. "Glorious!"

"So why hold back?" he says as the warning bell rings.

"Enjoy it!" Then he turns down the walkway to go about his business.

"Ya gotta love Cisco," I say with a laugh.

Billy nods as we start toward third period together. "Of all the people around here who think they're so smart, *he's* the one with keys to the universe."

At first I laugh and say, "You're right!" but then a strange feeling sort of floats through me. It's a vague feeling, but really unsettling. Like impending doom, only way off in the distance. Like something bad is about to happen way over . . . *there.*

And while this feeling of doom hovers over *there,* a little creepy-crawly tingle jumps right on me, going up my spine and into my brain.

It's a very icky creepy-crawly tingle, too. One that skitters all around my brain, making me go from one icky creepy-crawly thought to the next.

Who'd had to put up with Bad Mood Bob for *years?*

Who had keys to every building at school?

Who'd been eavesdropping on Foxmore and Vince?

Who was the first one to notice that Mr. Vince's car had been vandalized?

Who was free to roam around during the fire alarm?

Who probably set traps for rats in the storage sheds around school?

And who was the very last person you'd think would do such mean, threatening things?

Cisco Diaz.

I really did not want to be thinking what I was thinking,

217

but the thought wouldn't leave. And the more I thought it, the more sense it made, until pretty soon my heart's all fluttering and my head's feeling woozy, and I really want to blurt out what I'm thinking to Billy.

But then we round the corner.

Now, Billy had led us the back way to Mr. Vince's classroom. You're supposed to use the walkways, but people cut between the buildings all the time. So even though it's kind of secluded, it's not a *shock* to run into people.

Unless the people you run into are Lars Teppler.

And Sasha Stamos.

And you witness them . . . *kissing*.

TWENTY-FOUR

I grab Billy by the arm and yank him back around the corner. We both look at each other like, OH-HO-HO!

"Whoa!" Billy whispers as we take a sly peek.

"I would *never* have guessed!" I whisper back.

We duck out of sight quick, though, when they break apart. And when we peek again, only Lars is there—Sasha has gone to class. Then Lars hurries to class, leaving Billy and me having to really race to get around the building and inside the door before the tardy bell rings.

The first person I run into is Heather. And I guess I'm kinda giddy with my new Sasha-rific secret, 'cause I give her a real big smile and say, "Sis-ta!"

"Shut up!" she hisses. "Don't you ever call me that again!"

I head over to my seat, still smiling. "I've always wanted bunk beds, how about you?"

"Stop it!"

"Pil-low fight! Pil-low fight!" I say, grinning away. "Wouldn't that be fun?"

"I hate you! I hate you so much, I—"

"What's this?" the shiny-nosed sub asks. "Are we fighting?"

"Not at all!" I say, sliding into my seat. "I'm just excited because Heather and I might become *sisters*."

Everyone's jaw drops, 'cause it's no secret that Heather and I are mortal enemies. And I don't know. It's like I'm possessed with giggles or something. I just flip a hand out and say, "Well, her dad's running off with my mom, so what can ya do?"

"No, he's not!" Heather screeches. "No, he's *not*."

I look around the room with a shrug. "Someone's in de-ni-al."

Heather comes flying at me, only before she can lay a finger on me, the Shiny Sub lunges forward with a wooden ruler like Don Quixote attacking a wild-haired windmill.

He doesn't actually *touch* her, but he inserts himself between her and me, stares her right in the eye, then points to the door with the ruler and says, "You. Outside. Now. When you've composed yourself, you may come back in."

She slinks out, giving me the evil eye the whole time.

"And, you!" he says, pointing his ruler at me. "Stop pouring salt in her wound."

I almost say, "But—" but instead I look down and nod. "Yes, sir."

"All right, then," he says, taking a deep, calming breath. He goes back up to the podium and looks out at the class. "In case we haven't already met, my name is Mr. Derringer, and I'll be your teacher while Mr. Vince is out on medical leave."

Lars—who has not even looked at Sasha since he sat down—raises his hand and says, "Did he really have a nervous breakdown?" And Sasha—who hasn't looked at Lars, either—asks, "How long will he be gone?"

The Shiny Sub does a little uncomfortable shifting, but then nods and says, "I won't be divulging any personal information about Mr. Vince, but you have a right to know what to expect." He rearranges some papers on the podium. "And what you can expect is to see me for some time to come." Then he looks up and says, "I don't plan to be your babysitter, either. I am certified to teach history, and I intend to do just that."

Billy raises his hand.

"Yes?"

"Uh, how do you feel about guest speakers?"

The Shiny Sub laughs. "I *love* guest speakers." He tilts his head a little. "And how do you feel about me coming to class dressed as, say, Benjamin Franklin or Robert E. Lee or John Wilkes Booth?"

Billy jumps out of his seat. "I love *you*," he squeals.

The whole class busts up, which makes Heather curious enough to come back inside and take her seat.

Now, while everyone's settling back down, I notice Lars give Sasha a sly grin. It's almost like a wink, and it seems to hold a lot of unspoken meaning.

And that's when it hits me.

That's how he knew I had the chin-up record in my PE class—Sasha had told him!

Maybe the two of *them* have been doing this Die Dude thing together.

After all, Sasha was ticked at Mr. Vince and said someone should do something about him. Maybe she decided to be that someone. There was no doubt about it— she was tricky. Very tricky!

Plus, her family lives out in the boonies, where there are probably lots of rats.

And those times Lars came up to me? Maybe he was like a decoy, keeping me occupied while Sasha planted rats or got back to class or whatever.

Maybe one of Sasha's homeschooled brothers called in the fake fire!

And maybe she put Heather's phone in the outhouse to distract everyone.

Maybe *Lars* had left the Die Dude voice mail.

And maybe he'd spread rumors about me keying Mr. Vince's car because *he* had done it. He'd been late to school that day, and it sure would explain why he was so hot to frame me with all this stuff about "upper-body strength" and seeing me at the pet store.

And that's when something *else* finally clicks.

If Lars had seen me at the dog tag machine, then *he'd* been at the pet shop that day, too! *He* could have made the Die Dude tag!

My mind was going crazy, trying to piece together everything that had happened, and I was kicking myself for not paying any attention earlier. So for the rest of the day I racked my brain, trying to remember things.

Who was where when the dead rat reared its dog-tagged neck?

Who was where during the fire alarm?

Who was where when Vince's car got keyed?

I actually drew diagrams. I wrote things down. I even listed motivations:

Heather: hates me; is psycho.

Sasha: hates Vince and is miffed at me. (And is maybe kinda psycho.)

Lars: Sasha.

Cisco: hates Vince.

Between classes I also looked around for Cisco. And Lars and Sasha. And anytime anyone was gossiping about Mr. Vince, I eavesdropped.

"I heard he's not coming back!" "I heard he's in a psych ward!" "I heard he's suing the school!" "I heard he threatened to kill Mr. Foxmore!"

And I was so wrapped up in trying to figure out which pieces fit in this puzzle and which belonged in some *other* puzzle that I forgot all about putting Billy's name in the mix.

Or mine, but of course that was because I knew it didn't belong.

And because my name wasn't on my list, I guess I started thinking that it wasn't on Mr. Foxmore's, either.

Until drama, when a note came from the office.

Teri Nostern was the office aide, and I knew the minute she walked into the room that the slip in her hand was for me.

Her looking right at me sorta gave that away.

But office aides are supposed to give messages to the teacher, not the student, so Teri walks up to Mr. Chester, delivers the note, and looks at me *again* before leaving.

And, yeah, big surprise, Mr. Chester checks the note and calls out, "Samantha!"

So I grab my backpack and trudge up to the front of the class and take the note. And I'm halfway out the door when I finally realize that it's not a summons to the office.

It's a phone message.

> Don't forget:
>   Pick up shoes.
>   Go to Deb's.
> Call my cell if you need a ride (748-2000).
> GB

I kind of stare at the note 'cause, yeah, I'd completely forgotten about the shoes. And since I don't have to report to the office after all, I go back to my spot next to Marissa.

"What's up?" she whispers. I show her the note, and she says, "He gave you his *cell*? Easy to memorize, too." She snickers. "Maybe I'll crank-call him sometime."

I backhand her with a grin.

"You want me to come with you?" she asks.

I nod. "Sure."

So after school we head over to the mall. It's about ninety degrees out, and before Marissa can even think about taking her ridiculous house-stalking longcut, I distract her by showing her the notes I'd made during the day.

"Cisco?" she says after she's looked them over. "You think it might be *Cisco*?"

"He's got a key to every single room, he doesn't like Mr. Vince, we caught him eavesdropping on Vince and the Fox, and he's the one who 'discovered' that Mr. Vince's car had been keyed."

"But he's *Cisco*. He's the sunshiniest person at school. He wouldn't *do* things like that."

"I know," I grumble. But then I add, "But you know what he said about Vince calling him Nacho. And what do we know about him, really?"

"We know he's a sunshiny guy." She points to the paper. "You've got Sasha Stamos and Lars Teppler as suspects? And working together? Is that what this means?" She looks at me. "What were you on when you put this together?"

So I tell her about the Kiss.

"No!" she gasps.

"See? A little information changes everything."

Marissa's brain starts whirling away. "Sasha lives on that farm."

"It's a farm?"

"Or whatever. I'm sure she mentioned a barn, so there's got to be rats, right?"

"And this thing was *huge*, Marissa. Like something from the boonies."

She nods a bunch as she hands back my paper. "You need a calendar. Order of events. Who was where when."

I snort. "Thanks for the assignment, chief."

"*Or . . . ,*" she says after she thinks about it some more, "just drop the whole thing. Do we really care who freaked

Mr. Vince into leaving school? As long as you and Billy are off the hook, what does it matter?"

"But I'm not off the hook! Officer Borsch says I'm Foxmore's number one suspect! He thinks Billy and I are in this together!"

"That's ridiculous."

"*I* know that, and *you* know that, but he's convinced it's us!"

She scowls, then says, "Look, you didn't get called into the office today, and neither did Billy. And it's not like we're being followed by the police or anything."

Suddenly we both stop and look at each other, then glance over our shoulders and all around.

"Nope," she says. But as we're walking along again, she keeps checking over her shoulder. "Unless they're undercover."

It did make me feel a little paranoid. Especially since I'd let myself get ambushed *and* spied on by Heather. I mean, maybe we *were* being followed by some undercover cops. Maybe they were hoping they'd catch us red-handed doing some after-school Die Duding. Maybe they were hoping that we'd lead them to our Die Dude lair.

Or wait—maybe they were hoping we'd lead them to a Die Dude *ranch* where we raised our Die Dude rats.

Whatever. I had nothing to hide. If they wanted to follow me to the mall and see me pick up lavender high heels, fine.

So as we crossed Broadway and cut over to the mall, I changed the subject by asking Marissa what was going on with her parents. What I got back from her was a big, fat

"Who knows?" followed by a rant about how her mother hadn't bothered to check in with them yesterday, and why even have kids if you're not going to be good parents, and how she wished she and Mikey could stay at Hudson's forever.

"You don't mean that," I told her as I pulled open one of the mall's big glass doors.

"Yes, I do!" she said, but her chin was quivering. "I used to feel sorry for you because you don't know who your dad is, but you know what? I'm starting to think you're lucky. At least he can't let you down." She swiped away a tear. "And he won't drop you in the dirt in the middle of your life."

A bunch of thoughts ran through my head.

The first one was You have no idea what you're talking about! followed by It's better to have been held and dropped than never to have been held at all.

That, of course, made me think of the original cliché: It's better to have loved and lost than never to have loved at all, which, of course, made me think of Casey.

And this may seem weird, but to me there was some sort of connection between my dad never having been in my life and Casey now being out of it.

In both cases it felt like I'd been robbed.

And then, right there in the middle of the mall, I connected the dots.

Both times, it was my *mother* who'd robbed me.

It was like she *was* a soap character. One who kept secrets. One who manipulated. One who timed her interruptions for maximum dramatic effect. And Casey and

I had been like two characters in her soap—held apart by forces beyond their control . . . finally on the cusp of getting together . . . finally in each other's arms . . . inching closer and closer for their first kiss . . . when suddenly the Diva of Destruction enters the room and drops a bombshell that flings the characters apart forever.

I don't even remember getting to KC Shoes. I was too busy getting lost in Lady Lana's soap opera. But then Marissa's voice breaks through the daze. "Aren't you going in?"

"Huh?" I blink at her. "Oh. Oh, right."

Kenny's leaning against one of the Plexiglas displays like a mannequin. "Hello!" he says, coming to life when we step inside. Then he recognizes me. "Oh, yay. Debra will be so relieved. I'm under strict orders to tell you to go over to her house *immediately.*" He hurries behind the counter and produces a shoe box. And as he hands it over, he says, "As a matter of fact, I think I'll call her now and tell her you're on your way."

"You're sure a full-service shoe store," I grumble.

"What was that?" he asks, giving me an oily smile.

"Nothing." I open up the shoe box, and what I see kinda startles me. I mean, I was expecting lavender shoes—and these are definitely lavender—but I wasn't expecting the little glass beads that were glued over the toe area in the shape of a heart.

"Wow," Marissa says. "Those are little princess shoes."

"Did you want to try them on?" Kenny asks as he punches at the phone keypad.

I tell him, "No!" but it comes out in a ridiculously

228

desperate way, so I take it down a notch. "I mean, no, I'm sure they're fine." I scoop up the box and head for the door, calling, "Thanks!"

"So I guess we're off to Debra's?" Marissa asks once we're back in the main mall corridor.

"She lives on Elm. About a block away from that little white church on Constance Street. You want to come?"

She says sure, and since I'm now lugging around a backpack, a skateboard, *and* a big shoe box, we go the coolest way possible—through Cheezers.

Trouble is, as we're filing through, I look over at the dining area and see the same three guys the Vincenator had been hanging out with over the weekend. Bad Mood Bob doesn't seem to be with them, but on impulse I snag two menus off the counter, grab Marissa by the arm, and head for the dining room.

"What are we doing?" she whispers.

"Just be cool," I whisper back.

Then I drag her inside.

TWENTY-FIVE

I slip into a seat near the bikers and hold a menu in front of my face.

"Why are we doing this?" Marissa whispers around the side of her menu.

It's a good question, and to tell you the truth, my real answer is pretty lame.

It's just a *feeling*.

So instead of telling her that, I shrug and say, "So we can tell Spy Guy that we were tracking Captain Evil?"

"Captain Evil's not even here! And he's not going to *be* here! He's home having a nervous breakdown, remember?"

"Shhhh!"

She rolls her eyes and disappears behind her menu but pops out an instant later. "And I don't have money for a pizza, do you?"

I shake my head. "I don't even have money for a Coke."

She gives me a stern look. "Then I suggest we go!"

The biker guys are laughing and joking and passing around a pitcher of beer, but there are only three glasses, and Marissa's right—it's not like the Vincenator is any-where around. Plus, the bikers are talking *stupid* stuff.

"Do you think Mantrap Marcie will be back this year?"

"You can have Marcie. I'm goin' for Skullcap Sue!"

"Man, it's about the ride, not the chicks!"

"No, man, it's about the ride *and* the chicks!"

"Kick-start my heart! Can't wait to get outta here!"

They all laugh and clink their mugs together. "Hogto-berfest!"

Marissa gives me a disgusted look, then leans forward and whispers, "So, you're planning to report all this to Mikey?"

I sigh and put down my menu, and I'm about to get up and leave when the one with the blocky granite face opens his ringing cell phone and says, "Yo, Curveball, update me, man." And after a couple of minutes of uh-huh-ing, he goes, "I'm with Flash and Bones—we're at Cheezers." Then he's back to uh-huh-ing for another minute before saying, "When do you take delivery on that?" He gives the other guys a thumbs-up and says, "Awesome!" into the phone.

One of the Evil Eye manager guys checks us over as he brings the bikers a pizza. And since Marissa's obvi-ously right and since I don't want ol' Evil Eye to ask what we're ordering, or Flash and Bones and Gargoyle—or whoever the granite-faced guy is—to notice us, I just grab my stuff and we scoot out of the dining room, then hurry to the back door of Cheezers.

"What was that all about?" Marissa asks once we're outside. "Those guys are total *losers*."

And, yeah, I'm feeling kind of stupid and pretty defensive. So I say, "Hey, just because they're bikers doesn't mean they're losers."

She looks at me like I've lost my very last marble. "It's three in the afternoon and they're sucking down beer. Obviously, they don't have jobs!"

"Maybe they work the night shift?"

"So they're getting hammered *before* work?" She flashes a look at me. "And did you hear the way they were talking about women? They're disgusting losers!"

She was right, and I knew it. And even though I'd always thought of Mr. Vince as being disgusting and kind of a loser, he seemed miles more responsible than his buddies inside Cheezers.

Which got me to thinking that maybe they weren't even his friends. Maybe they were just, like, *acquaintances* he'd run into there and had hung out with for a little while.

Marissa's squinting at me. "What were you hoping to *do* in there?"

"I don't know, okay? I don't know!" And as we pass by the same three Harleys we'd seen the day we'd been to the mall with Mikey, I'm *feeling* like I'm Mikey—like I'm in some make-believe world where I can spy on people and figure things out. Only instead of spying on someone who might actually have something to do with what's been going on, I'm spying on middle-aged men who call themselves Bones and Flash and make toasts to "Hogtoberfest."

Whatever *that* is.

We trudge along in silence clear across the mall parking

lot until finally Marissa says, "Sorry. I didn't mean to come down on you like that."

"Hey, I was being an idiot."

She laughs. "That's usually *my* role."

"No, it's not. Your role is to wreck things that have wheels." I grin at her and pull away. "So don't *even* think you can borrow my skateboard."

"I am so done with skateboards," she says. And since we're real near Cypress Street, she asks, "Hey, can we drop our stuff at Hudson's before we go over to Debra's?" So we cut down Cypress, dump everything but my lavender shoes at Hudson's, and *then* head out.

"Her house is so *cute,*" Marissa says as we go up the walkway. But the minute Debra answers the door, the word *cute* vanishes, and what we're thinking instead is some combination of *Holy smokes* and *Ouch* and . . . *She's a carrot!*

"I know, I know!" Debra says, and then bursts into tears.

"What happened?" I ask, following her inside.

"I went to the tannin' salon, but it was my first time and I didn't think I looked dark enough, so I bought some Quik Tan, and . . . and . . . now I look like this!"

"Will it wash off?" I ask.

"No!" she wails. She shows me her palms, which are bright orange. "And the weddin's *tomorrow.*"

I try, "Maybe it'll fade into a perfect tan by then?" but she just bursts into tears again, crying, "No, it won't!"

"Where's the tube?" I ask, looking around. "Does it give any directions about how to *undo?*"

233

She collapses onto the couch. "I don't think so. . . ."

So I search, and when I find the tube, what's it tell me? A whole lot of nothing.

"Maybe there's a site on the Internet?" Marissa says, standing by a small desk near the couch. "Do you want me to try to find something?"

"Go ahead," Debra hiccups.

"By the way, I'm Marissa," Marissa says as she types at Debra's laptop. "You probably don't remember, but I've met you before at the police station."

Debra sniffs hello and after a minute asks, "Did you find anything?"

"How to Fix a Tanning Cream Mistake," Marissa reads aloud.

Debra sits up a little. "Really?"

So Marissa skims the article and says, "Basically, you soak for an hour in the tub, exfoliate, then apply baking soda paste, rinse, and apply baby oil, then dab on lemon juice, take a shower, and moisturize."

"I don't have *time* to do all that! The rehearsal's at eight!"

I put out my hand to help her off the couch. "You don't have time not to."

"But I've got to hem your dress!"

"Just show me how and I'll do it." I couldn't believe the words actually came out of *my* mouth, but they did.

She takes my hand. "Are you sure?"

I pull her up. "Sure I'm sure. Marissa'll help me. We'll do it while you're soaking in the tub."

So she brings out the Mountain of Lavender, which makes Marissa's jaw drop. "That is a lot of dress," she whispers in my ear.

When I've burrowed my way into it, I let Debra triple-zip me up, then I step into my stilettos and stand completely still while she sits on the floor and pins the hem to the right length.

After she's cut off some extra fabric, she sets up Marissa and me with needle and thread and shows us how to do a slip stitch. And since the skirt is about a mile of fabric around, it's like Marissa and I are hemming in our own little universes.

"You got it?" she asks.

"No problem," I tell her.

"Got it!" Marissa says. "Now go in there and light some candles! Turn on some music. Relax!"

"Oh, that sounds so nice!" And after clicking through a stack of cases in a bookshelf, Debra pulls out a CD and says, "You girls ever heard of Darren Cole?"

Marissa starts bouncing up and down. "I *saw* him! In Vegas! With my mom!" She laughs. "My mom *loves* him."

Debra chuckles and says, "Yup," like, Who doesn't? But all of a sudden I'm totally down in the dumps. Long story short, there's a Darren Cole song called "Waitin' for Rain to Fall," and it's, like, my "Casey" song.

Anyway, once Debra's in the bathroom with the door closed, Marissa whispers, "She looks *horrible*."

I force away thoughts of Casey. "Shhh!"

"And she really clashes with this dress!"

"She's not wearing this dress," I whisper back. "*I* am."

Marissa looks up from her sewing. "How *do* you get yourself into these things?"

I shake my head. "One wrong step at a time?"

Anyway, we sit there and sew, and although I do prick my finger hard a couple of times, I don't die, or fall into an enchanted sleep, or anything like that. By the time Debra's emerging from the bathroom, we've made it all the way around the bottom of the dress.

Well, Marissa's done about three-fourths of it, and I've done the rest.

"Nice job!" Debra says, inspecting Marissa's stitching. Then she sees some of mine and pulls a little face.

"Hey! It'll hold it together."

She kisses the top of my head like Grams might have and laughs. "I suppose it will."

"So baking soda's next, right?" Marissa asks.

"You know, I can do the rest myself. Soakin' in the tub was so soothing. Thank you, girls."

She's looking as orange as ever, but at least she *feels* better.

So we head out the door, only at the last minute she calls, "Wait! Your dress! And your shoes!"

I stop and blink at her because, really, I don't know how I'm going to haul them up the fire escape without being seen. "Uh, I can't leave them here?"

At first she says, "No," but then I can see the wheels turning in *her* head. And I don't know if that's because Officer Borsch has told her about my living situation or because she's thinking she could really use some help, but she says, "Uh . . . the other girls, Brandi and Tippy? They're meetin' here tomorrow before the weddin' to help me out."

"Brandi and *Tippy*?"

"Mmm-hmm," she says, like these are real names and not nicknames or something. Then she just goes on with, "I'm takin' my dress over to the church after they show up. Would you like to come by here, too? We could take your dress at the same time."

Well, that sure beat hauling a mountain of lavender up the fire escape, so I tell her, "Sounds like a plan."

"All right. So I'll see you at the church tonight at eight."

I start to say okay, but then I stop cold. "You'll what?"

She cocks her head a little. "For the rehearsal?"

"Uh . . . what rehearsal?"

"The weddin' rehearsal?"

"I don't know anything about it."

She covers her face with her hands. "Oh, Sams, I'm so sorry." She peeks out at me. "Please tell me you can make it."

"But . . . why do we have to *rehearse*?"

Marissa looks at me. "How else will you know what to do?"

"I don't know! How should I know? I've never been in a wedding before. I've never even been *to* a wedding before!"

Debra eyes me. "Which is why we need to rehearse!"

I point to the dress. "Do I have to wear *that*?"

"To the rehearsal? No, hon," Debra says. "It's just a run-through. No dress code requirements. I know eight o'clock is late, but Tippy and Brandi are flyin' in today, and it's the only time that worked for everybody. It'll be quick, I promise." She gives me a pleading look. "There'll be refreshments afterward . . . ?"

I let out a deep, puffy breath. "Okaaay."

Then I grab Marissa and get out of there.

TWENTY-SIX

By the time we get back to Hudson's, it's almost six o'clock. "I should have called Grams from Debra's," I tell Marissa. "She's probably worried."

Sure enough, Hudson greets us with, "You better call home, Sammy."

So I do, and what I find out from Grams is that my mother has been waiting around the apartment so that she can spend some "quality time" with me.

"She's just trying to get out of painting and cleaning," I grumble.

Grams sighs. "Samantha, honestly. You need to be a little more gracious about these overtures."

"They're more like over*dues*," I grumble.

"Samantha!"

"I know. I'm sorry. But it's not like she asked if I was, you know, *available*. All of a sudden *she* decides she needs to spend some time with me, and I'm supposed to drop everything? I've got a wedding rehearsal to go to tonight."

"You do?"

"Yes, I do." Then I add, "How else am I supposed to know what to do?"

"But—"

"So, see? If the world revolved around something besides Lady Lana, she might have checked with me ahead of time."

"But . . . why didn't *I* know about it? When is it? What time will you be home?"

Now, I don't exactly want to get into the *facts* about this, so I start giving her *other* information. "Oh, Grams, you wouldn't believe what we've been going through today. Debra went to a tanning place but didn't think she came out dark enough, so she got some of that tanning lotion, and it turned her completely *orange*. So Marissa and I have been picking up shoes and hemming dresses and trying to help her get the orange off her skin."

"You were *hemming*?" she gasps.

"All in the line of duty," I tell her. Then I throw in, "So, see, the bride-to-be's a basket case, and it's been a pretty intense afternoon for the bridesmaid. I know I should have called earlier, but this was the first chance I had. And now I've got to eat something and get over to the rehearsal."

"Oh my," she says, then after a pause she asks, "How orange is she?"

"Carrot orange."

She sighs. "Poor dear. Poor, poor dear."

"So tell Mom sorry, but I really have no 'quality time' to spend with her tonight. I'm probably not going to be home until nine-thirty or ten."

"That late?"

"Yup. Don't worry. I'll be fine." Then, 'cause I know

she *will* worry that I'm *not* fine, I add, "I'll ask Officer Borsch to give me a ride."

"That would be good. And by the way, Warren does not know that you're living here, so that secret's still safe."

I hesitate, then ask, "So where does he think I'm living?"

There's a kinda long pause, and then Grams says, "With your father."

"With my— Oh, you've got to be kidding me!" Then something hits me. "So he *does* live in Santa Martina?"

"Uh . . . I didn't *say* that," Grams says, and I can tell she's really uncomfortable being tangled up in my mother's secret. She drops her voice and says, "You know I can't get into that." Then she adds, "And I agree with you—I don't like what she told Warren, either, but we'll just have to deal with it. At least she had the good sense not to put us in jeopardy."

"But Casey knows! What if he talks to his dad?"

"You see how unfortunate that is now?"

I knew she was right, but still, the whole situation felt wrong. I got off the phone thinking my mom and Warren were doomed. I mean, she already had huge secrets from him! Wasn't that the beginning of the end?

And maybe I should have felt happy about that, but I didn't. I felt like I was living in the shadows of secrets. It felt cold. And dark. And . . . *sad*.

I tried to forget about my mom as I horned in on dinner at Hudson's, but that was kind of futile. And staying for dinner turned out to be awkward. Not because I'd invited myself but because Mrs. McKenze showed up with

Chinese takeout and acted like everything was perfectly normal. Like, Oh, isn't this fun, having little white boxes of food all over someone else's dinner table.

Hudson tried to keep the conversation going, but Marissa and Mikey were quiet, and I sure didn't feel like I had anything to say. And then when Mrs. McKenze finally says she has to be going, Mikey chases after her and *clings* to her.

"I'm sorry, sweetheart," she says, trying to pull away from him. "You and your sister can't come home quite yet."

"I don't want to go home," he says, and now he's crying. "I want *you* to stay *here*."

Mrs. McKenze seems stunned by this, and after looking around at the rest of us, she pries herself free from Mikey and dashes for the door.

Seeing this puts an awful lump in my throat because it sends me straight back to the day my mom left me with Grams and moved to L.A.

It's a panicky, heart-crushing feeling.

One that makes you think you'd rather die than have your mother leave.

Marissa hurries over and promises Mikey that their mom will be back, and I'm sure that she will be.

Still, inside I know—things will never be the same.

It turns out that the Community Presbyterian Church only holds about a hundred people. It's *small*. And even though I was five minutes early, I was still the last one to show up, so there was this big flurry of introductions when I walked in. I had my backpack on and was holding my skateboard, and everyone else had a few more, you know, *years* under their belt, so I felt a little out of place.

Make that a *lot* out of place.

"So you're *Sammy*," they all said, and with a little too much gusto. Like they'd heard stories.

"Uh, yeah," I said, shaking their hands.

Officer Borsch's groomsmen were all obviously cops. You can just tell. Something about the hair or the moustache or the way they dress . . . it just says cop.

And Debra's bridesmaids looked a lot like Debra, only less orange. They weren't sisters, but they all had bleached hair and long, painted fingernails and lots of eye shadow.

A man up near the altar called "Good evening!" and everyone turned to look at him. He had combed-back hair and wore aviator glasses, and the bottom two buttons of his sweater were popped open, leaving room for his pooching belly. "I'm Reverend Doyle," he said with a smile. "Is everyone assembled?"

When Debra told him that we were, he started conducting us around, showing us where we'd wait, where we'd walk, and where we'd stand. It was actually pretty painless, and really simple—especially for me, since I didn't have any real *duties* except making it down the aisle without tripping. But we still had to go through the whole thing three times.

So I was more than ready to dive into the "refreshments," which were on a small table near the front door.

They were actually just donuts, but they looked a whole lot better than the half of a cake donut that I'd snagged in the teachers' lounge.

The one I'd never had the chance to eat.

And having to march past this spread of jelly-filled and maple and glazed buttermilk bars over and over and over, I felt like I was being tortured by donuts. So when the rehearsal dissolved into a discussion about rings and paperwork and the organist, I slipped away from the others and helped myself to a nice, fat maple bar, thinking that my part in all this was done.

Trouble is, I've taken only two bites when Debra calls my name and waves me over to a side door. So I take another quick chomp, and once again I hide a donut in my hand the best I can, then I join everyone else outside.

The minister turns on a floodlight, and Debra announces, "The reception'll be back here." She smiles at the men. "We're having tri-tip barbecue, with Ray James at the grill."

There's a chorus of "Mmmm!" from the men, so I guess this Ray James guy is some hotshot barbecuer or something.

Anyway, we all look around at what's really just a big backyard. "There'll be tables and chairs out here, the DJ'll be there, and our table will be right along here," Debra says, pointing around all over the place.

Everyone nods like, Yeah, okay, and then Debra says, "Parking's going to be really tight, but Gil's got a friend who's offered to valet-park in the side lot, so we've got that covered." She looks around. "Any questions?"

No one seems to have any, so she says, "Well, I think that's about it, then. Go on and help yourself to refreshments!"

So while people file toward the refreshment table, I polish off the rest of my donut, grab my stuff, and then ask Debra, "What time do you want me to be at your house tomorrow?"

"How's about eleven?"

I'm thinking, *For a two o'clock wedding?* but I just nod and say, "All right. See you then."

"You're not stickin' around for refreshments?"

I shake my head, hoping there's no maple frosting on my face giving me away. "I've really got to get home."

"Do you need a ride?"

"Nah," I tell her with a wave as I head for the door. "I'm good."

But I'm not even halfway home when a white car pulls up alongside me. It's an older model. Sort of big, with lines that are sharp instead of rounded.

"Get in," Officer Borsch says through the passenger window.

"Hey, go back to your friends—I'm fine."

"You're getting in," he says. "I don't like this neighborhood, and I don't like you riding through it at night."

"I'm fine!"

"Get in."

I roll my eyes and say, "Whatever," as I get inside with all my stuff. His police scanner is still on, chattering under the dash, so I laugh and say, "Don't you ever turn that thing off?"

He shakes his head and drives forward. And neither of us says anything, even though I know *I've* got lots of questions shooting through my mind.

Questions like, Are you really going to wear a lavender cummerbund tomorrow?

Did you notice how orange your bride-to-be is?

And You're so calm. Aren't you supposed to be freaking out or something?

But then Officer Borsch points with his cast hand to the sidewalk on the other side of the street and says, "Isn't that your friend?"

"Huh?" I say, following his point.

And then I see him.

On his skateboard.

Cruising along slowly in the opposite direction, all by himself, the breeze pushing back his hair.

Casey.

I watch through the front window, then the side windows, then the back window. I watch as he gets smaller and smaller behind us.

"You want me to go back?" Officer Borsch asks.

I shake my head and face forward. "No."

It's a lie, but all I can hear are Casey's words in my head.

Stop calling. We're done.

TWENTY-SEVEN

I had trouble falling asleep that night. I couldn't get the picture of Casey rolling by on his skateboard out of my mind. I just wanted to grab him. Stop him. *Talk* to him.

But he was gone.

Rolled out of my life.

When I finally did fall asleep, I had weird dreams. *Really* weird dreams. There was a wedding, with Reverend Doyle at the altar. He wasn't wearing minister robes or anything—he was wearing a black cardigan, and the bottom buttons kept popping off. So he'd chase after them, then run back to the altar and push them on while people walked up the aisle.

Only it wasn't Debra and Officer Borsch getting married.

It was my mom and Casey's dad.

Casey was there, and Heather was there, and Grams was there, and we were all trying to block them, but they walked right through us.

Like ghosts.

But Reverend Doyle's buttons kept popping, and he couldn't stay at the altar long enough to read the vows.

And then all of a sudden rats were storming the church. Big, black, hunchy-backed rats in white tuxes and wedding gowns. They were running around all over the place—underfoot, on the altar, up the walls. . . .

My mom started screaming and jumping from pew to pew while Heather screeched, "Get her, my pretties. Get her!"

And I could hear my mother calling, "Samantha! Samantha!"

I couldn't see her anymore, but it sounded like she was drowning.

"Mom!" I called, and I was looking all over for her. But it was like I was blind. I couldn't see anything anywhere.

"Samantha!"

I shot straight up, gasping for air, and there was my mother, sitting at the foot of the couch. She was wearing a pale yellow sweater and white capris.

There wasn't a wedding dress in sight.

"I think you were having a nightmare," she said, stroking my leg through the blanket. "Why were you calling my name?"

I flopped back down and panted for a minute. "I don't remember," I lied. Then I sat up a little and asked, "What time is it?"

"It's after nine. I've been here for about an hour. You must've been exhausted."

Now, the couch is plenty small enough without someone sitting on it while you're trying to sleep.

No wonder I'd been having bad dreams.

And then I saw *why* she was sitting there instead of the chair—so she could get a better view of herself on TV.

The sound was barely on, but still, there was a *Lords* tape running.

I wanted to shove her off with my feet. Get her away from me. But then she scooped up my feet and put them in her lap. "Better?" she asked.

I grunted and closed my eyes, trying to give her a hint.

Which, of course, she didn't take. "I heard you've been catching up on *Lords,*" she said, her focus on the TV. "I appreciate that."

I grunted again, sneaking a peek at her through slits in my lids.

"Oh, this is the scene right before Jason got hurt." She leaned forward a little and shook her head. "Poor guy."

"Are you talking about Jason Kruger?" Grams asks, handing my mother a cup of tea. Then she sits down in the chair with a cup of her own and says, "I was wondering why they'd replaced him—he was so good!"

So my mom tells her, "A light fell on him and crushed a bone in his shoulder."

Grams gasps. "That's terrible! Will he be coming back?"

"He's supposed to, but it's obviously taking a while. I heard they're having to do another surgery."

"So what happens in the meantime?" Grams asks, sipping from her tea. "If something like that were to happen to you, how would you make ends meet?"

Lady Lana does a regal little nod. "It's a good question. And in a way he's lucky it happened at work. If he'd been hurt at home, he'd be in real trouble. But since it was a workplace injury, he's still drawing a paycheck." She picks up the remote to fast-forward to another scene. "Still, I'm sure he'd rather be on-screen than on workman's comp."

I sit up a little. "You're talking about a real person, not a character on the show?"

My mother looks at me. "That's right."

"So he got hit by a light in real life? Sounds like something that would happen on your soap."

She laughs. "Yes, it does."

"What time do you have to be at the church?" Grams asks me.

"I have to be at Debra's at eleven."

My mother's eyes pop. "Eleven! I thought the wedding wasn't until two!"

I swing my legs down and sit up, saying, "But I'm a bridesmaid, and I'm supposed to be helping out."

"Is she still orange?" Grams asks.

"Pretty much, yeah."

My mother rolls her eyes and shakes her head. Like, Wow, how stupid can a bride-to-be be? But Grams tisks and says, "Poor dear."

I stand up and say, "Anyway, I'd better take a shower." I look at my mom. "Thanks for visiting."

It came out kinda sarcastic. I didn't *mean* for it to, but it did. And c'mon. Who could blame me? We'd talked about her soap and some guy she works with who'd been hit by a light and was now getting paid for staying home. Another thrilling conversation orbiting around Lana's World.

As usual.

And, really, I wasn't expecting her to hang around while I took a shower and dried my hair, but when I stepped out of the bathroom, there she still was.

"I thought it would be fun to help get you ready," she says, and that's when I notice that the kitchen table is covered with makeup and mirrors and hair spray bottles and curling irons. There are three curling irons, all different sizes.

"Uh, that's *nice*," I say, trying to be diplomatic, "but I'm not into that."

"Oh, come on," she coos. "Just a little."

"Uh . . . thanks, but no."

Grams is standing behind her, giving me granny signals with her face and her hands telling me to sit down and let my mother have at my face with her pots of paint.

"No!" I snap at her, which makes my mother turn around and say, "She doesn't have to if she doesn't want to." Then my mother looks back at me and says, "We could just do your hair?"

Well, I'd feel like a real brat saying no to that, so I plop in a chair and shrug. "If you really want to."

Her face gets all . . . sparkly. "So, what's your dress like? Simple? Elaborate? Clean lines? Frilly?"

I scowl. "It's lavender."

"Lavender?"

"Mm-hmm. And it's"—I ruffle my hands around me—"poufy and frilly."

She and Grams exchange grins as she says, "Okay, then!"

So for the next twenty minutes she sprays and curls and clacks those irons around my head. And it seems so ridiculous that we're not talking about anything *real,* but I don't want to start a fight with her by asking about my father or how she thinks she can be in love with a guy she can't trust with her secrets. So I just sit there.

And, really, I can't believe it can take so long to do someone's hair, so I finally pick up a mirror, and when I see myself, I jump out of my seat. "I look like Little Bo Peep!"

She laughs and takes away the mirror, then pushes me back into the chair. "You won't when I'm done with you, I promise."

So I just sit there some more while she clacks and combs and sprays and rats, and when she's finally all done, she presents me with the mirror and says, "Well?"

I just blink at myself for a minute. She's put my hair *up,* with a little bump at the back, but there are long, soft ringlets coming down at my temples and at the nape of my neck, and she's pinned in fake pearls here and there.

"It would look so much more balanced," she says, "with just a *little* makeup. Maybe a wisp of mascara?" And before I know it, she's whipped out the mascara tube.

Now, I would have just stopped her, but as she's unscrewing the brush, she says, "I really wish you'd patch things up with Casey. There's no reason we both can't be happy, you know. Even if the circumstances are a little . . . *unusual.*" The brush rakes through my lashes, and she says, "He's miserable, and there's no reason for it."

I push her hand away. "He's not miserable! He told me to quit calling him!"

Her perfect skinny eyebrows arch way up. "He told me *you* broke up with *him*."

"I did not! I called him over and over, and he never called me back. And finally he sent me a text and told me to quit bugging him."

The mascara brush hovers in the air a moment before it comes toward my other eye's lashes. And I want to slap it away, but my mom gives me a stern look and says, "You'd look ridiculous with only one eye done."

So I let her swoop through my other lashes, and while she's doing that, she says, "A text, huh? To one of your friend's phones?"

"Yeah. Dot's. But it would be nice if I could have my *own* phone."

She pretends not to hear that last bit. "And when was this?"

I think back. "On Tuesday."

She pulls away a little. "This past Tuesday?"

"Yeah."

She pushes the mascara brush back inside its tube and screws it closed. "That's odd. Warren just took both Casey and Heather out for new phones. Seems Casey lost his during the move, and there was some issue with Heather's."

"During the move?" I ask, blinking my sticky eyelashes at her.

She's coming at my face with a blush brush. "Mmm hmm."

My brain is rewinding at lightning speed. "That was last weekend."

She nods, pushing the brush against one cheek, then the other.

"But then—" And that's when I remember. "What was that message you told Grams to give me? Something about a note? That I didn't have to write that note?"

"He showed it to me," she said, looking through her lipsticks and glosses.

"What did it *say?*"

"That you didn't want to see him anymore."

"No!" I cry, jumping out of my seat. "I never wrote him a note!"

A lipstick comes at my mouth like a homing missile. "It looked like your handwriting to me."

"But it wasn't!"

"Hold still!"

And that's when it hits me—Heather!

I collapse into the seat, and while my mother's busy painting my lips, everything's snapping together in my head:

My missing homework in Vince's class—Heather must've taken it from the in-basket for a sample of my writing!

Casey not answering his phone or calling me back—Heather probably stole it the weekend he'd moved in. All this time, *she'd* had his phone!

And the text—Heather sent it!

And Heather spying on us through Hudson's window—she hadn't followed us home, she hadn't even been at school that day. She'd done a reverse lookup after Marissa had left Casey a message!

"Oh my God," I mumble. "Ohmygod, ohmygod, ohmygod!" I jump up. "It was Heather! Heather stole his phone! Heather sent that text! Heather forged that note. It was Heather!"

My mother looks shocked. "Are you sure?"

I snort. "Oh, I am *so* sure."

"But . . . I have to say—she's been very nice to me."

"Well, watch your back."

Grams nods. "That girl is vicious, Lana. You have no idea."

"Well," my mother says, "regardless of how it happened, if this is all some big misunderstanding, you need to call Casey. Call him right now."

Trouble is, he has a new number, and I don't know what it is. So Mom tries to call Warren to get it from him, but his phone rolls over to voice mail.

She leaves a message, but after fifteen minutes of him not calling back, she takes a deep breath and says, "I'm loath to call Candi"—then she looks at me—"but I will."

"Really?" It seemed a very *brave* thing for her to volunteer to do. And believe me, my mother does not do brave well. Or often. "You have her cell number?"

"No, but let's try their house." And after looking it up, she very calmly punches the number into her cell phone.

Too bad for her, Heather's the one who answers.

"Good morning, Heather," my mom says sweetly. "Does your brother happen to be around?"

She shakes her head at me, relaying that Heather said no.

"How about your father?" Then she adds, "Or your mother?"

Another shake, and then, "Do you have your mother's or brother's cell numbers? Maybe I can reach them that way. It's pretty important."

But of course Heather's not about to give them up, so after another short minute, my mom says, "Well, thanks anyway," and clicks off.

"Of course she knows them!" Grams snaps.

"And now she knows yours, too," I say, looking at my mother.

My mom gives me a puzzled look. "Is that a problem?"

I snort and shake my head. "Oh, you have no idea."

But at the rate things were going, it wouldn't be too long before she did.

TWENTY-EIGHT

Casey's dad still hadn't called by the time I had to leave. And since my mom had been dropped off at the Senior Highrise, and since my grams doesn't have a car, I grabbed my skateboard and made for the door.

Trouble is, Grams steps in the way. "Wait a minute," she says. "Why don't we call Hudson to give you a ride?"

"Because I'm already late!"

"You can't ride a skateboard there," my mother says. "Your hair will be completely ruined!"

"It'll be *fine*. It's, like, shellacked."

And, really, Mrs. Tweeter would be happy, 'cause I have, like, *helmet* hair. But my mother produces a red silk scarf and whips it over my head. "There," she says as she ties it under my chin. "That will keep it from blowing away."

"I am not wearing this!" I tell her as I try to untie it. "I look like Red Riding Hood!"

"Oh, you do not!" She smiles her movie-star smile. "Red Riding Hood did not wear jeans, and she did not ride a skateboard."

"Well, she should have," I grumble, fumbling with what is now a knot under my chin.

Grams hurries in with my sweatshirt. "Here," she says. "Put this on over."

"It's *hot* outside!"

"Just wear it," Grams says, and before I know it, she has my arms in and the hood up over the silk scarf. "Just tie it, and no one will even notice."

Both of them are blocking the door, and I know I'm not getting out of the apartment without protecting my foo-foo hairdo. So I grumble, "Oh, good grief," and tie down the hood. "There. You happy? Now can I please go?"

They step aside, and after we're sure the hallway's clear, I zip over to the fire escape door, slip outside, then charge down the steps and *out* of there.

I actually thought about going by the Acostas'. I mean, knowing Heather, Casey *was* at home. Probably in the room right next door to where she'd been lying to my mom through her teeth.

My ridiculous hair is what stopped me.

That and the fact that I was already half an hour late.

Anyway, when I get to Debra's, the door's half open, so I put my skateboard on the porch and walk right in. And since I'm *hot,* the first thing I do is dump my sweatshirt.

Debra sees me and does a double take. "Sams?"

"Yeah, it's me," I grumble, wrestling with the knot under my chin. "Can you undo this thing?"

She comes over and has it off in a flash. "Wow," she says, taking me in. "I was not expectin' *this.*"

"Blame my mother," I grumble.

"Oooh, I like your mother!" she says with a laugh, then calls, "Tippy! Brandi! Come here!"

The other two bridesmaids appear and start making a fuss. And with their blond hairdos and the way they're clucking around me, I feel like I'm cornered by a scary bunch of oversized chicks.

"Hey!" I tell them, backing away. "It's just hair!" I look around. "Isn't there work to do?"

"There sure is," Tippy Toes says. "We are behind on everything!"

Debra checks the clock. "Someone's got to get over to the church. The flowers and cake are supposed to be delivered any minute."

"I still need to redo that broken nail for you," Brandi says.

"And I'm still tying ribbons on the favors," Tippy Toes says.

I look at Debra. "So that leaves me. What do I do?"

"Just go down there. The cake goes in that little back kitchen—make sure it's nowhere near the window—and the florist'll know where to put the flowers. I'll just feel a lot better knowing they've arrived."

So off I go on my skateboard, down Elm to Constance Street, where I hang a right and head for the church. And really, I'm taking it easy. I mean, there *is* wind in my hair, but I'm making sure it's not, you know, *gusty* or anything. And because I'm not going very fast or having to focus too hard on what's ahead of me, I'm able to do a little looking around. And what I see as I roll past the second house on Constance Street is an SUV in the driveway.

A dirty blue SUV with three faded oval stickers on its chalky, dinged-up bumper.

259

Now, I don't exactly fall off my skateboard, but I do slow waaaay down. I mean, running into your teachers around town is plenty strange enough. Especially when they're wearing do-rags and sucking down beer with a bunch of bikers. But even when you run into normal teachers, it just throws you to see them someplace besides school. It's like they're haunting you. Spying on you. Reminding you that you have homework.

Of course, they always act like they don't want to see you, either, so maybe it goes both ways.

Anyway, running into a teacher in the mall or in a store is one thing.

Finding out where they live?

That's just . . . weird.

So I'm not quite believing that this house I'm cruising by is where ol' Scratch 'n' Spit actually lives, but the SUV is the only car there, and it's parked smack-dab in the middle of the driveway like it owns the place. And as I pass by and look over at the driver's door, it's easy to read the DIE DUDE that's scratched into the paint.

I come to a stop and just stare at it. Sure, I'd seen the scratched door on Officer Borsch's computer, but seeing it in real life made it seem even more, I don't know, *vicious*.

Anyway, as I'm looking at it, I notice the area around the DIE DUDE that Officer Borsch had pointed out on the computer. Maybe it's the way the sunlight is hitting it, but the patch over and *around* the DIE DUDE is very visible. Not obvious, but definitely there. It's rectangular and slightly darker. Cleaner. Like someone's vacuumed off every third particle of dirt or something.

But I'm supposed to be checking on flowers and cake and stuff, so finally I make myself get going.

When I reach the church, I start up the steps, only before I get to the little front porch, a lady in jeans and a polo comes hurrying out. "You in the wedding party?" she asks, checking out my hair. I nod, and that's good enough for her. She hands me a clipboard and a pen and says, "Sign right here."

"What am I signing?" I ask.

"Just that I delivered the flowers," she says. "They're right inside."

Now, I've never signed for anything before, but I can't image she's *lying* about delivering the flowers, so I take the clipboard and sign away.

"Thanks!" she says, and hurries off.

So inside the church I go. And I do find a bunch of flowers—some are in little clear plastic boxes, some are in vases, and there are all sorts of bouquet-y things—but they're just kind of stacked on and around the table where the donuts had been the night before.

I look inside the main part of the church and see Reverend Doyle up near the altar. He's not wearing a sweater, so at least *that's* good. "Hey," I call over to him. "Do you know what's supposed to be done with these flowers?"

"Uh . . . no," he says as he walks toward me. And then when he sees the heaps, he raises his eyebrows and says, "Not good."

"What do you mean?"

"Usually, the florist positions them. At the end of the pews, up by the altar . . . that sort of thing." He looks out the front door. "Has she left already?"

I run outside in time to see a van peeling out of the little side parking lot. It's got a crooked sign on the sliding door that says:

BLOOMIES

Your Fast and Friendly Florist

Well, obviously, the delivery lady is taking the "fast" part of their motto seriously because she roars up the street and around the corner before I can yell, Hey, wait! So I hurry back inside and tell Reverend Doyle, "She's already gone."

"Hmm," he says. "Well, I guess you'd better get busy." Then he walks away.

Now, I don't know where the flowers are supposed to go, but how hard can it be? Plus, I sure don't want to go running to Debra like a little kid and *ask*. So after the cake gets delivered, I start putting the flowers around the church where *I* think they look good. Trouble is, after about fifteen minutes Reverend Doyle sees what I'm doing and says, "Uh . . . you might want to get some help with that."

I look around. "Am I doing it wrong?"

He eyes a statue near the altar. "I don't think the bride's bouquet is supposed to go around Jesus' neck."

Oh.

So I hop on my skateboard and head back to Debra's, and after I explain the situation, there's five frantic minutes of discussing what to do. And finally they decide that Brandi will walk back to the church with me while Tippy and Debra load the dresses and party favors and who knows what else into Debra's car.

"This is craziness," Brandi grumbles as we head back to the church. "I told Tippy we'd need a car, and here were are, needin' a car."

She's acting pretty stressed, so I tell her, "It's not far."

"That's easy for you to say," she says, eyeing me on my skateboard. "You just roll along and it's nothing! That's like one of those movin' walkways at the airport. And I'm like the fool walking alongside."

"You want to ride?" I ask, jumping off and offering her my board.

"And break my neck?" she laughs. "That's all Deb needs." Then she notices the Vincenator's car and stops dead in her tracks. "Would you look at that!" she gasps.

"Yeah," I say, taking in the DIE DUDE again.

"Do you have biker gangs around here?"

I cock my head at her. "*Biker* gangs? Why'd you ask that?"

She starts walking again. "The Sturgis stickers."

I get back on my board. "I don't even know what Sturgis is."

"Oh," she says with a laugh. "Well, if you were from South Dakota like I am, you'd know that it's a biker rally. Sturgis is actually a town, but when you see stickers like the ones on that bumper, it's referrin' to the rally. It happens the first week of August every year. The whole Black Hills area is crawlin' with bikers. Half a million of them come to town. It's ridiculous, but good for business."

"So . . . bikers have gangs?"

"Well, sure. Although it's not like it used to be. Seems like every man over forty owns a Harley now, but biker gangs used to be very dangerous. My brother, Duane, got caught up in one for a while, but he's mellowed out a lot." She laughs. "Not that he's given up his Harley. His big thing now is Hogtoberfest."

My head snaps to look at her. "What *is* that?"

"It's another rally, but bikers stretch it out for the whole month of October. They start from everywhere and meet up with other bikers along the way, road-rallying across the country. By the time they roll into Texas, which is where they all meet, they're dominating highways and whole cities. Then they have their week of drunken debauchery and all ride home. My brother *lives* for Hogtoberfest. He works his whole life around it."

I was so busy listening to her I almost rolled right past the church. "Hey, we're here," she said, laughing. "Let's go figure out those flowers."

So I picked up my skateboard and followed her up the steps, but my mind wasn't on flowers. It was on Mr. Vince.

And Sturgis.

And motorcycle gangs.

I may have seen him in a do-rag, but I still couldn't picture Mr. Vince as a biker. I mean, come on—he'd fainted at the sight of a dead rat.

What kind of bad-boy biker does that?

And he may have the stickers to prove it, but I still couldn't picture Mr. Vince going to a biker rally.

A fart rally, yeah.

A scratch 'n' spit rally, yeah.

A biker rally? No.

Which got me thinking . . . maybe Mr. Vince bought the SUV from someone who *was* a biker and *had* been to Sturgis. Maybe those stickers weren't his at all.

Still. What about his biker friends at Cheezers? They all had tricked-out Harleys—were *they* in a gang?

And that's when it hit me that maybe they *weren't* friends with Mr. Vince at all. Maybe he'd been *arguing* with them the day we'd seen him at Cheezers.

Wow. That was a whole new thought.

Were *they* the ones who had done all the Die Dude stuff?

And *that's* when I remembered about the pay phone that was used to call in the fire alert to our school.

It was at the mall.

Right near Cheezers.

I could feel goose bumps spreading across my back.

But . . . how *could* the guys from Cheezers be behind the Die Dude stuff? They couldn't get into school and leave a rat in his drawer! How would they even have heard about Billy's little prank so they could run with the whole Die Dude thing?

I mean, it just didn't make any sense.

Still. I couldn't stop trying to find a way to *make* it make sense. The whole time Brandi was sorting through the flowers and telling me what to put where, I played with all the little pieces in my mind, trying to find some way to fit them together. I kept trying to find a place for Heather. Or Lars and Sasha.

Was one of the bikers Sasha's dad?

Lars' dad?

A biker uncle?

Did *Cisco* know any of them?

Were they connected to *Heather* somehow?

I felt like I had little chunks here and there, but I couldn't find a way to connect them, and it was driving me crazy.

What was I missing?

What *piece* was I missing?

TWENTY-NINE

It's a good thing I was wearing my high-tops and not my foo-foo shoes, because for the next hour I ran around like crazy trying to get everything ready. First there were the flowers, then we had to unload Debra's car, and I don't know why, but somehow I got elected gofer while Brandi and Tippy "took care of things" in the changing room.

I didn't really mind, because the changing room was tiny. So going back and forth to the car was way better than listening to them complain about the "cramped quarters" and cluck around like worried chickens. But after all the dresses and shoes and gloves and makeup cases and mirrors and bows and *hair spray* were inside, Debra started dispatching me to "check on" things. "Oh, Sams! Could you check on the DJ?" and then "Oh, Sams! Could you check on the cake?" and "Oh, Sams! Have you seen the photographer?" and "Oh, Sams! Could you check on the weather?"

The rest I just walked around and brought back an "Everything's fine," but the weather? She was obviously having a nervous breakdown. "What do you want to know about the weather?"

"It's awfully warm! Do you think we need fans out there?"

"No, but we could sure use one in here." So I got Reverend Doyle to lend me a portable fan from a little office in back, and when I had it plugged in and blowing air around the changing room, Debra started up with the dispatching again. I put out the guest book. I spread wedding-bell confetti on the tables that had been put up out back for the reception. I put the little candy almond favors in place. I laid a DEB & GIL, NOW & FOREVER wedding-bell napkin at every setting.

By the time I was finally done running around like mad, Debra's carrot face was caked over with makeup, and she was cinched into a high-collared white dress that had long sleeves with buttons from the wrists all the way up to the elbows and a train that looked like it was longer than the church. There was also a veil attached to her beaded headpiece. It was folded back, but if she was going to wear it *forward*, she would be totally covered in white.

My first thought was, You look like the Matterhorn! but what came out of my mouth was, "You wanted to be tan because . . . ?"

Lucky for me, they all thought that was funny, and after they laughed, Debra asked me, "Are people arriving? Have you seen Gil?"

"Yup and yup," I said. "I think everything's set."

Music was drifting inside our little changing closet, and we could hear people's voices out in the foyer. "You girls need to get dressed!" Debra said.

So I triple-zipped Tippy and Brandi into their mountains of lavender, and then it was my turn. I kicked out of my jeans and was about to toss them aside when something fell out of a pocket.

Now, if I'd known what it was, I would have just left it there, but I *didn't* know what it was, so I picked it up, unfolded it, and came face to face with Spy Guy's Jiffy Print receipt:

12x18mgntsn . . . $19.95

I blinked at it a minute, *then* crumpled it up and tossed it in the trash.

"Get in this thing, girl, come on!" Brandi tells me, holding out my dress. So they zip me in it, and when I turn around, Debra is holding three silver chain bracelets, a little silver heart dangling from each. "Thank you for being my girls," she says, and starts clipping them around our wrists. "I don't know how I could have done this without your help." She wraps mine around my wrist and smiles at me. "You have been a godsend, Sams."

"Way more helpful than Robyn," Tippy mutters.

"You can say that again," Brandi says.

"Way more helpful than Robyn," Tippy mutters, and they all laugh.

But then all of a sudden Debra's looking around saying, "Oh no. The ring."

"What ring?" Tippy asks.

"Gil's ring! His weddin' ring!"

Well, while they're figuring out who's got the ring, I step into one toe-pinching, glass-beaded lavender high heel.

"Don't look at me," Brandi says to Debra. "I sure don't have it."

I step into the other toe-pinching, glass-beaded lavender high heel.

"Neither do I," Tippy says. "I never even saw it."

I feel like I'm on stilts with alligators nipping at my toes.

"It was . . ." Debra's eyes get enormous. "Oh no! It's still at home! On my dresser! I was so worried about losin' it, and here I forgot it! I can't believe I forgot it!"

"Calm down," Tippy says. "I'll drive right over and get it."

So Debra hands her a small ring of keys and Tippy tippy-toes out of there in her high heels to save the day. Trouble is, Debra's car is blocked by a bunch of other cars, and no one seems to know who they belong to. And since the groomsmen's cars are blocked, too, and Debra's about to have a nervous breakdown, I grab my skateboard and say, "I can be back in five minutes." I put out my hand to Tippy. "Let me have the house key."

"I'm sure we can find—"

"Let me have the house key!"

So she turns it over to me, and I hurry out the front door and down the church steps. Trouble is, there's just no riding a skateboard in three-inch heels. So I peel them off and *then* I jet out of there, looking like a giant lavender sail on top of a skateboard as I hold on to my ridiculous high heels and push along in bare feet.

Now, you'd think I'd be used to Mr. Vince's SUV, but when I sail by his house, there it is, still parked in the middle of his driveway, still vandalized, and I don't know—it's like a gnarly car wreck or something—I can't seem to look away.

And again I notice the dust pattern. Or the missing-dirt pattern. Or whatever you want to call it. And as I'm rolling past it, I can hear Officer Borsch's words in my head. *Once you notice it in one of the pictures, you start seeing it in all of them. . . . It's very uniform. Maybe a foot by a foot and a half. . . . Maybe someone held something up to the door to prevent leaving fingerprints.*

For some reason it keeps looping through my head. It's like I'm trying to figure out a riddle without there actually *being* a riddle. I try to shake it off. I try to say, Forget it! You've got a ring to find! A wedding to get to! But it won't stop looping through my head.

Anyway, I get inside Debra's house, no problem.

I find the gold ring sitting on her dresser like she said it would be, no problem.

And since I'm already carrying my bejeweled shoes *and* a skateboard *and* keys, and since the ring is way too big for even my thumbs, and since in all the miles of fabric around me there's not one pocket and I'm afraid I'll lose the ring or drop it and watch it roll down a sewer grate or something, I take off the heart bracelet, thread it through the ring, and latch the bracelet back around my wrist.

No problem.

I'm feeling pretty secure about it, too.

Like I've just handcuffed the perp.

No way this little gold ring is gonna get away from me!

So I hurry and lock up the house, then take off toward the church. The *problem* happens when I turn from Elm Street onto Constance and something in my brain goes *click*. It happens so loud and so fast that I actually gasp and go, "No!" as I'm rolling along. It seems so crazy, so out there, so *impossible,* but all of a sudden a bunch of *other* pieces start clicking into place. "No!" I gasp again, and my mind is now going click-crazy.

In science last year we did a lab on measurements. We learned why a foot is twelve inches, why horses are measured in hands, and how you can get a fairly close measurement of most things if you know (a) how long your stride is and (b) how many inches it is from the tip of your pinky to the tip of your thumb when your fingers are spread apart.

My stride is three feet.

My hand spread is six inches.

Almost exactly.

Anyway, as I'm remembering this, I'm telling myself it'll only take a minute.

Half a minute, really.

I mean, Officer Borsch had just guesstimated, but now I want to know exactly.

Or as exactly as I can.

All of a sudden it *matters.*

So when I get to Mr. Vince's house, I leave my skateboard and lavender high heels at the fence near the sidewalk and tiptoe my little bare feet up to his SUV.

Up to the scratched driver's side door.

Then I measure, from the edge of the "clean" spot over.

It's three hands wide.

Inside my mountain of lavender, my heart starts hammering away.

I measure from the base of the clean spot up.

Two hands.

Exactly.

"Holy smokes!" I gasp, and then I start looking inside the SUV's windows.

The front seats are a mess. There's trash on the floors and junk all around.

I don't see what I'm looking for, so I move back a window.

The rear windows are slightly tinted, but it's still easy to see inside, and what I discover is more junk. Sweatshirts. Binders. Store flyers. Tennis shoes. An umbrella. A dash protector.

And then all of a sudden I think I spot it—on the floor behind the passenger seat, lying there like a floor mat.

I pull up the back door handle.

It's unlocked.

So I open the door and reach over, still not quite believing that the thing on the floor is what I *think* it is. Only I can't reach it, so I lift up my skirts and get one knee inside the SUV and *stretch*.

So there I am, in a big, poufy lavender dress, halfway inside Mr. Vince's SUV, when I hear something scary.

Something with a deep, very powerful growl.

Something that's getting closer.

Fast.

Something that I'm afraid is about to turn up the driveway and catch me breaking into Mr. Vince's SUV.

I tell myself I'm crazy.

I tell myself that everything's okay.

I tell myself to just be cool—that there are no biker gangs in Santa Martina.

But my gut is screaming RUN, and since it's way too late for that, I do the next best thing.

I pull in my skirts, close the door, and *hide*.

THIRTY

I've barely had a chance to close the door and duck when, one by one, three motorcycles dip and roll into Mr. Vince's driveway.

One's dark orange with flames painted across the gas tank.

And one's royal blue with screaming eagles.

One's a blackish purple with laughing skulls.

It's the three guys from Cheezers, all right—Bones, Flash, and Gargoyle. And even though it's got to be eighty degrees outside, they're all decked out in black leather and wearing black half helmets that look like they're straight out of World War II Germany.

"Oh no!" I whimper, because I'm surrounded. Two of them have come to a halt on the left side of the SUV, and one is on the right. And the window tinting isn't dark enough to keep them from seeing me if they looked.

So I stay low while they're out there revving up their motorcycles. It's like the call of the wild, only they're letting their Harleys do the howling.

I keep one eye on them as I reach for the thing that had lured me into the car in the first place.

A magnetic sign.

It's like the one on the Bloomies van, only this one has been spray-painted blue—the same color as Mr. Vince's SUV.

My hand is shaking as I measure it, and sure enough, it's twelve by eighteen.

And now I know for sure—"12x18mgntsn" stands for a twelve-by-eighteen magnetic sign, the same dimensions as the clean spot on the DIE DUDE door. And since Mr. Vince had bought the magnetic sign the day *before* his car got keyed, Mikey's little receipt was proof—*Mr. Vince* is the missing piece.

He could have done *all* of it.

Plant the rat.

Use Billy's phone to call in the Die Dude threat.

And key his own car—something he must've done at home the night before, then concealed with the magnet until he got to school.

And with all his fainting and freaking out, plus the viciousness of the threats, he was also the one person no one would ever suspect.

After all, what kind of person keys their own car?

The revving outside quiets to a loud purr, and when I take a peek, I see Mr. Vince coming out from under his opening garage door.

Gargoyle calls, "Curveball! Yo, man! Are you ready?"

Mr. Vince has a duffle bag in one hand and is holding a helmet in the other. Seeing the helmet is a relief because I figure he's going to get on the back of one of his friends' bikes and ride away, leaving me free to escape the SUV and get down to the church. But instead, he motions Gargoyle—who's one of the two guys on my left—to park his bike inside the garage.

That leaves one bike on each side of me, so I'm still stuck. But when Vince and Gargoyle come out and close the garage door, it looks like they're each going to get on the back of the other two bikes. Vince is walking to the left side of the SUV, and Gargoyle is heading to the right.

Only they don't stop at the motorcycles.

They come toward the car.

"Oh no!" I gasp, then grab my lavender skirts and crawl around the middle seats as fast as I can, hiding behind them. And I've barely got my dress smashed down and out of sight when both doors open and Gargoyle and Vince get in.

"See you there!" Vince calls out his window. Then he fires up the SUV and backs out of the driveway.

Now, I'm not just worried that they're going to find me, or that they'll see my shoes and skateboard parked by the fence and say, What's this? and *then* find me.

I'm worried about messing up the wedding!

I've got Officer Borsch's ring!

And I promised I'd be right back!

I feel like such an idiot. I mean, why couldn't it have waited? Why couldn't I have just gone back to the church and told Officer Borsch what I was thinking, uncrumpled the receipt, and let *him* take care of things?

Why did I have to get inside a car that was now going who knows where?

"You stoked, man?" I can hear Gargoyle asking.

"Hell, yeah!" the Vincenator says. "I am free, man. *Free*."

"So they bought it?"

Vince laughs. "They're so confused, they'll never figure it out. I've got 'em going in ten different directions."

Gargoyle laughs, too. "You keyed your own car, man. That's pretty extreme."

"That was the whole point! It had to be something no one would think you would do to yourself. And the beauty of it is, insurance will cover it, so it's no skin off my nose."

Then Gargoyle says, "Remember—don't get cocky. You gotta keep up appearances. It's the number one thing."

"Why do you think we're doing this whole park-at-your-place thing, man? I'm tellin' nobody."

Gargoyle laughs. "Although since you're going for a *psychological* disability, you could make the case that gettin' a Harley's therapy, man."

Mr. Vince laughs. "Yeah, but no way am I riskin' it. Unless I'm on the road, I am layin' low." They're quiet for a while, and then Mr. Vince says, "I could never have done this without you, man. You went *way* above and beyond by calling in that fire."

"Hey, it was a phone call. Got your go-time text and did a little ring-a-ling-ling. No biggie. Besides, Bones helped me set up my disability, and Flash helped him set up his. Just doin' my civic duty of payin' it forward. Besides, you've been hatin' on that job for *waaaay* too long. It's about time you ditched it." He laughs. "And it's about time you got a Harley!"

While we're driving along, I can hear Bones' and

Flash's motorcycles growling down the road ahead of us. And as we're driving away from the church, I'm wishing more and more that I had a cell phone.

In my head I'm screaming, WHY DON'T I HAVE A CELL PHONE?

I could text Officer Borsch right now.

I could let him know what's going on.

I could maybe even save my own life!

I mean, who knows what's going to happen to me if Gargoyle and his gang discover that Vince has got a stowaway? If they're all doing some kind of get-paid-for-not-working scam, are they really going to risk letting me blow the whistle on them?

No!

They're going to tie me up in biker chains and throw me in the lake!

Okay, so we don't have a lake. But at this point I'm one big, freakin'-out pile of lavender, and my head is spazzing with some really bizarre thoughts.

Like, I don't want to die with Officer Borsch's wedding ring handcuffed to me.

I don't know why I'm thinking that, but I am.

And I don't want Debra to hate me forever. Here she's waited forty years to get married, and it's going to be totally ruined 'cause I've gone missing. They'll find my skateboard and shoes, but who knows if they'll ever find me wrapped up in biker chains, buried in a lacy lavender coffin at the bottom of some lake somewhere?

But mostly I'm thinking that if they wrap me in biker chains and throw me in the lake, I'll never see Casey again.

And I really, really, *really* don't want to die without seeing Casey again.

So there I am, in the middle of freaking out about dying, when all of a sudden we stop. It's not at a stoplight, either, because Mr. Vince cuts the motor, and the Harleys go quiet, too.

"Let's do it!" Gargoyle says, and a second later both doors are slamming, and I'm all alone again inside the SUV.

"Oh, thank God!" I whisper, but then I start wondering if there really is a God, 'cause when I peek out the window, there's Bones and Flash just hanging out on their bikes, real near the SUV.

We're at the Harley-Davidson shop, and I don't know why they're not following Vince and Gargoyle inside, but they're not. And after a few minutes of *willing* them to go inside, I'm deciding that I just need to make a break for it. I mean, they won't know who I am. And what are they going to say to Vince? Hey, dude, an oversized purple fairy just flew out of your car?

So I'm just reaching for the door handle when something buzzes.

Then it stops buzzing.

Then it *starts* buzzing.

It takes another stop and start for me to realize that it's Mr. Vince's cell phone vibrating in the cup console between the front two seats.

I sneak forward and grab the phone, watching Flash and Bones the whole time. They may be off to the side and a little forward of the SUV, but one glance over their shoulders and I'll be wrapped in chains and heading for the lake.

Lucky for me, they don't do any glancing, and by the time I've grabbed it, the phone's stopped buzzing. So I duck back and punch in Officer Borsch's number.

It never even crossed my mind to call anyone else.

After one ring, I hear his voice. "Borsch here."

It's intense.

Commanding.

Worried.

I whisper, "It's me."

"It's Sammy!" I hear him call over the phone.

"Listen," I tell him, keeping my voice down, "I'm really, *really* sorry I'm messing up your wedding, but it was *Vince*. The whole time it's been *Vince*. He did all that Die Dude stuff to *himself* so he could get a psychological disability! The phone call, the rat, the scratched-up car—he did it to fake a nervous breakdown! It's why he didn't want Foxmore to think it was Billy and me. Oh, he loved torturing us, but in the end he wanted people to think he was in real danger! And you were right—the fire alarm wasn't a coincidence. One of his biker friends called it in! And that clean spot on his car door? It was caused by a door magnet! You know, one of those big ones that people use for businesses? Like Bloomies? When they delivered your flowers, the sign was on all crooked, and—"

"Sammy! Stop talking! Where are you?"

"Uh, trapped inside the Die Dude Mobile at the Harley shop on Main Street."

"He kidnapped you?"

"No! Well, not on purpose. I . . . uh . . . I accidentally stowed away."

"How do you accidentally stow away? And on my wedding day!"

"I know! I'm sorry! And I *do* have the ring! But I'm stuck, 'cause I'm surrounded by bikers who are probably gonna wrap me up in chains and toss me in the lake when they find out I'm here!"

There's a second of silence. "What lake?" And then, "Never mind! Hold tight. I'm on my way."

So I hold tight.

And I sweat bullets.

Pop, pop, pop, out they burst, one at a time.

But as Bones and Flash get off their bikes and stretch their legs and come in close to inspect the DIE DUDE on Vince's door, those bullets start *machine*-gunning out of me. I mean, Bones and Flash are right there. One good look inside and I'm doomed.

Then all of a sudden a brand-new cherry red Harley comes growling from behind the shop and onto the parking lot. The Vincenator's on it, wearing chaps and a fringed leather jacket. "You monsters ready?" he shouts.

Gargoyle's coming at the SUV, and since there's no escaping, I crawl as far as I can, then dive into the cargo space behind the backseats, thinking that maybe I can sneak out the hatchback. But I'm barely there when Gargoyle gets in the driver's seat. He shouts, "That is one tough ride!" out the window, then fires up the SUV. And since I can't find a lever that opens the hatchback, I'm stuck.

Gargoyle puts the SUV in gear and follows Bones, Flash, and Vince out of the parking lot, down the street, and around a corner. And in my head I'm going, No! No-no-no! I mean, *now* what? Officer Borsch will never find me in time, 'cause in my hurry to hide I'd made the insanely stupid mistake of leaving the cell phone behind.

But then I hear a siren.

It's not a full-blown honking or wailing siren.

It's more a single siren.

Or maybe a *toy* siren.

And it does seem to be getting closer and a *little* bit louder, but Gargoyle sure isn't pulling over for it. So I peek out the back window, and there's Officer Borsch's white car with his little portable flashing red light on top, starting through the intersection we'd just crossed, going toward the Harley shop, and away from us.

So, okay. Maybe there was a better way to handle this, but I'm a panicking purple fairy in a Die Dude Mobile with a gargoyle driving. And what panicking purple fairies in Die Dude Mobiles with gargoyles driving *do* is pop up and wave like crazy through the back window.

Lucky for me, Officer Borsch's head whips a double take, and he skids and squeals, making the turn to follow us. But up front Gargoyle's shouting, "What the *hell*?" and when I turn around, his face in the rearview mirror is terrifying. It's like a big gray rock with bloodshot eyes, set to catapult.

And then he sees that a white car with a little flashing light and a toy siren is tailing him. "Who *are* you?" he shouts. "And what are you doing back there?"

"Uh . . . your fairy godmother? Here to say bibbity-boppity-boo?"

And that's when I see that the traffic in front of us has stopped for a red light. I point and shout, "Watch out!" but it's too late. Gargoyle crashes the SUV into Mr. Vince's brand-new Harley.

Which smashes into Flash's bike.

Which falls onto Bones'.

Officer Borsch screeches to a halt behind us and runs his lavender cummerbund and bow tie up to the Harley carnage in front of us. "Robert Vince!" he shouts. "You are under arrest!"

Gargoyle's out of the car now, and ol' Scratch 'n' Spit isn't even paying attention to Officer Borsch. He's screaming at Gargoyle, cussing up a storm. "You *totaled* my brand-new bike!"

Officer Borsch grabs one of ol' Scratch 'n' Spit's wrists with his cast hand and slaps a handcuff on it with his good one. "What are you *doing*?" Vince shouts at him, and believe me, everyone around is squinting hard at the Lavender Lover.

But the Borschman sure isn't *acting* lavender. He pulls Mr. Vince out of the mess of motorcycles by the scruff of his biker jacket and says, "You have the right to remain silent. Anything you say can and will be used against you in a court of law." He hauls him over to the SUV. "You have the right to have an attorney present during questioning. If you cannot afford an attorney, one will be appointed for you." He claps the other half of the handcuff onto the Die Dude door handle. "Do you understand these rights?"

"What are you *doing*?" Mr. Vince shouts.

"*Do you understand your rights?*" the Borschman shouts back.

"Yes! But . . . what are you arresting *me* for?"

"How about we start with for perpetrating fraud, *dude*, and I'm sure we'll have at least a dozen other charges before this is done, *dude*."

"But . . . I'm the *victim*."

Police sirens have been approaching, and as two black-and-white units with racks of flashing lights zigzag through stopped traffic to reach us, I open the back door of the SUV and step out.

When Mr. Vince sees me, his jaw drops. "*Sammy?*"

"Yeah, Curveball, it's me."

He blinks at me a minute, then wails, "No! No! No! No! No!" and starts beating his free fist against the SUV.

When the on-duty cops arrive, Officer Borsch turns the arrest and accident reporting and all that over to them and then hustles back to his own car, calling, "Hurry up, Sammy! I've got a wedding to get to!"

So I jump in, and off we go, the little red light flashing and toy siren wailing.

THIRTY-ONE

I tell Officer Borsch again that I'm sorry, but all I get out of him is a grunt. And I'm thinking he's *completely* ticked off at me until he says, "I don't know why I didn't peg him. The guy's an obvious lemon." He shakes his head. "I just didn't get his angle." He glances over at me. "Disability for a nervous breakdown?"

"Crazy, huh? And really sleazy."

"How long was he expecting to milk that one, I wonder."

"Forever?" Then I shrug and add, "Or at least through Hogtoberfest?"

He gives me a quick look. "How do you know about Hogtoberfest?"

So while he blazes a path with his toy siren and portable flashing light, I tell him about my little eavesdropping at Cheezers and then what Brandi had told me on our walk over to the church.

Officer Borsch frowns. "Guys like that give the rest of us a bad name."

At first I don't get what he means, but then it hits me. "*You* have a Harley?"

He eyes me. "Don't lump me in with those losers, all right?"

I laugh. "Never!" Then I eye *him* and say, "Like any of them would have the guts to bust a biker gang wearing *lavender*?"

He scowls at me.

"Hey, you look spiffidy-doo-dah."

"I look like a damn fool," he grumbles.

And that's when something *else* hits me. "You must really love her," I say softly.

He ducks past two cars that have pulled to the side out of our way. "I must." Then he lets out a deep, puffy sigh and says, "I swore I'd never get married again. The first two were disasters. Let's hope I've learned something in the last couple of decades, huh?"

Now, I had no idea that the Borschman had been married before, let alone *twice* before. And hearing this makes me wonder why so many people split up. I mean, you don't get married unless you love someone, right? So how come so many people go from being in love to getting nasty divorces?

Officer Borsch sees me thinking. "They were my fault for the most part. I wasn't exactly a communicator. I'd bottle things up, and it caused a lot of problems." He shrugs. "Deb is the sweetest, kindest, most understanding woman I've ever known." He takes a tight turn. "And it helps that she's at the station. She knows what she's in for, marrying a cop."

We're blasting down Constance now, real near Vince's house. "Oh!" I cry. "My shoes!"

"Your shoes?"

"Stop right here!" I say, pointing to Vince's house.

He nose-dives to a halt, and I jump out, only my shoes and skateboard are nowhere to be found. "Oh no!" I say, spinning around. And even though the shoes being stolen is not good, it's really my skateboard that I'm upset about.

"Get in," he shouts.

So I dive back in and slam the door. "Someone stole my skateboard! And the shoes! Debra's going to hate me forever."

"Sorry about your skateboard," he says, then chuckles. "I *told* Deb it was risky having you in the wedding." He eyes me. "You *do* have the ring, right?"

I hold up my wrist.

His gold band is still handcuffed to my bracelet.

He nods. "I think she'll forgive you." Then he screeches to a halt in front of the church, throws the gearshift in park, and bolts out the door. "Let's get this show on the road!"

"He's back!" someone in the group of people on the front porch shouts into the church.

Now, Officer Borsch goes around the back of the church, but the changing room where I figure Debra is waiting is closer to the front of the church. So I hike up my skirts and charge my bare feet up the steps as fast as I can.

The people who are gathered on the steps move aside for me, and I'm so busy trying not to trip on my skirts that I don't really look up until I reach the top. And when I finally *do* look up, who do I see?

Casey.

He's, like, two feet in front of me, just standing there,

looking amazingly handsome in a long-sleeved button-down shirt and skinny black tie.

I gasp, and my heart goes positively wacky in my chest.

He smiles, then produces my glass-beaded shoes from behind his back. "I've been looking for the girl who fits these shoes."

I laugh and put my hands out to take them, but instead of handing them over, he gives a little grin and says, "They were next to a skateboard on the side of the road," then drops to one knee.

Everyone around us falls quiet as Casey reaches out, scoops my left heel forward, and slips a shoe onto my foot.

He smiles up at me. "It looks like I've found her." Then he takes my right foot and slips on the other shoe.

I'm now three inches taller, and when he stands, I just blink at him, eye to eye, with a big Oh! on my face.

People around us start whispering like mad, but Casey just grins like they're not even there. "I think they're waiting for you in back," he says, then steps aside with a half bow and a sweep of the arm, ushering me through.

I'm feeling totally light-headed and breathless, but when I stumble into the changing room, I get snapped back to earth.

"Sams!" Debra cries when she sees me. "What happened? Where's the ring?"

"You really don't want me to explain it now," I tell her, and the minute I hand over the ring, she instantly forgives me. "It doesn't matter," she says. "You're here, Gil's here, we've got the ring . . . everything's okay."

I sort of laugh and say, "Officer Borsch told me you

were the sweetest, kindest, most understanding woman he's ever known, and I think he's right."

Her eyes get teary. "He *said* that?" She looks around at Tippy and Brandi. "Girls, let's move! I need to marry that man!"

So we grab our bouquets and line up, and after a short break in the music that's been droning in the background, the organist goes *dun-da-da-da, dun-da-da-da* and begins the wedding march.

I start feeling a little heady again as I walk up the aisle. Like I'm floating or about to fall or . . . I don't know what. It's not from being three inches taller, either. And I *am* trying to take the walk slow like I'm supposed to, but it's making the whole trip even more strange. It's like I'm in a dream. And I know the church is packed, but the people in it are just a blur to me. I'm, like, in my own little cloudy world just moving forward, step by step by step.

It isn't until we're all lined up at the altar and Reverend Doyle has announced, "Dearly beloved, we are gathered here . . . ," that I actually see people in the crowd. Some of them look vaguely familiar to me. Like I've seen them around town. Or at the police station. But most of them are strangers. People I've never seen before in my life. And there's one *ancient* couple sitting in the front row that I keep looking back at. The man's skin is mottled, and his hair is like sparse dried grass sticking out of a boulder. The woman is twitching like she might have Parkinson's, and her dress looks like it's draped over a collapsing hanger.

But the reason I keep looking at them is their hands. Their spotty, knotty hands.

She's holding his, and he's covering hers, and something about that mound of spotty, knotty hands makes me choke up.

A million years ago they said "'til death do us part," and they meant it.

They *lived* it.

Right there in front of me is proof.

It *can* be done.

Well, I don't want to be standing up in front of all these people getting weepy about a mound of spotty, knotty hands, so I force myself to look away. And that's when I see my mother. She's sitting next to Grams, and she's smiling at me as she dabs the inside corner of her eye with a tissue.

I just blink at her.

She's crying?

Why in the world is she crying?

She can't even see the old people up in the front row.

But my grams is all weepy, too, which I can tell 'cause her nose always runs when she cries, and she's out there pinching at her nostrils with a Kleenex.

And then I see Casey. The pews are all full, and I guess there's no room for wedding crashers, 'cause he's standing by himself in the back of the church. He gives me a little smile. So I smile back, but then I feel all embarrassed, so I look down.

And what do I see when I look down?

The toes of my shoes, peeking out from under a mountain of lavender.

Seeing them makes me think about Casey slipping

them onto my feet, which makes me feel heady and happy and . . . I don't know . . . *twinkly*-toed.

The ceremony seems to fly by. There are no readers or singers or interludes. It's just Reverend Doyle talking and reading passages from the Bible, and before I know it, Debra and Officer Borsch are exchanging rings and kissing and everyone's cheering.

Then the organist starts up again, and we file out in the opposite order we came in, with Mr. and Mrs. Gilbert Borsch leading the way.

Now, in no time, the area outside the front of the church is milling with people, and I'm scanning the crowd for Casey.

Instead, I find my mother and Grams. "Oh, Samantha!" my mom says, holding my cheeks. "You looked like a princess up there!" Then she starts pushing at the little pearl pins in my hair and fussing with my curls. "You must not have worn your scarf."

"Lana . . . ," Grams warns gently.

I laugh. "My hair is fine, Mom. Actually, it's amazing. I can't believe it held up this well."

"Why, *thank* you," she says, looking very pleased. Then her face flutters a little, and she says, "I hope you don't mind, but I did manage to get in touch with Casey, and I explained what you told me. I . . . I also told him you'd be here, and I *thought* he was going to come, but . . ."

Her voice just trails off. And I don't know, all of a sudden I love her to the ends of the earth and back. I mean, despite everything, if it wasn't for her, Casey and I might never have figured things out. And I want to tell her that he's here . . . somewhere . . . and about what he did with the *shoes,* but it all still feels like a dream to me.

Besides, how in the world could I explain about the shoes?

What kind of guy *does* that?

And then suddenly a hand slips into mine, and when I look over, there's Casey.

"Well!" my mother says, suddenly all rosy-cheeked. "I'm glad you could make it!"

"Thanks," he says back to her, then smiles at me. "You think it'd be okay if I stick around?"

"You can take my place," my mom offers. Then she wrinkles her nose a little and says, "Tri-tip barbecue is not my thing."

Grams looks at her like she can't believe what she's hearing. "But it's Ray James at the grill!"

My mother rolls her eyes. "You can stay, Mother, but I've got other things to do." Then she adds, "And I'm sure Casey will enjoy my seat a lot more than I would."

But in the end, Grams leaves with her. And the truth is, I kinda wanted to leave, too, and just hang out with Casey somewhere and catch up, but I knew it would be really tacky of me.

Turns out, I'm glad I stayed. For one thing, I loved seeing Debra so happy. She was just glowing, holding on to Officer Borsch everywhere they went. And Officer Borsch looked like a happy little boy.

In a blustery don't-mess-with-me kind of way, but still . . .

And the toasts were funny, and the speeches were

tearjerkers, and the food was amazing, and the DJ was great. Everyone danced, and believe me, it was very entertaining to see grown men in lavender cummerbunds getting *down*.

Casey and I danced, too. We danced a lot. But every time a slow song started, we had just sat down or had just gone to get something to drink. And even though we talked a ton and he held my hand, like, nonstop, I started wondering if maybe I had a big, nasty piece of tri-tip stuck in my teeth or something.

Finally I excuse myself and go into the bathroom to check my teeth in the mirror and what do I see?

Nothing. No tri-tip, no pepper, no bits of lettuce, nothing.

So I yank open the door, only when I step out into the hallway, I jump back 'cause Casey's standing right there.

"Hey," he says with a little grin. "Any chance we could maybe get out of here?"

"Uh . . ." I think about it a minute. I mean, we've been there for *hours*, and, really, what do they need me for? Cleanup?

I did way more than my fair share of *set*up.

"Sure," I tell him. "But I need to get out of this dress and these shoes first, okay?"

He nods. "I'll meet you out front."

So I go to the changing room and switch back into my jeans and high-tops, thinking that the minute I get home, I'm going to find my little horseshoe charm and lace it back on. Then I remove all the little pearl pins and totally brush out my hair and pull it into a ponytail.

And I'm just leaving when I remember—the receipt.

Who knew if they would actually need it to convict Mr. Vince?

So I dig through the trash until I find it, and stuff it back into my pocket. And I'm on my way out *again* when I see my glass-beaded shoes tossed to the side.

I think about it a minute, then snatch them off the floor. I mean, I know I'll never wear them again. I know they're ridiculous. But still. Something inside tells me I'll be keeping them forever.

Anyway, when I finally get out of the church, Casey is waiting for me at the bottom of the steps with both our skateboards.

"Hey, it's *you*," he says, smiling. "Don't get me wrong—the princess look is cool, but I like the real you better."

I laugh and say, "Me too!" and take my skateboard from him.

But before I can toss it down, he stops me and locks eyes with me. "I *promise* never to let my sister or my father or your mother or *my* mother or anyone else come between us again."

His eyes are so clear.

So . . . honest.

I nod. "Me too."

"And I *promise*—no more keeping secrets from you. And if something's wrong, I will *talk* to you. No notes, no texts, no messages . . . I'll talk to you face to face."

I nod again. "Me too."

Then we look into each other's eyes, and he slowly

leans forward. And when he's just inches away, my eyes drift closed.

And then . . . his lips . . . touch . . . mine.

They're soft.

And sweet.

And somehow . . . *electric*.

And when we finally pull apart and open our eyes, my cheeks are totally on fire and I'm feeling pretty wobbly. And what I'm thinking is, That was definitely worth waiting for! but what comes out of my mouth is, "It's about time!"

"Yeah," he laughs. "It's about time!"

Then we get on our skateboards, and he grabs my hand, and we roll down the sidewalk, side by side.

Have you read
sammy keyes and the night of skulls
yet?

Turn the page for a sneak peek.

PROLOGUE

I love Halloween.

And I'm sorry, but trick-or-treating is *not* just for little kids. It's for anyone who likes to dress wacky and tear through neighborhoods in search of free candy.

Which definitely includes me and my friends.

And since last year was sort of a disaster because my friends and I wound up going into the scariest house in town to put out a *fire* and discovered a guy inside all bound and gagged and conked over the *head*, and since we had to deal with police and perpetrators and all of *that*, I swore that this year we were just going to have a fun, carefree Halloween, where the worst thing that would happen was we'd eat too much candy.

But then Billy wanted to cut through the graveyard.

And I made the mistake of going along.

ONE

Hudson Graham may be seventy-three, but he's the coolest old guy you'd ever want to meet. I mean, how many "seniors" will offer up their house to a bunch of teenagers to use as their Halloween headquarters? Most old people zip up their homes, shut off their lights, and hide in a back room until Halloween is over. They don't even hand out candy, let alone lend out stuff to help you transform into scar-faced zombies.

Dressing up as a zombie was new for me. I usually go as the Marsh Monster, with ratty green hair and marshy-looking clothes, but this year Casey and Billy were going trick-or-treating with Marissa and Holly and me, and they wanted to use super creepy makeup and blood capsules and fake scars and stuff, so just painting myself green seemed pretty lame in comparison. And after I jumped on the scar-faced zombie wagon, Marissa and Holly got on board, too.

Our friend Dot didn't want anything to do with our little death brigade. She said she was going to "reprise" her bumblebee costume from last year and take her little sisters around their neighborhood instead, but I think she just didn't want to risk another Halloween like last year.

Anyway, Holly, Marissa, Billy, Casey, and I all met at Hudson's house and had a blast painting and spraying and plastering scars onto each other. It got uuuuuugly! And even uglier when we put in our fake rotten teeth!

"You look hideous, darling!" Billy says to Marissa in a Count Dracula accent.

"And you're revolting!" Marissa says back with a laugh.

Then Hudson comes in with some old, worn flannels and a pair of scissors. "Seems you could use some tatters to go with those faces."

"Are you serious?" Casey asks him.

"Rip away," he says with a laugh.

So we put on shirts, then we tear and tatter and, you know, *destroy* them, which really does a lot to complete our zombie look.

"Very gruesome," Hudson says as he lets us out. "You look like you're straight from the grave."

Billy hunches over like Quasimodo as we go down the porch steps, then makes a horrifying sound in his throat and says, "Let's go, my pretties!"

So off we go, racing from house to house, collecting candy in our pillowcases, and it didn't take long for Billy to really start hamming it up.

"Aaaaah," he'd gurgle when someone answered the door. "I think I'm . . . dyyyyyyyyying!" Then he'd grab his throat and stagger around, finally collapsing onto the porch. "Caaaaaaandy!" he'd gasp, holding up his sack. "Save me!"

The person who answered the door would always

laugh, then give all of us two or three pieces instead of just one.

"You're the master at this," Casey tells him after about the sixth performance.

"And you, my pretty, are my slave!"

Casey laughs, "Dude, there's no way I'm your pretty."

"My pretty ugly, then!" Billy rasps. "But still my slave."

So we're all laughing and chasing after Billy as he scurries back onto the sidewalk, but we quit laughing quick when we find ourselves doing a domino-style bump-up into a *cop*.

It's pretty shadowy right there, so it takes a second for me to realize that it's not a real cop—it's just a guy in costume. And *then* it hits me that this fake cop is none other than Danny Urbanski.

Now, let's just say that Danny Urbanski doesn't need to dress up for Halloween. Anyone with two eyes can see that he's a snake. Trouble is, Marissa's two eyes don't focus where Danny's concerned. She's had a crush on him *forever*, and even though she knows he's a slithering sneak, she still can't seem to shake him.

"Dude!" Billy says to him. "A cop?"

Danny laughs. "Best way to stay out of trouble, man." He checks us all over. "You, on the other hand, are dead meat!" Then he laughs really hard at his own joke.

I hate the way Danny laughs. It's one of those forced, kind of hacking laughs that sounds like a lawn mower that won't start.

Ha-ha-ha. Ha-ha-ha.

Like he needs a new spark plug.

Anyway, Danny and Casey used to be really good friends, but not anymore. And I think Danny knows that Holly and I aren't exactly his biggest fans, so it was kinda awkward standing there in the middle of the sidewalk. Especially since Marissa was mortified to be looking so drop-dead ugly.

"Hide me!" she whimpers, then slouches behind me and Holly.

But Danny knows that Marissa and I are usually together, so he sort of leans around and says, "Marissa?"

Marissa spits her nasty yellow teeth into her hand and smiles at him. But all those white teeth flashing through warts and scars and peeling skin looks weird.

Like, *extra* creepy.

Danny laughs again. "Hey, beautiful. Wanna be my *ghoul*friend?"

Now, he says this all, you know, *suave*-like, but there's also a hint of sarcasm to it and it's hard to tell—is he making fun of her? Or is he actually saying, You want to hang out with me tonight?

Or maybe this is his snarky way of apologizing for sucking face with that nasty Heather Acosta and flirting with every hot girl who walks by.

With Danny you just can't tell.

Anyway, Marissa obviously doesn't know what to say because she just *stares* until Casey comes to the rescue, asking him, "So who you hangin' with tonight?"

"I'm meeting up with Nick and some of the guys at the haunted house on Feere Street." Then he kinda throws a smirk at the rest of us and says to Casey, "I can't believe you're trick-or-treating, man."

What's totally implied in this is, I can't believe you're hanging out with these *babies*. See, even though we went to the same junior high, Danny and Casey are both freshmen in high school now. Billy would be, too, only he got held back a year, so he's stuck in eighth grade with us.

And I'm sure Casey's at least a *little* embarrassed by Danny's comment, but he doesn't show it. Instead he moves past Danny saying, "Hey, if I'm ever too cool for free candy, I really will be a walking dead man."

Danny lets out another one of his stupid fake laughs, then says, "Whatever, man. I'm heading over to the haunted house," and he takes a few steps before calling over his shoulder, "There'll be people from *high* school there."

So he went one way and we went the other. And even though we tried to act like Officer Urbanski had never crossed our path, he had definitely put a damper on our fun. Oh, Billy did the whole die-on-the-doorstep thing a few more times, but his performance went from great to lame pretty quick, and before you know it we were back to straight trick-or-treating.

And then we got caught in the Invasion of Little People. I don't know if it was the neighborhood or what, but little Luke Skywalkers and ghosts and teddy bears were suddenly everywhere, scampering up and down the walkways, blasting past us or squealing at the sight of five big zombies in their way.

So finally I say what I know everyone else is thinking. "Why don't we go check out the haunted house?"

Everyone's quiet until Holly shrugs and says, "I've heard it's pretty cool."

Marissa nods. "Me too."

Casey shakes his head. "Yeah, but I really *don't* want to go, you know that?"

I grab his arm and give him a deathly smile. "Yes, you do."

Somehow this pushes the reset on Billy's mood. He grabs Casey's other arm and says, "Yes, my pretty ugly, you do!"

So we duck out of that neighborhood and head for Feere Street, and pretty soon we find ourselves on the corner of Stowell and Nightingale waiting for the light to turn green.

"Perfect!" Billy says, pointing across the street. "Bonesville!"

Casey gives him a grin. "The old side, too!"

Now, the Santa Martina Cemetery is big, and is basically divided into two sections—the old and the new. And the whole thing's separated from the rest of the world by a stone wall that's topped with wrought-iron fencing. So it's not like you're actually *next* to graves as you go by, but still, there's no ignoring that there are people buried on the other side of the wall—especially when you're going past the old part. It's hilly and has big gnarled trees, and there's everything from life-sized angels on huge podiums, to marble grave markers that look like tall skinny pyramids, to the Sunset Crypt—a full-blown mausoleum with Roman pillars and flower urns and a shiny black threshold that says DISTURB NOT THE SLEEP OF DEATH.

The *new* part, on the other hand, was leveled before they started burying people and has only flat grave markers with built-in holes for flowers. Nothing sticks up so a riding mower can drive right over the graves.

When I first found out about the riding mower, it really bothered me. But now I try to think of it as a sort of gentle massage for dead people. I mean, they're six feet under and in a box, right? So they probably barely feel the big ol' lawn mower rumbling around above them. And if they *do,* it's gotta be a pretty quiet, soothing vibration, right?

Anyway, when the light turns green we start to cross Stowell, but jump back quick when a silver minivan looks like it's going to barrel right through the light. It nose-dives to a halt at the last second, and as we cross in front of it Holly says, "Another idiot breaking the law."

At first I don't know what she's talking about, but she's looking at the driver, so I do, too, and what I see is a woman with ruby red hair talking on her cell phone.

"Everybody does that," I tell her.

"Which is why there are so many crazy drivers!"

So we cross the street and as we walk away from the traffic on Stowell Road and down the cemetery side of Nightingale Lane, we pass by a crooked old gate. It's just a single-person gate and it's got a chain and lock around it, but I know from experience that it's definitely not kid-proof.

Now, I'm not about to mention this little fact, but Billy figures it out for himself. "What are we *thinking*?" he cries. "We're zombies! We need to join our brethren!" and in a flash he's squeezing through the gate.

"No!" Marissa cries. "I do *not* want to go into the graveyard!"

"Uh, why?" Casey asks as he follows Billy. "Are you afraid you'll scare the ghosts?"

"I . . . I just don't!"

"It's a shortcut," Billy singsongs. "It'll save us at least ten minutes."

"Will not!"

Holly steps forward, following Casey and Billy. "Come on, Marissa. It's Halloween. It'll be fun." Then she adds, "You don't believe in ghosts, do you?"

"No, but . . . !" Marissa looks to me for help, and the truth is, I'm kinda torn. I mean, I'm not crazy about the idea, but it *is* Halloween, and we *are* dressed up like zombies, and something about doing it sounds fun.

In a heart-in-your-throat kind of way, but still.

"You're kidding me!" Marissa says, watching me think. "You're going to abandon me? What kind of friend are you? Why are you always dragging me places I don't want to go? Do you remember the last time we took a shortcut? Do you *remember*?"

"Yeah. Through the mall. Nice cool air . . ."

"No! The time before that!"

"Uh, let's see . . . I remember the last time we took a *long* cut . . ."

"No!" she says, pointing a finger at me. "Don't you *even* bring that up!"

"Bring what up?" Holly asks through the gate. Then she says, "Oh. That you go by—"

"No!" Marissa cries, because there's no way in the

world she wants Casey and Billy to know that she's so obsessed with Danny Urbanski that she takes the long way home from school, just so she can walk past his house.

And she's so desperate to shut us up that she grabs my wrist and before you know it, we're squeezing through the graveyard gate.

WENDELIN VAN DRAANEN was a classroom teacher for many years before becoming a full-time writer. The Sammy Keyes mystery series has been embraced by readers and critics alike, and *Sammy Keyes and the Hotel Thief* received the Edgar Allan Poe Award for Best Children's Mystery. Ms. Van Draanen is the author of many other award-winning titles, including *Flipped, Swear to Howdy, Runaway, Confessions of a Serial Kisser,* and *The Running Dream.*

Wendelin Van Draanen lives with her husband and two sons in California. Her hobbies include the "three R's": reading, running, and rock 'n' roll.

YEARLING MYSTERY!

Looking for more great mystery books to read? Check these out!

- ❏ *The Case of the Cool-Itch Kid* by Patricia Reilly Giff

- ❏ ENCYCLOPEDIA BROWN SERIES by Donald J. Sobol

- ❏ *Harriet the Spy* by Louise Fitzhugh

- ❏ I SO DON'T DO . . . SERIES by Barrie Summy

- ❏ *Key to the Treasure* by Peggy Parish

- ❏ *Last Shot* by John Feinstein

- ❏ *Mudshark* by Gary Paulsen

- ❏ *The Mysteries of Spider Kane* by Mary Pope Osborne

- ❏ NATE THE GREAT SERIES by Marjorie Weinman Sharmat

- ❏ *Nightmare* by Joan Lowery Nixon

- ❏ OLIVIA SHARP: AGENT FOR SECRETS SERIES by Marjorie Weinman Sharmat

- ❏ THE RED BLAZER GIRLS SERIES by Michael D. Beil

- ❏ SAMMY KEYES SERIES by Wendelin Van Draanen

- ❏ *The Séance* by Iain Lawrence

- ❏ *The White Gates* by Bonnie Ramthun

YEARLING BOOKS

Since 1966, Yearling has been the

leading name in classic and award-winning

literature for young readers.

With a wide variety of titles,

Yearling paperbacks entertain, inspire,

and encourage a love of reading.